MW00945594

# SPIDER SILK

## KEEPER OF PLEAS BOOK 2

### ANNELIE WENDEBERG

Copyright 2017 by Annelie Wendeberg

Paperback Edition

This is a work of fiction. Names, characters, places and incidents are the product of the author's imagination or are used fictitiously.

No part of this book may be reproduced in any form by any means, electronic or mechanical, including photocopying, recording, or by any information storage and retrieval system, without the written permission of the copyright owner.

Cover design by Nuno Moreira

Editing by Tom Welch

ALSO BY THIS AUTHOR

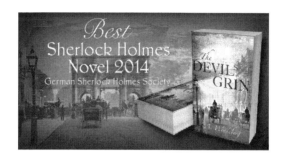

www.anneliewendeberg.com

*This book is dedicated to all the people who helped us save our small farm:*

Marcus Anhäuser, Katrin Scheller, Pete S. Wolfsson, Gitta & Tom Welch, Ursula Kania, Kim Wright, Melissa Petrilla, Christine Mckinley, Charlotte & Rainer Hartwig, Luke Kuhns, Thomas Goldberg, Christiane Hesse, John Doyle, Ruth Powell, Patti Hauge, Robyn Montgomery, Chris Allar, Linda Koch, Ele Brusermann, Anja Bagus, Alex Jahnke, Josef Zens, Steffen Müller, Sarah-Lena Gombert, Merrily Taylor, Hélène Vrot, Matthias Montag, Deb Stidham Avery, Ruth Poirier, Maribel Lorenz, Michaela Majce, Cathy Pillower, Ulla Buthe, Karin Schumacher, Andrea Reinhardt, Lars Fischer, Maria Begoña Zertuche Aizpuru, Terry Kearns, John Lurie, Shannara Johnson, John Della Pia, David Hunter, Zabrina Claire, Giovanna Donnithorne-Tait, Gaila Gutierrez, Deanna Stearns, Dennis Fink, Nigel Franks, Anja Bagus, Stacy Snyder, Frederik Zinken, Mike Gorry, Margaret Graham, Debra Manette, Sabrina & Ben Herrera, Marc Adams, Lou Valentine, Elke Allers, Carola Schwarz, Karen Grear, Sigrid Malessa, Pat Rhodes, Walki Tikanesh, Michael G. Morrison, Terry G.

*Wilson, Merrily Taylor, Linda Koch, Martin Ballaschk, the many anonymous donors, and all the lovely humans who helped spread the word, who thought of us, and prayed for us.*

*THANK YOU!*

# FIRST ACT

*for we all have*
*our own twilights*
*and mists*
*and abysses*
*to return to*

Sanober Khan

## BAIT

*R*ose bunched up a handful of dirty-brown hair she'd snipped off the neighbour dog's wiggly backend, added four matches, and wrapped it all up in paper.

As she worked, a warm evening breeze sneaked through the window and lifted her hair. The tip of her tongue poked out of her mouth, curling up, snakelike. She caught herself, tucked her tongue between her teeth to hold it still, and gazed out the window. Standing on tiptoe, she surveyed the courtyard.

Higgins was grooming the horses. The sun had slipped behind the houses.

Everything was in place.

She struck a match and put it to the crumpled paper, then held her breath and let the burning missile fly. She watched its trajectory, a grin dimpling her cheeks as it landed in the courtyard with a dramatic *poof*.

The chestnuts jumped.

'One. Two… Three.'

'Aaaaaalf!' Higgins bellowed from below.

Alf being the kitchen boy. He sported two very large ears, of which the left was more lopsided than the right. This condition alone had earned him Rose's distaste when first they'd met.

He would get those ears pulled in a moment. She hated Alf, he was… Well, silly, clumsy, and naive was how one could best describe him. He was two years her senior and a brat. The feeling of dislike was mutual.

Alf often took a beating for things he hadn't done. What a dumb boy! No one suspected her, of course. Not ever. Girls don't build stink bombs, they don't climb out of the attic's top window, and traipse about the roof. And a girl would *never* throw a dead cat down the chimney.

Ever.

Rose loved being a girl.

She waved whiffs of the stink bomb's aroma out the window, then shut it, and tiptoed down the dark stairwell to the third floor, to the second floor, and — after making sure the servants weren't around — she slipped into Olivia's room.

'Where have you been?' Olivia asked, squinting at Rose through the looking glass.

The girl grinned, her gaze traveling up and down Olivia's form. 'You look horrible!'

'As I should.'

'Are you catching thieves and murderers?' Rose asked, eyebrows perching high on her brow.

Olivia patted her mutton chops, and spoke with a dark and dramatic voice, 'That, my dear First Mate, is my destiny: to save mankind, to stop evil from spreading. Damn, this itches.'

Rose giggled, and Olivia shooed her away, 'Off with you to the kitchen, landlubber! Cook hates it when you let your dinner go cold.'

A toothy grin, two fingers to her temple. 'Aye, Captain!' And Rose dashed from the room.

---

'HE'S NOT COMING,' Olivia whispered and looked up at Sévère, who said nothing in reply. 'At least I know now what a rhinoceros is going through.' She crossed her eyes toward the putty on her nose that was in the way wherever she looked. She decided on the spot to never mock anyone with old potatoes for noses. It was a miracle they could walk straight, considering their obstructed vision. Tentatively, she pressed her fingers to the fake enlargement, then yanked her hand away as the putty began to wobble.

Sévère threw an irritated glance at her, and hissed, 'Stop it already! It's coming off.'

She stuck out her tongue, then directed her attention toward the house across the street. Windows spilt murky light onto the pavement and a lone, stubborn whore.

'I wonder why business is so slow to…to—' Olivia held in the sneeze, else she might shoot her fake nose off her face. Perhaps even the prickly mutton chops. Damn that vile shoe polish she'd put on her eyebrows! And damn this entire investigation!

She curled her fists so as not to claw at her disguise

and throw it into the nearby piss puddle. She coughed once, then said gruffly, 'What do we do now?'

'Patience,' Sévère whispered, and leant against a lamp post, right hand in a trouser pocket, the left lightly tapping the knob of his cane against his hip.

Olivia's gaze touched upon his face that was partially hidden by his cap, partially lit by the cigarette that smouldered at the corner of his moustached mouth.

She huffed. If investigating a crime meant to wait *months* for something — anything — to happen, hoping that it could be used in court, then she wasn't made for this. She lacked Sévère's calm patience, and doubted she'd ever attain it. She'd reached the point of "shoot first, ask later."

'This isn't working,' she grumbled softly, and then louder, 'Well then, my dear chap,' as she elbowed Sévère, and motioned toward a woman across the street. 'Shall we be on our way, or are you *still* lusting after that foxy girl?'

'I wonder if she might like to see the both of us,' he said casually, a dark glimmer in his eyes. He scanned the brothel's windows once more, its entrance, the street. The redhead smiled at them and lifted her skirts to show her ankles.

Olivia whistled and set off across the street, ignoring Sévère's muffled protest.

She stopped as a group of youngsters came running, and stepped aside to avoid collision. Without success.

A boy bumped into her, and his hands probed her trouser pockets as swift as fleas. She pulled up her knee but missed his testicles. Her right arm swung. Her fist made contact with his cheekbone.

A moment later, she was on the ground, stomped by a herd of furious young men.

———

'GODDAMMIT, Olivia! Would you please allow them to pick your pocket next time? There wasn't much to steal anyway!' Sévère's finger brushed the tip of her bleeding nose, then plucked off the putty that hung from her nostrils. 'This might hurt.' He pulled at the left mutton chop.

'Ouch,' Olivia said.

'One more.' And off came the other mutton chop. He extracted a handkerchief from his pocket, and dabbed at her nose and the cut on her upper lip. He was worried about her right eye. It was swollen shut.

'Can you move your jaw?' he asked.

She tried to open her mouth, and winced.

'What about your ribs? Might anything be broken?'

Olivia laughed. Or grunted. He wasn't quite sure which.

Sévère stood. 'Cabbie!' he called to a nearby hansom. 'To Sillwood Street!'

'Let Johnston sleep. I'm all right,' she spoke through clenched teeth.

'I will not discuss this.'

'I won't, either!'

'Excellent.' He helped her up and into the waiting cab.

Once the horse had fallen into a fast trot, he said, 'We need to revise our tactics. For three months we've been tailing this…subject.' He was so furious at Olivia, he'd almost let slip the name of the man they were working so hard to apprehend. The cabbie might be able to hear their conversation over the rattling of wheels.

Sévère ground his teeth. 'The handful of witnesses we have managed to talk to are unwilling to give statements. Honestly, considering their position and the position of the subject in question, I would be reluctant, too.'

From the corner of his vision, he saw her sitting up straighter.

'Go on,' she said, her voice dangerously soft.

'What I mean to say is…' He balled his hands to fists. 'Damnation! This is not what I envisioned to happen!'

'If you give up now, I will do it alone.' She sank against the back rest. 'I don't have to abide by rules set for men like you.'

'Dammit, Olivia! Have you ever seen me give up? No. I said we have to revise our tactics. There's nothing wrong with that. Ah, here we are.'

'I don't need a doctor. I'm all right, really, Sévère.'

He squeezed his eyes shut and exhaled. 'Humour me. Just this once.' As he tapped his cane to the hansom's roof, he heard Olivia mutter something that sounded much like *overbearing weasel brain*.


A SLEEPY SERVANT opened the door for them and beckoned them in. Sévère apologised profusely to her, and to Johnston who came descending the stairs in robe and tattered slippers

'My goodness,' Johnston muttered, eyeing Olivia. 'What the deuce happened? Why are you in men's clothing?' And then to Sévère, 'And when did *you* grow a moustache?'

'We were tailing a suspect.' Sévère ripped off his moustache and tucked it into his waistcoat pocket.

'We?'

'Oh, it's fun,' Olivia said, and flapped a dismissive hand at Johnston. He seemed not to hear her remark.

Johnston led them to the drawing room and held a candle to Olivia's face. 'My bag and the leeches.' He snapped his fingers at the waiting servant, who rushed out of the room and returned a moment later with the requested items.

'You may retire.' Johnston waited until the servant had shut the door, then dropped his voice and said to Olivia, 'How did you come about your injuries?' He flicked a sideways glance at Sévère that wasn't any too trusting.

'You don't believe…I would…' Sévère stammered.

Ignoring Sévère, Johnston gazed gently but enquiringly at Olivia.

'I had a disagreement with a band of pickpockets,' she supplied, and shrugged.

Johnston nodded as though such occurrences weren't unusual in the least, and beaten up wives of coroners paid him visits at least twice a week.

He rubbed the bridge of his nose, nodding once. 'My apologies, Sévère. The husband is always the first suspect. To me, and to you.' Johnston went to turn up the gas light at the wall, then lit an oil lamp and moved it closer to his patient.

Sévère mumbled agreement, and watched the surgeon

run tender fingertips over Olivia's face. When she flinched, Sévère grabbed her hand.

'You can let go of me, Sévère. I won't run away, I promise,' she said.

He dropped her hand.

'I feel no bones shifting, my dear,' Johnston said softly. 'But I would like to see the swelling around your eye lessen. Two leeches should do. It won't hurt.'

Olivia smiled up at him. 'Don't worry. I've had worse.'

Johnston froze. 'You've had worse? When was that?'

'When I was a child. There was that boy in the neighbourhood…'

Johnston's gaze was sharp, but Olivia's expression was so innocent that one could not but believe her.

Sévère observed the interaction, and found himself quite surprised that his friend was fooled by his wife.

Johnston placed the leeches onto Olivia's swollen eye, disinfected the cut on her upper lip, and then excused himself to find a cup of tea for her.

'I know how we can apprehend him,' Sévère said in a low voice.

'You do?'

He nodded. 'We've been doing it all wrong. He's always a step ahead of us, and we've allowed it. We've chased him. This time we'll set a trap.'

Olivia's healthy eye narrowed.

Sévère continued, 'Unfortunately, for this to succeed, we have to enter into rather…shady areas of legality. We'll need a young girl as bait.'

'No! *That* we won't do.'

'Why ever not? Call a prostitute into the witness stand

instead? The jury won't believe a word she says. But a young girl that hasn't been ruined...' Slowly, he nodded. 'Why didn't I think of this earlier?'

'If you do this, I will divorce you. What do you believe will happen to the girl after you and the court are through with her? Even if Frost never touches her, she'll be ruined. Her name and her face will be public property. *The girl who was almost raped.* I have a better idea for you, Coroner.'

Sévère straightened his shoulders. Whenever his wife called him *Coroner*, he knew to prepare for battle.

'Why not simply change your lovely legal system so that the voice of a woman is given as much credit as the voice of a man?'

'That would be like trying to convince people God does not exist,' Johnston's voice sounded from the door. 'You cannot fight belief with logic. And I can't believe what I just heard. Should I apologise for overhearing your heated discussion on how to lure a young girl into prostitution?'

Groaning, Sévère rubbed his brow. Olivia touched his hand, and said, 'Allow me.'

He nodded.

'Dr Johnston,' she began, and sat up straight. 'We've been trying for months now to obtain evidence against...a man with considerable political power. We know he is paying seductresses to gain access to underage girls. And we know he has been doing this for years.'

Johnston sat down in a chair opposite Olivia. He completely ignored Sévère.

'How do you know?'

'I know because…' She flicked her gaze to Sévère who shook his head minutely. 'We just know. And we can't tell you all the details. I hope you understand.'

'No, I certainly do *not* understand. What I *do* understand is that an injured woman is my guest, and so far she's been telling me only half-truths. Or half lies. I am not quite sure which. I do understand that her husband is the Coroner of Eastern Middlesex — a position of political power, although not considerable. And both have been arguing about forcing a young girl into prostitution.'

'It's not what you think—'

'How, then, is it, Mrs Sévère? Your husband is about to lose my friendship, and I do wonder if I have enough evidence to report him to the authorities.'

'Johnston, listen to me,' Sévère interjected.

Johnston stuck his index finger in Sévère's face. 'I am not talking to you, lad. I am talking to the lady. So, Mrs Sévère, I'm listening.'

Olivia lifted a hand to rub her brow, but remembered the injury. She sucked in a breath, held Johnston's gaze, and told him about her abduction at the age of nine, the various boarding houses and brothels she'd called home, that her marriage to Sévère was a mutual business agreement, and that her past was to be kept secret, so that she could work as his assistant without damaging his reputation. And she told him about Chief Magistrate Frost's appetites.

Johnston stood, placed the saucer he was still holding onto a nearby table, and left the room without a word.

Sévère stared at Olivia, about to speak, when Johnston returned with three glasses and a bottle. He poured whiskey, and handed a glass to Olivia, and another to Sévère.

With a grunt, Johnston tipped his drink into his mouth. His Adam's apple bounced, and he smacked his lips. 'Well, then. May I assume your knowledge of Chief Magistrate's illegal and, I must say, extraordinarily disgusting activities stems from personal experience?'

Olivia dipped her chin.

Johnston harrumphed, refilled his glass, and hurried the contents down his throat.

'By the Queen's mammary glands,' he muttered. 'I agree with your wife, Sévère. Do not use an innocent as bait. Do you have a trustworthy midwife at your disposal?'

Sévère shook his head no.

'In that case, you will need a surgeon or physician whom you can trust. And I don't mean to stitch up your wife every time she's injured. Well...that, too. But what you need is a medical man who is discreet and ever at your disposal. One who is qualified to testify at court that a girl's maidenhead is no longer intact, and that physical evidence clearly shows she's been taken against her will.'

Sévère coughed. 'Are you volunteering?'

'Of course I am. Why else would I venture such a forthright speech?'

'I think the swelling is going down,' Olivia said. A fat leech let go of her brow and dropped to her lap with a soft *plop*.

# EDWINE

*E*dwine's gaze hurried across the note. Her hand twitched and the small paper fluttered to the floor. Hastily, she picked it up. Had she read correctly? Yes, she had. There was no doubt. After all, he had typed it:

*Wear this and meet me by the tigers.*

She felt herself blushing. Her gaze dropped back to the package. Her fingers brushed the shimmering fabric. She lifted the garment from its wrappings and gasped. Rupert had sent her the finest chemise she'd ever laid eyes on. Embroidered silk in shades of rose and pink. The sheer garment would reveal more than it hid. Outrageous!

Edwine's blush grew hot.

The room tilted. She sank to the mattress and clapped a hand to her heart, whispering softly to herself, 'He will propose today. Oh my god! Did he speak to father already?'

She looked up, wondering if her sister knew. She probably did. 'You should have warned me, Frances! *He* should have warned me.'

'About what?' Frances was oddly flushed. Much like an overripe apple. Her hair was in disarray and stuck to her sweaty temples.

'What in all the heavens is *wrong* with you?' Edwine asked. 'Are you upset?'

'The boy was rather rude.'

'What boy?'

'The boy who gave me the package, you goose! Rupert's boy.' Frances tried a smile, but it slipped off her mouth and her trembling chin.

Edwine's fickle attention drifted back to Rupert's present. The chemise. Oh gods, the chemise! How much had he paid for it? She picked up the chocolate that lay on a purple, heart-shaped paper, sniffed at it, and stuck it into her mouth. Almond flavours burst on her tongue. Marzipan was her favourite.

'Fetch Ella,' she said. 'I need to change.'

'If she's to help you with *this*,' Frances indicated the chemise as though it were a fat and hairy spider, '...she'll tell Mother before we can make it to the coach.'

Edwine eyed her sister, her triumphant, but strangely nervous expression, and wondered if Frances begrudged her her happiness.

Edwine brushed the thought away, and put on a friendly face. 'Would you, dear sister?'

Frances pulled up a shoulder, as though she didn't care either way.

WHEN THEY REACHED THE ZOO, Edwine could barely contain herself. The prospect of seeing Rupert and being asked for her hand in marriage was making her skin prickle. Her heart felt unusually heavy, and she wondered if she were quite ready for him.

She clicked her tongue. Of course she was ready! She'd been wondering for a month when Rupert would finally ask her. In fact, their parents must have met and come to an agreement already. The thought made her stop in her tracks.

Why hadn't anyone told her? Perhaps Rupert had asked her parents and her sister to keep it a secret until he could talk to her in person? So as not to impose on her?

That might be it.

She smiled to herself, feeling lucky to have found such a thoughtful man. All of a sudden, she grew hot. The chemise clinging to her bare skin was giving her impure thoughts. Bawdy, even! As if Rupert were already laying his beautiful hands on her. Her breath shortened. Was this what a woman felt in such moments? Odd. It was almost…painful.

She spotted the building where the large cats were kept. The stink of urine burnt in her nostrils. How could Rupert possibly consider this place romantic? What *was* he thinking?

A wave of nausea ripped through her. The corset was hurting her, squeezing her, stretching her skin too tight.

Unbearable. Her legs felt like water. She stumbled, and her sister caught her elbow.

'Frances?' she whispered as her vision blurred, grew yellow around the edges, and finally winked out. 'Why does it hurt so much?'

The darkness around her did a backflip, and Edwine could no longer control her limbs.

———

'WE HAD ANOTHER INCIDENT,' Sévère said when Olivia entered the dining room.

'Is that so?'

He looked up, his gaze touching upon the bruises around her eye and her mouth. He decided to say nothing, for she very much disliked his fussing. Instead, he tried humour, 'I see. You were fraternising with the enemy.'

She flicked an eyebrow at him — the one that wasn't bruised — then she sat, and reached for the tea. 'Thank you for last night. It was very refreshing and enjoyable.'

'It was?' He folded the morning papers. 'I thought it was rather…painful. By the by, why do we sound like a married couple?'

'I'm working hard at keeping up the pretence.'

He stopped chewing.

'That's…not how I meant it, Sévère.'

'To keep up the pretence it would rather help if you addressed me by my given name.'

She signalled neither agreement nor disagreement. The word *Gavriel* clung to her tongue, reluctant to slip out. She'd called him that when they'd consummated their marriage.

She gazed at the shimmering film that floated on her tea, and wondered why she couldn't say that one word to him. Perhaps referring to him by his family name — her family name — created the distance she needed in order to feel safe? Was she afraid of him? No, she certainly was not. But feeling close to a man was something she couldn't imagine. Not in a hundred years.

Through her lashes, she stole a glance at him. His hair had an odd shade between brown and blonde, and currently needed a cut. He had shaved this morning, for the stubble from the previous night was gone. His cheekbones and nose seemed sharper than usual, and shadows clung to his eyes.

Had he slept at all? Had he gone out again after they had returned from Johnston's? How often did he enjoy other women? She didn't even know if he had a lover, or if he visited prostitutes. No, he wasn't the type of man who took a lover. It was…impractical, too intimate and time consuming.

She cocked her head. How often did he think of her as a whore? How often did he wonder what it would take to get her into his bed? Would he try the stick or the carrot?

Upon her scrutiny, Sévère looked up from his papers, frowning. 'Were you saying something?'

'We do indeed sound like an old couple.'

He shrugged. 'There are worse things, I'm sure. Now, I would appreciate it if you would tell Rose to cease her stink bomb assaults on Higgins and the horses, else I shall find myself unable to hold off an assault on the…erm…

What might that thing up in the attic be called? Her dinosaur cave? A witch's hovel?'

'It's a *castle*. I thought that was obvious. She and I conquered it. We drove out the evil king and his soldiers with cannon fire from our pirate ship.'

Sévère blinked. 'You did what?'

Her mouth twitched.

'Excuse me,' he continued, '...but aren't you a grown woman?'

'You know, Sévère, sometimes I think a laugh would do you good. Shake off etiquette and do something silly from time to time.'

He opened his mouth, shut it, and smirked. 'How, then, would you describe our nightly activities?'

'Useful.' She decapitated an egg with a swing of her butter knife. 'Adventurous, reckless, and wonderful. Definitely not silly.'

He sighed. 'Well, then. Let me be responsible for adventurous, reckless, and wonderful while you are responsible for silly and...whatever it is a woman feels the urge to do.'

Her shoulders stiffened. She placed the spoon aside, and cleared her throat. 'Funny. I have an entirely different view of what distinguishes man from woman.'

'Predator and prey, I know.' He feigned a yawn.

Her jaw clenched.

'You do know this is your weakest spot, do you not?' he said. 'Whenever I wish to discombobulate you, I let out an idiotic *men are so and women are so* statement. And every time you jump at it right away. You fluff up your plumage and look at me as if I were the epitome of prejudice. But it's you who can't overcome prejudice, not I. Otherwise, I would hardly have found myself able to marry you.'

She gifted him a sweet smile. 'Oh, well. Fret not, *husband*, for you will be rid of me in but two and a half years. Then you can marry a decent woman who warms your bed whenever you tell her to.'

'Whatever you wish, *wife*. Now, let us finish our breakfast in a civilised manner. We are meeting Johnston in a few hours and it would look suspicious if my eyes were gouged out. Besides, we still have to get through said two and a half years without murdering each other.'

---

'She collapsed yesterday at noon,' Johnston said, and leant against the doorframe to his ward. 'She and her sister visited the zoo. You've read the witness statements?'

Sévère grunted confirmation. The police had taken Miss Edwine Mollywater's body to the morgue before anyone had thought to notify the coroner. Naturally, a herd of onlookers had trampled the crime scene before evidence could be secured.

'She being young and healthy, the police wished to consult a physician. Dr Edison examined her. You've probably read his report.'

'We did.'

Johnston flicked his gaze to Olivia. He still felt a slight discomfort whenever Sévère mentioned discussing post-mortems in detail with his young wife.

'The results of my examination differ insignificantly from Dr Edison's. The cause of death appears to be natural.'

'"Appears" is not a word one often finds in your conclusions.'

'I couldn't find anything, Sévère. That's the truth. You know me to be thorough.'

Sévère nodded, a frown carving his brow. 'My intuition tells me someone sped up her demise.'

'Well, my dear lad, I had the same feeling. But evidence is lacking. Perhaps she was killed by witchcraft.' With a wink, the surgeon bade his farewell.

## JOHNSTON

'Dr Johnston, sir?' A sharp *rat-tat-tat* of knuckles against wood accompanied the warbling voice.

Johnston's fingers slipped off his waistcoat buttons.

His wife closed the last two buttons for him, and said, 'She probably forgot to take her medicine.'

'What is it?' he called, squinting at the milky looking glass.

'Dr Johnston! You must come quick! Mrs Frank is dying!'

'Yet again.' Johnston puffed up his cheeks, and took the bowler his wife held out to him. He stopped before placing it on his head, and tried to flatten his unruly hair. To no avail. 'It's getting worse with age, it seems.'

'I like your mop of wires.'

He lifted an eyebrow. 'Mop of wires?'

Molly Johnston reached up, and tweaked a corner of

his moustache. 'I wish you a pleasant evening with the Coroner. But don't forget Mrs Frank is dying.'

'How could I with the racket her housekeeper is making?' He gave Molly a soft kiss, and brushed his whiskers across her cheek. 'It certainly is one of those days,' he mumbled.

One of those days when half the neighbourhood claimed to be at death's door.

They usually weren't — the crying and kicking were good indications of life wriggling through flesh unabated. It was the quiet ones who worried him.

Mrs Frank's *dying* didn't worry him in the least. On several occasions she had tried to convince him that her being short of breath was proof of an impending heart attack, and the inability to pass wind a sure sign of cancerous growths in her guts.

Unhurried, he grabbed his doctor's bag from a chest of drawers, opened the door and clapped eyes on the Franks' housekeeper. She wrung her hands as if she felt no need to keep her fingers functional and attached.

With a gentle but firm voice Johnston said, 'Please lead the way, Miss Appleton, and tell me what ails your mistress this time.' Over his shoulder he called to his maid, 'Send notice to Coroner Sévère,' and, seeing the shock on Miss Appleton's face, he added, 'Not to worry. The Coroner and I share a glass of brandy from time to time, and it seems I must keep him waiting tonight.'

They crossed the street and went into Mr Frank's house, all the while the housekeeper providing a flood of information on her mistress's complaints: There's a great weight on her chest. She can barely breathe. Her heart again. Couldn't he give her more of the medicine? Shouldn't he forbid her to tie her corset so tight? Wouldn't it be better if…

Johnston entered the bedroom and almost stumbled. A chandelier was fully lit. Candles — ten or fifteen — spilt golden light across bedside tables, windowsills, and a coffee table. Mrs Frank lay prone, dressed in what seemed to be her finery: a dark-green velvet dress with lace at the throat and wrists, lace gloves, leather boots strung around slender ankles. Her ribcage barely moved. Her husband knelt at her feet.

That was when Johnston knew he should have hurried.

'Open the windows!' he said sharply, and bent over his patient.

'Mrs Frank?' He patted her cheek. She opened her eyes and focused on him with some difficulty. Her skin was clammy, her face pale.

He asked her about her symptoms, and she attempted to speak but it seemed her tongue was too heavy.

'Did she complain about pain in her chest?' he asked Mr Frank, to confirm what the housekeeper had told him.

'Y-yes.'

Breath crawled lazily through Mrs Frank's windpipe, and Johnston lost no time with etiquette. He rolled her onto her side, unbuttoned the back of her dress and, with the help of Mr Frank and the housekeeper, swiftly peeled off dress and corset.

The damp chemise stuck to her skin. Her ribs sharp against the silk. He palpated her through the fine fabric, examined her eyes and mouth, and pressed his wooden stethoscope to her ribcage. Two quick beats, and then silence. One beat. Silence. Three beats. Silence.

Her chest stopped moving.

'Rub her legs!' He barked as he bent Mrs Frank's head back, and opened her mouth wide. There were no objects blocking her airway. Mr Frank was frantically patting his wife's feet. 'Harder, bloody damn! Rub the whole length of her legs. Help her blood circulate.'

At that, panic seemed to grab Mr Frank, and he rubbed and kneaded, his rough palms tearing holes in Mrs Frank's expensive silk stockings.

Johnston lifted her upper body and slammed his flat hand against her back three times, then laid her back down and blew breath into her mouth. He searched for his stethoscope. It must have rolled under the bed. He pressed his ear against her breast, massaged her chest, breathed for her, and listened again.

Their efforts continued for a while — for how long precisely, neither man could have said — but when Johnston stopped and straightened up, wiped the perspiration from his brow, and tapped his index finger against Mrs Frank's eyeball to ascertain there was no reaction and the patient was quite dead, Mr Frank still rubbed and rubbed.

Johnston squeezed the man's shoulder until he ceased his desperate attempts at resurrecting his wife. He slumped forward, head low, hands wrapped around her ankles.

'I will give the certificate of death. Will she be laid out here?'

Mr Frank nodded and wiped his eyes. 'I wish... I wish we'd had more time.'

Johnston picked up a small brown bottle, labelled *Tincture of Digitalis,* from the night stand and checked its contents. Almost full. He nodded to himself. The symptoms weren't those of a digitalis poisoning anyway. Mrs Frank's heart had simply given up its long struggle.

DR JOHNSTON PAID THE CABBIE, and caught his breath. You are getting too old for this, laddie, he told himself.

The summer heat wasn't doing him any good. His palms were itching, and a peculiar burn was spreading to his wrists. His face felt too hot. An odd sensation filled his mouth. As if a wad of cotton were stuffed under his tongue. He pressed two fingers to his carotid artery. There was a stutter. He wondered if he should consider retirement.

But the thought of a comfy armchair, a drink, and a stimulating discussion with his friend distracted him from the shortcomings of his ageing body. Besides, what else could one expect at fifty-seven?

He knocked at the door to Sévère's house, and was admitted. Netty took his hat, brushed it off, and placed it onto the hatstand. He climbed the stairs, his breath becoming shorter the farther he ascended. The door to Sévère's smoking room stood ajar.

'Did someone die?' Sévère asked with a twitch of his mouth.

'Indeed she did. A matter of time. The patient has had a weak heart for years.'

Sévère's expression sobered. 'I apologise for the poor

jest. Would a brandy improve your mood? Or a coffee? Tea?'

'I've been thinking about that excellent brandy of yours for hours now.' He took the offered glass and tipped it down his tingling gullet. His tongue felt like a dead fish, his throat clenched, and his skin was all drawn up. He looked up at Sévère.

'You look ill, Johnston.'

Johnston pulled at his collar. 'I must have caught influenza. The hospital is full to the brim. You wouldn't believe how many patients were brought in today.' He touched his brow. Sweaty. Clammy. His hands felt as though he'd dug into a nest of ants. A queer symptom.

'Influenza? Really?'

Johnston blinked, looked down at his hands, and curled his fingers. 'Strangely intense.' A mere mutter. His gaze flickered to the brandy. 'I might be needing a holiday.'

Sévère stood. 'I'll arrange for the carriage and tell Netty to call a doctor for you. Is there anyone you prefer?'

Johnston waved Sévère's concerns away. 'Pour another brandy and allow me a few moments of respite from this…utterly mad day.'

'Johnston, you should see yourself. You looked like death when you walked in, and now it's even—'

'I'm a surgeon, I know what I need,' Johnston protested, a little too loud. He cleared his sticky throat, blinking the wavering black spots from his vision. 'I need rest. Don't bother your driver. I'll catch a hansom.'

He grabbed the armrest and pushed himself up. God, if only his skin didn't feel so tight. When did the symptoms appear? This afternoon? He couldn't quite recall. He rubbed his neck and decided to seriously consider retirement, when suddenly, the room tipped aside.

A hand grabbed his elbow and steadied him.

'Dammit, Johnston. You pigheaded old bastard! At least allow me to walk you downstairs, get you into my brougham and drive you home.'

'I hate it when people mother me.' His voice sounded far off.

They made it out to the corridor, and Johnston was surprised at how fast he was deteriorating. What was the mortality rate of influenza this year, he wondered. One percent? Three percent? The hold Sévère had on his arm was painful. His skin felt as if it was tearing beneath his grip. 'God, how my hands burn! Sévère, you are hurting my arm.'

At once, Sévère let go of him. 'Johnston, I don't care what you think this is, or how much of an expert you are. I'll call for a physician as soon as—'

From the centre of his failing vision Johnston spotted the stairs. He felt as though a giant had picked him up and let him float a few inches above the world. His vision blurred. The walls turned a strange greenish yellow, wobbled, and the stairs approached slowly. He didn't know what was up and what was down. His chest and head hurt. He wondered how he had reached the bottom of the stairwell. And his skin! God, how his skin was smarting.

Sévère's face appeared. Eyes big as saucers. Johnston knew this expression all too well. He looked like someone whose friend was dying. How curious.

Johnston opened his mouth to speak, but words wouldn't come. Darkness closed in on him like a fist. All he felt was the weight, the burning and prickling driving him to madness. And this one, all-important thought that kept him tied to life for a stuttering heartbeat longer: *Molly*.

OLIVIA

*T*he sound of running feet. Down the corridor, and a short moment later, back up. Olivia stood, and Rose's fingers slipped off her braid. Her thick black hair unfurled as she walked to the door and opened it. The corridor was empty. At the far end, Sévère's door stood ajar, agitated voices sounding from the stairwell beyond it.

Olivia pulled the lapels of her night robe close, and exited her room, Rose in her wake. The first thing she saw was Sévère hunched at the bottom of the stairs, a hand wrapped around a prone man's throat.

Her feet faltered.

Johnston.

'Go back to your room, Rose.'

A gaggle of servants stood behind the two men, pale-faced, hands pressed to mouths.

Olivia forced her feet forward, down. Goosebumps prickled on her arms, her neck. Her eyes stuck firmly to the two men, she realised that Sévère's fingers weren't wrapped around Johnston's throat, but lingered softly at his carotid artery.

'The brougham is ready, sir,' Higgins announced.

Sévère showed no reaction.

'Sir?'

Olivia stepped over Johnston's legs, avoided looking at his open eyes, the gaping mouth.

She touched Sévère's shoulder, and said with a voice so hoarse she barely recognised it as her own, 'Gavriel, we need to take him to hospital.'

For a long moment, he did not answer, and the silence rang louder in her ears than a sharp cry. And then Sévère whispered, 'Six minutes.'

'Six m… What?'

'Six minutes!' With a growl, he chucked his watch against the wall. 'His heart stopped beating the moment he hit the floor, perhaps already before he fell. It hasn't been beating for a full six minutes.' He looked up at her, and the paleness of his eyes made her think of a knife's edge, well honed.

'We need to inform his wife,' she said.

His gaze flickered toward the servants and back to Johnston. A slow nod. 'Netty, send for Dr Taylor of London Hospital. Tell him the coroner requires him to perform a postmortem at once. Someone please inform the mortuary that we'll be needing a table. Olivia, be so kind as to inform Mrs Johnston.'

'What happened?' she whispered.

Sévère swallowed and shook his head as though not quite sure how to answer. Olivia knelt and placed a hand on his arm. 'I can't just tell her that her husband is dead. She'll want to know what happened.'

He inhaled, and sat up straighter. 'He looked unwell. Very pale. He said he might have caught influenza. I didn't believe it, because he seemed to be getting worse by the minute. I told him I'd put him into my brougham and send him home. He complained about me mothering him.' A low chuckle slipped from his throat. He lowered his head, and continued. 'I helped him walk down the corridor. Then he complained about pain in his hands and arm. When we reached the landing, he... His body stiffened and he...fell. I believe he must have been unconscious already.'

He shook off her hand and stood with some difficulty. His weak leg had been curled up under him for too long. The knuckles of his hand turned white as he leant heavily on his cane. A trembling ran through his left side.

She rose to grab his elbow for support and helped him sit on the stairs. 'The crutch?' she asked.

He nodded. 'In my bedroom.'

---

OLIVIA STARED AT THE DOOR. She'd been there a few times. Johnston was refreshingly unconventional and humorous. Had been. His wife was quiet and reserved, but friendly. Practical. Both feet on the ground. Never pretentious enough to seem the wife of a leading expert in medicine. Somehow, Olivia managed to lift her arm and rap the knocker against the door. The housekeeper opened. 'Mrs Sévère?'

'I need to speak to Mrs Johnston.'

The housekeeper peeked over Olivia's shoulder, then pushed the door open to admit the late guest. 'Is anything the matter with the doctor?'

'I need to speak to Mrs Johnston,' she repeated, hoarse. 'I'll wait in the parlour.'

A few moments later, Mrs Johnston sat down on the couch next to Olivia. She didn't say "hello," or "what is it," didn't enquire about the bruise on Olivia's face. She just sat and looked her full in the eye.

Olivia opened her mouth, and shut it again. Her throat clenched shut and a tear rolled down her face. Puzzled, she touched her cheek.

'Well?' Mrs Johnston said. There was ice in her voice, as though she knew or suspected what was to come.

Olivia reached for Mrs Johnston's hand, and was rewarded with an incredulous stare. It felt like a slap.

'Is he hurt?'

'He's dead.'

Mrs Johnston stood abruptly. A strand of her greying hair slipped from her severe bun. It made her look fragile, about to shatter into many pieces. 'I knew it would happen this way.'

'What… What do you mean?'

'That one night someone would come to my door and tell me he's gone.' Mrs Johnston unfurled a fist, and looked down at her trembling fingers. 'And that nothing would prepare me for it.' She cleared her throat and straightened her spine. 'How did he die?'

It took Olivia a moment to collect her thoughts. She took in Mrs Johnston's carefully guarded expression, the effort it took her to keep up the facade of the hostess. The effort to not sink to the floor, weeping.

'I… I don't know the particulars,' Olivia began. 'I saw him lying at the bottom of the stairs, Sévère kneeling by his side. He said that your husband had been looking quite ill, and had complained about pain in his arm. That he had helped him walk out. He wanted to send him home in the brougham. They made to descend the stairs, and then…your husband lost consciousness and fell down the stairwell. My husband found no heartbeat.'

A long moment of silence. And then, 'He has a healthy heart. It cannot just stop beating. He's a healthy man. He cannot just…' Mrs Johnston set her jaw and turned to look out the window. A lone street lamp pierced the dark.

'Sévère has ordered a postmortem examination. It will be performed tonight. My heartfelt—'

Mrs Johnston's spine snapped to attention. 'I don't wish to hear *heartfelt* words from a woman who doesn't know what *heartfelt* means. You don't know love.' She pressed her fists against the window sill. 'I wish to be alone now. Tell them to send Peter… Tell them to send my husband back home as soon as they are…done. I wish to see him in the morning. Latest.'


A FETID SUMMER breeze pressed through the windows as Olivia took the brougham back home. She wondered if it had always been obvious to Mrs Johnston that her marriage was an arrangement. She doubted Dr Johnston had mentioned the truth to his wife. Or maybe he had. Olivia couldn't bring herself to worry about it.

She entered Sévère's house — her home, although she didn't see it that way, not truly. A temporary arrangement, valid for another two and a half years. Had she ever felt at home anywhere? Yes, when she was little. But she couldn't remember much of what it was like.

The hallway was empty. Voices seeped up from the basement. She walked down and met an agitated scullery maid. 'They are in the laundry room,' the maid squeezed out, and fled toward the kitchen.

Alf raced through the corridor, his cap flapping in one hand, hair on end, eyes gleaming. 'The morgue is full! They'll cut him up right here!'

Olivia grabbed his shoulder and turned him around. 'If I see a hair of you tonight, you'll regret it bitterly. Now, off with you!'

'You can't watch, either. They sent the womenfolk away.'

She ignored him, and set off for the laundry room. Sévère would be there.

Wearily, she turned the knob and pushed the door open a crack.

'Rigor mortis is setting in. Temperature in the rectum is—'

A rushing noise filled Olivia's ears. She felt sick to the bone.

Pull yourself together. Three deep breaths. There, now. Only forward, no looking back.

She slipped into the room, grateful to find Sévère's back blocking most of the view. She found herself able to take one step farther in. She glued her gaze to the stone tiles, but she couldn't shut her ears. Most of what was being said was terminology she could recall from her nights with Simon.

Do not think of that now.

She heard the questions directed at Sévère, and his brief answers.

The sounds of bone giving way under the teeth of a saw.

The howling in her ears intensified. Icy cold coated her skin like a wet blanket.

She knew that her knees would fold soon. She bit the inside of her cheek, her tongue, the pain helping her to remain upright. She placed her left index finger onto her right wrist and counted the pulse.

Wet noises. The doctor — what was his name? — spoke of stomach contents, lung and liver, spleen. No signs of a poisoning. Sévère insisting that something must be amiss, and the doctor answering gruffly, 'If you say so, coroner.'

A rivulet of blood crawled into view, with dark red clumps lazily drifting along. She tried to look away, but where to lay her eyes instead? Sévère's back perhaps?

She bit her tongue so hard that blood formed a puddle in her mouth. A mistake. Blood on the floor, blood in her mouth, the sounds of knife and saw. Screeching in her ears.

A hand fastened around her arm and she was led out of the room. The door shut. She sank to the floor and buried her face in her hands, a sob erupting from her chest.

The feeling of relief lasted only a moment. Anger followed. She slapped her face and pinched her cheeks, then pressed her knuckles against the cold floor, stood, opened the door and entered again.

Sévère whipped his head around, his expression incredulous, irritated. She held up her hand, and stepped around him.

Her eyes took in the sight. She told her mind to analyse, only analyse, and to put a damper on her heart. 'Do you believe he has been poisoned?' she asked.

'It's a possibility.'

'Explain it to me.' Johnston's ribcage gaped. There was blood in the coarse salt-and-pepper hair that covered his chest, part of his belly, and his pubes. His mouth was slack. Saliva wetted his lips. Buckets held organs. The lungs, the liver, and smaller ones that she guessed must be kidneys, spleen, and—

'He has never complained about a weakness of the heart,' Sévère answered. 'He mentioned influenza. But the symptoms came on too fast and were too violent. I can't know how long he'd had them before he arrived, but when he entered the house, he looked pale, ill.'

He directed his attention to a row of brown glass bottles standing on a chair nearby. Clumps of tissue samples shone through. 'These will be analysed by a toxicology expert of London Hospital. If Johnston died of poisoning, we'll know it in a fortnight.'

He did not ask her if she was all right. But he moved a step closer to her. She bent forward a little, pointing to a dent at Johnston's cheekbone. 'Was he hit?'

'He fell down the stairs.'

The doctor cut along Johnston's hairline and pulled down the upper half of his face, then sliced into his scalp and pulled it aside, too. He cut the bone with a saw, then used a small hammer to crack the skull along the groove he'd made. The skull cap came off. Olivia thought of a breakfast egg. Her stomach grumbled in protest. A flood of bile filled her mouth, mixing with the blood from her tongue. She swallowed, and cleared her throat.

'Olivia.' A warning. Don't waste my time, it seemed to say.

'I am well, thank you.' She broadened her shoulders and held her chin high.

'Anything yet?' Sévère asked the surgeon.

'As far as I can see, the man was as healthy as a horse. I assume you will want a second opinion? Of course you do. I'll call for a colleague and send the samples to Dr Barry.'

---

OLIVIA FOUND him in his smoking room. The door stood ajar, and cigar smoke quivered over the threshold. Sévère's gaze was firmly attached to a spot behind her.

'Will you be all right?' she asked.

'Why did you do it? There was no need for you to attend the postmortem.' His focus slid toward her face.

'Wasn't it you who said that I must educate myself on all facets of criminal investigation?' And then, softer, 'He was your friend. No one should have to do that alone. I'm… I'm sorry.'

He gave her a small nod. 'I need to be alone now, Olivia. Good night.'

Dawn began to creep through the windows.

# SECOND ACT

*Rage,*
*rage against the dying*
*of the light.*

Dylan Thomas

# AFTER THE BLOOD

*R*ose slid aside the door of the laundry closet. Every time it snagged in its rails, her heart hiccuped. Her stomach felt hollow, and she was sure she'd never be able to put food into it again. Ever.

She kept her eyes fastened to the tiles. Her face felt numb. Everything felt numb, except for the horrible buzzing in her head and chest.

For the first time in her short life, Rose wished she hadn't been so nosy, hadn't wanted to see the dead man. The one she'd seen back at her mother's hadn't looked so bad. That one had looked like someone asleep, deep asleep. But this man here… All the blood and entrails were too much to bear. She wished she could burn the images from her mind.

With a hand pressed over her eyes, and the other to brace herself at the edge of the sliding door, she climbed out of the closet.

But Rose being Rose, her small hand acted on its own

volition, and spread her fingers just a little, creating a gap large enough to peek through.

She stopped in her tracks.

He didn't look all that bad anymore. The doctor had stitched him back together, and a sheet covered him up to his chest. The seams were ugly and thick, especially around the head. She turned away, pressed her body to the wall, and proceeded toward the exit. Her hand was already touching the doorknob when she thought, perhaps he shouldn't be all alone in the laundry room. It was cold and awfully uncomfortable.

But she was so tired. She hadn't slept the whole night. Her body ached, and she had to go to school soon. Her stomach was grumbling. Perhaps she could eat a bite after all.

But she should at least say farewell to Dr Johnston. Yes, that she could do. He'd been kind to her.

Once the decision was made, it was easier to look at him and view him as who he was: not a bloody husk of a man, but Dr Johnston, Mr Sévère's friend. She approached him respectfully and took his hand in both of hers. There was a drop of blood on his palm.

She spat in her hand, and rubbed at his skin. She didn't want to use her dress to wipe the stain off. Blood was so difficult to wash out. And although his flesh felt so cold and stiff that the hairs on her neck prickled with revulsion, Rose rubbed her small hand over Johnston's big one until it was all clean and dry.

'I'm sorry,' she whispered. She didn't know what one was supposed to say to the dead, and she certainly wasn't going to kiss his cheek in farewell, so she simply wished him a good night, curtsied, and slipped through the door.

Once she reached the stairwell, she found she had no stomach for eating, or talking about what she had done, or anything at all but curling up next to Olivia.

She rushed up to Olivia's room and entered quietly. Olivia was sitting on her bed, chewing the inside of her cheek. A candle stump was guttering on the bedside table.

They exchanged a silent glance. Rose kicked off her shoes and sneaked into Olivia's bed, pulled up her knees, and pressed her back against Olivia's warm side.

'Where have you been?' Olivia asked softly.

Rose shrugged, pressed closer, and rubbed her prickling hand. She felt the touch of Olivia's fingers on her hair, felt how it helped her unclench her stomach. She shut her eyes and tried to think only of the soft touch and the rhythm of shared breaths.

A few moments later, she retched on the bedside carpet.

---

THE WARM and buttery taste of fresh rolls went unnoticed by Sévère. He could have eaten sawdust; it wouldn't have made a difference. The morning papers lay next to his plate, untouched.

Olivia entered and wished him a good morning. He automatically nodded and sipped at his tea. When she asked him how he was doing, he didn't know how to answer, so he talked about what was occupying his mind.

'The postmortem examinations rendered no evidence

which could adequately account for the death. All organs were found to be healthy.'

'Hmm,' said Olivia and took her seat.

It was this "hmm" that nearly threw him off. Had she asked him how he felt, or told him she was sorry, he could have dealt out a blow of sarcasm, and then carried on with his own thoughts.

His fist hit the table. The cutlery bounced to the floor.

'I know. To have to wait for the results of the toxico-logical analyses for two weeks is...' She groaned. 'It makes me itch all over. Did Johnston have enemies?'

Sévère squeezed his eyes shut for a moment, collected himself, and said, 'None that I know of. We have to track his every move from the moment his heart stopped beat-ing, all the way back to where and when he met his killer. At present, everyone is a suspect.'

'Even his wife?'

'Even his wife.'

'I don't think she did it,' Olivia said as she stuck her knife into the *pate de foie gras* and spread it on her roll.

'Never disregard a potential suspect because of your emotions and limited experience. I've met Molly three times. You've met her four times. Everyone is a different person unobserved.'

'Did *you* do it?'

An unexpected grin flickered across his face. 'I am the only person I can exclude as a suspect.'

'I didn't do it, either.'

'You have no motive. Well, we could construct a motive of jealousy. *My husband spent more evenings with him than with me.* Which is untrue, of course. How does your eye feel?'

'Fine, thank you.' She caught his gaze. 'Rose watched the postmortem.'

'Excuse me?' It took him a moment to take in what she'd said. 'How?'

'She hid in the laundry closet and slipped out only an hour or so ago. She's taken ill. I allowed her to stay in my bed.'

'Where does this girl get her mad ideas? An eight-year-old attending postmortems?' Sévère huffed and shook his head.

'She was curious to see what had happened to Johnston. She had no idea he was to be cut up.'

'She didn't make a peep.' He frowned. 'I wonder why.'

'Her mother taught her early on how to be quiet. Rose was repeatedly locked in the closet of her mother's room and told to peek through the keyhole, so she would learn how to satisfy a client.'

The pulse on Sévère's throat visibly quickened. His hand holding the tea cup shook. He set the cup down and cleared his throat.

'Which brings me to a question I meant to ask you last night,' Olivia said. 'Did the Home Secretary respond to your request for a new decree to protect children from abduction?'

He pulled in a deep breath. 'Yes, he did. It was his usual "We are looking into the matter." Letters are of no use, obviously. I will pay him a visit next week. Would you join—'

A knock interrupted him. Netty stepped in, kneading

her apron. 'Sir, the police wish to talk to you. They are waiting in the parlour. Would you like me to offer them tea and biscuits?'

'That won't be necessary, thank you, Netty. Please inform the gentlemen that I'll join them shortly.'

After Netty had left, he addressed his wife, 'Remember, we are not only witnesses. We are suspects, too. That is, if the police are any good at investigating a crime. Keep this in mind when you speak to them.'

SÉVÈRE ENTERED THE PARLOUR, Olivia one pace behind him. Everyone took a seat. Inspector Height whipped out his notebook and pencil. He was the only man in the room who knew of Olivia's past. Other than Sévère himself, of course. Height had given his word to keep her secret — that is, until the law should require him to do otherwise.

Courtesies were exchanged, and Sévère gave Height an account of what had occurred, and the results of the postmortems.

'Will you be holding an inquest?' Height enquired.

Puzzled, Sévère said, 'Of course I will. Do you see any reason why I should not? If you believe I am unable to conduct an investigation into Dr Peter Johnston's death, say so now, and send notice to the Home Office to ask for a replacement.'

'I was referring to the cause of death.' Height tapped his pencil against his notes and read, 'No evidence for death by violence or poison.' He looked up at Sévère. 'I can't see anything suspicious about Dr Johnston's death. Can you?'

Sévère arched an eyebrow. 'Is there anything else I can help you with, Inspector?'

Height produced a soft groan. 'When do you plan to hold the inquest?'

'As soon as I have the results of the toxicological analyses.'

Height nodded, shut his notebook, and stood. 'My constables and I will now take the statements of other household members. A mere routine. You understand, I hope.'

'I do. And I'd appreciate if you began with my wife. We have work to do. Olivia, meet me in my office when you've answered his questions. Gentlemen, you will excuse me now.' With that, Sévère pulled himself up on his crutch and left the parlour.

He climbed the stairs, entered his bedroom, and locked the door. Hastily, he opened the drawer to his night stand. There was the small jar he wanted. He pushed down his trousers and sat, uncapped the jar and spread the unguent onto his aching leg. The prickling of a thousand small needles was followed by numbness and the sensation of his limb being wrapped in clouds.

He sighed in relief, pulled his trousers back up, and went down to his office.


WHEN OLIVIA ENTERED, she was unusually pale. 'Height asked me to show him where Johnston fell. The stairs, your smoking room. He even examined the bottle of brandy. And he pocketed a sample.'

Sévère gazed at her through a curtain of smoke. His cigar was, as usual, smouldering in the crystal ashtray, untouched. 'Hmm,' he said.

'Molly Johnston said she wants the body. This morning, if possible. Is he…presentable?'

Sévère gazed at the desk, took a deep breath and slowly let it out again. 'He's stitched back up and dressed. I'll have Higgins deliver Johnston to his wife after we return.'

'Return from where?'

'From Johnston's home. We'll first pay his wife a visit and then the household of the patient Johnston treated before he came here. We will find the cab driver who drove him. We will see everyone he met in the hours before his death, visit every place he went.' Sévère rapped his knuckles against the armrest of his chair. 'I want to know where and when he ate and peed, whom he saw and who saw him. Stripling will deal with the Medley and the Bartlett cases. He'll be delighted to be given more responsibility again. You and I will focus our efforts on finding Johnston's murderer.'

She lowered her head and crossed her arms behind her back.

'Spit it out, Olivia.'

'I've learnt to trust your intuition. But in this case, I have to point out that your judgement might be…clouded.' She looked up, her expression softening. 'Your friend died. And you couldn't help him. It's hard for you to accept that nothing could be done, so you are desperately trying to find something to do now. Have you considered that you might be hunting a ghost?'

'I'm considering that every minute. The problem is that I cannot wait for the toxicological analyses. If Johnston was poisoned, we can't give his murderer time to destroy evidence and disappear. A hunt must begin while the tracks are fresh.'

He stubbed out the cigar, and stood. 'Grab your bonnet. We are leaving.'

───────

'HAVE YOU MY HUSBAND?' was the first thing Molly Johnston said when they entered her house.

'My driver will bring him in an hour,' Sévère answered, gaze flat. 'Mrs Johnston, I have reason to believe that your husband's death was not natural. Allow me to express my deepest—'

She slapped his face. 'Stop your gabbing, Sévère. Don't pretend Peter was a stranger to you. He was your *friend*. He spoke fondly of you. If someone has... If someone...' She swallowed audibly, her lips compressed to a sharp line. 'Find out who killed him and be quick about it. I want to see that monster hanged.'

Sévère took her hand into both of his, looked down, and nodded. A promise.

'Tea, Mistress?'

Mrs Johnston straightened her shoulders, told her maid that yes, tea and biscuits were required, and that they would be retreating to the sitting room.

Mrs Johnston sat opposite Olivia and Sévère, a table between them, flowery china and silverware tastefully arranged on the tablecloth.

'I'll tell you everything I know of Peter's day, but I'm afraid it won't help you much,' Mrs Johnston began. 'First, do tell me the results of the postmortem. And please, don't spare me anything.'

Sévère lowered his head in agreement. 'No physical signs to indicate death by violence or poison. He was healthy. But the symptoms I observed were viol…came on quickly. I found this suspicious. So I asked the surgeon to take samples of all his organs. They've been taken to London Hospital and will be tested for poison. I will get the results in a fortnight.'

She gave him a faint nod. 'He left early in the morning. As he usually does. Half past eight, that is. He took a hansom to Guy's, returned at noon — ten minutes past one, I believe — to take lunch with me.'

'Has he routinely done that?' Sévère asked. 'I remember him saying that he had a very busy day.'

'Yes, his afternoon was horrible. An omnibus accident on the Strand. Many were injured. Two…two children died.' She pulled a handkerchief from her sleeve and hurriedly dabbed her eyes. 'Most days he doesn't have the time to come home for lunch. Only once in a while, he… Perhaps two or three days a month.'

'What did he eat that day?'

'We had a light soup of chicken and vegetables, and bread with butter. Tea. And before you ask, he ate what I ate. If someone slipped poison into his food, it would have been in mine as well. And I'm not dead.'

'Did you feel sick?'

'Yes, after I heard that my husband died.'

'What was on the lunch table? A soup bowl, ladle, a plate or bowl for each of you?'

Her gaze dropped to the table cloth, lost and then regained focus. 'Yes.'

'It would have been possible to lace his plate or cutlery with poison. Were there animosities between him and the servants?'

'No. You know him. He is...' She picked up her cup and lifted it to her lips, but did not drink from it. Droplets spilt onto her dress. She set the cup back on the saucer, and placed a napkin in her lap.

'He was a kind and humble man. The servants loved and respected him.'

'What did Johnston usually eat at the hospital? Did he take sandwiches with him or did he buy from street vendors?'

She smiled at her hands. 'I make his sandwiches.' Then she cleared her throat. 'After lunch, he went back to work. A surgery was scheduled. A caesarean section, I believe is what he mentioned. I saw him next in the evening. We ate, then he was about to leave. To visit you.' She looked up. 'And then Mrs Appleton from across the street called for him. She said her mistress was dying. We didn't quite believe it.'

Sévère cocked an eyebrow.

'Mrs Appleton is known to be a tad melodramatic, as is her mistress, Mrs Frank, who has had a long history of minor heart problems. Every time Mrs Frank pales, Mrs Appleton believes she may be dying. Mrs Frank believes it, too.' A small smile lifted her lips. It was gone in a heartbeat.

'I see,' Sévère said. 'He mentioned that he might have caught influenza. Do you know anything about it? Did he show any symptoms last night? You mentioned you'd taken dinner together. What did he eat and was it the same you ate?'

'We had…fish for dinner. Yes, that's what it was. The food was arranged in tureens and platters on the table. If anything had been poisoned, I would be dead now, too. He mentioned that a few influenza patients have been transferred to his ward, because the infectious diseases ward was overcrowded. But he didn't say anything about feeling ill. He…seemed normal. Perfectly normal. Had I known…' Her chin trembled. She flicked her gaze out the window.

Sévère waited for her to regain her composure. Then he said, 'After he went to check on Mrs Frank, did he return or did he go directly to my house?'

'He must have left directly, because I didn't see him after that.' She kept avoiding Sévère's gaze.

'With your permission, I will speak to your servants now, and then visit Mr Frank.'

---

'Mr Frank, my name is Gavriel Sévère. I am Coroner of Eastern Middlesex, and this is my wife and assistant Olivia Sévère. We heard about the death of your wife. Our condolences to you and your family.'

Mr Frank held on to the doorknob, swaying a little. 'The Coroner?'

'We are here to enquire about the previous night. Can you tell us what occurred?'

A cough. A wobbling of knees. The man stepped back. 'The housekeeper is presently attending to my wife. W… washing her body. You don't think… You can't cut her up. I won't allow it!'

'I have not ordered a postmortem examination of your wife. Our enquiries relate to Dr Johnston. He died last night.'

'Dr Johnston? Ex…excuse me, but I am not feeling well.' Mr Frank leant against the wall, and Olivia wrapped her hand around his elbow and led him to a chair. 'Thank you, ah, Mrs…Sévère. My wife…and I were ill, and…' He looked up, a pleading in his eyes. 'Could you come back tomorrow? I promise, I'll answer all of your questions.'

'Would you like to lie down, Mr Frank?' Olivia said softly. 'You are very pale. Perhaps if you lie on the rug and put your feet up on the chair? Yes, like this.' She pushed a pillow under his head, and he shut his eyes. 'Are you feeling better?'

'Yes, thank you,' he whispered.

Olivia jerked her chin at Sévère, and he disappeared from the hallway. He found a set of stairs and walked up to where he assumed the bedroom might be. The doors to all the rooms stood open. Sounds of splashing water came from the farthest door. He entered.

'Mrs Appleton?'

A squeal, and a flannel sailed through the air. The housekeeper turned, and clapped a hand to her bosom.

Sévère introduced himself. His gaze scanned the body, the neatly folded clothes on the bedside table, the *digitalis* bottle, the boots at the side of the bed.

'Mrs Appleton, you called upon Dr Johnston late the previous night to attend to your mistress. May I ask if Dr Johnston ate or drank anything while he was here?'

She yanked a blanket over the exposed body of Mrs Frank, and answered, 'I had not offered him anything. And now that you mention it, I think perhaps I should have. He is ever so helpful.' She blinked, her gaze flew from the body to the coroner, and her mouth fell open. 'Will you cut her open?'

'Why would you think that?'

'Well, you are the Coroner.'

'You have an excellent gift of observation, Mrs Appleton. But no, I didn't come for your mistress. I wish to take your witness statement as to Dr Johnston's visit the previous night. Unfortunately, he died shortly after he left this house. We have reason to believe that he was poisoned.'

Mrs Appleton grabbed the edge of the bed, and sat down.

'Let us begin with the moment you went to fetch Dr Johnston,' Sévère said.

# POISON

*D*ear Coroner Sévère,

*I wish I could give you a positive answer, but neither I nor my colleagues have found a cure for infantile paralysis in its recurring form. However, it may relieve you to know that although several of my patients have experienced a return of all the paralytic symptoms they suffered in childhood, a greater number have experienced no recurrence of symptoms, or the recurrence of only a few of them.*

*This field of research is still very much in its infancy. However, I am presently collecting more data, especially as to the factors that bring on fatigue, pain, and muscle atrophy, as well as data on alleviating substances. Your physician did well in recommending* unguent aconitia *and frequent rest, and asking you to discontinue the use of arsenic, as I too have found it to be inadequate for the treatment of pain in joints and muscles. I fear, however, that the unguent will soon become ineffective, and that you may need opium to be able to sleep. To prevent injuries to joints of ankle and knee, I recommend you wear a brace in addition to your crutch.*

*I take the liberty of including in my letter to you a number of illustrations of the braces, crutches, and chairs manufactured for wealthier patients. The wheeling chairs are of excellent quality and might even be used outside your home should the weather permit.*

*Respectfully,*

*Dr Bedbrock, Edinburgh Medical School*

The letter sank to the desk. Sévère hadn't had great expectations. But, that Bedbrock had nothing useful to add to the diagnosis and bleak outlook that Johnston had already given him, was hard to digest.

Sévère's gaze touched upon the drawings of the wheeling chairs. Disgusted, he pushed the letter aside.

A brief knock and his officer, Stripling, stepped into the room. 'Mr Sévère, the witness statements of—'

'Not now, Stripling.'

'But the witness—'

Sévère slammed his hand flat on the desk. 'Not now, Stripling! Close the bloody door!'

Stripling was about to obey when Olivia squeezed past him. She scanned the desk, Sévère's face, and said, 'Coffee or brandy?'

'Both,' Sévère grumbled.

'You heard him,' she said to Stripling, smiled, and shut the door in his face.

'He hates you,' Sévère said.

'Of course he does. A *woman* stole his respectable position.' She produced a theatrical shudder.

'You didn't steal it. I gave it to you.'

'And the question remains: do facts matter when the ego is hurt?' She sat opposite him and indicated the letter. 'Is this what upset you so? May I?'

With an impatient flick of his wrist, he pushed it toward her.

She leant back and read. The paper in her hand began to quiver. She placed it back on the desk, holding it there for a moment lest it grow bigger and swallow the whole office. 'Would you like to visit Bedbrock?'

'And buy a chair?' he said acidly.

'To learn. To know what you should expect, so you can prepare yourself.'

'Not now.'

She dipped her chin.

There was a knock at the door. She stood and received the refreshments, placed the tray on the desk, but then thought otherwise and moved the brandy to the mantelpiece. 'We'll share a drink later tonight.'

'My merciless wife,' Sévère muttered, folded his hands over his stomach, and regarded her.

'Now,' she began, 'I've thought about what Mr Frank said this morning: Johnston appeared healthy when he entered the house to attend to Mrs Frank. Mrs Johnston made the same observation: Her husband appeared in perfect health when he left his home. Then he took a cab, arrived here, and looked like death. Whatever toxin he was exposed to, it acted extraordinarily quickly.'

She scratched a spot behind her ear. 'He must have ingested it either at Mr Frank's, in the cab, or…here. I believe you and I need to split up. I'll try to find the cabbie, and you talk to Dr Barry. We need to know what poison was used, and how. He *must* have a theory. Was it a powder? A liquid? When the poison is identified, we'll know how quickly it acts, and then we'll know precisely when and where Johnston took it. Sévère, are you all right?'

He blinked. 'My apologies. I wasn't quite...here. Yes, you are correct. Take Stripling with you. He can help to interrogate the driver.'

She snorted. 'No, thank you very much. Stripling is of no help whatsoever. Well, except for doing the tedious paperwork. Besides, interrogation is one of my specialities. Will you be...' She stopped herself. He hated being pitied.

---

A HAIRY FACE and a nose like a tree stump. Words came twisting around a pipe clamped between teeth. 'Gentleman with a doctor's suitcase and half-moon spectacles, you say? Mighta been midnight I seen him. Mighta been later.'

'Did you stop to take another passenger?'

'Nah. Went directly to where he wanted me ter go. Can't quite recall where.' The man scratched his stubbly chin, and pushed his pipe from one corner of his mouth to the other. 'Why you askin?'

'He was poisoned. My husband, who is the Coroner, and I need to find out who did it.'

'Poisoned you say? It wasna me!' He held up both hands.

She thought that a silly reaction, but narrowed her eyes at him, roasting him with a sharp glance and waiting for his mind to speed up the thinking process.

'No, Missus Coroner, I wasna doin it! I *swear!*' He wiped his big nose, spotted the snot track on his sleeve, and quickly rubbed it off on his trousers.

'How did he appear to you when he climbed into your cab? And how did he look when he alighted?'

'Looked like a docter. Both times.'

Olivia wanted to rip off her hat and slap it into the man's face. How did anyone ever solve a crime when witnesses were generally so unreliable? 'Was he all right?' she asked through her teeth. 'Was he tired? Did he say anything?'

'Said where he wants ter go. Dinna look any way paticlar, and I wasna askin. Mind my own business.'

Olivia produced a theatrical sigh. 'My husband won't be happy with me.' She shook her head and looked rather downtrodden.

'Warm his bed, lass, and he'll be all right.' He patted her shoulder, flashed his teeth in what must have been a smile, and tipped his cap. 'Must be off now.' He jumped back onto his cab, clicked his tongue, and winked at her. 'M'lady.' The whip flicked the horse's back, and off he went.

'Cockchafer,' Olivia muttered, and received a loud snort as an answer. A cabbie who'd been waiting nearby must have heard the exchange.

'Don't believe him, Missus. He has a head like a colander. Never remembers a thing, so he makes up colourful stories.'

Olivia looked up at the man. 'Do you, by any chance, know a cabbie who does *not* have a head like a colander?'

He grinned. 'It'll cost you something.'

'And how much would that be?'

'Depends what it is that you want.'

She extracted Sévère's warrant from her skirts, unfolded it, and read it aloud.

'Ah!' The man nodded. 'I just remembered that I have not heard or seen a thing. My apologies, Missus Coroner, but I can't help you. Most unfortunate.' He looked straight ahead, chewed his tobacco, than ejected a long string of brownish saliva onto the pavement.

She stuck her hand into the folds of her skirts and let her coins jingle. At once, the cabbie's attention was drawn back to where she needed it.

Interrogation is much like prostitution, Olivia mused.

---

SÉVÈRE SAT AT HIS DESK. The morning sun shone through the window behind him, lending his head a halo. 'You look terrible.'

'Why, thank you,' Olivia answered, snatched up his coffee cup, tipped the cold contents into her mouth, and placed it back on the saucer. She unlaced her boots, kicked them off, and curled up on a chair. 'I feared you would be sleeping still. I'm glad you aren't. I hate to barge into your bedroom.'

Sévère didn't mention that he, too, had spent the night working. 'I assume chasing down the cabbie proved difficult.'

'Indeed it did. But at last I found him. He took John-ston directly from the Franks' to here. No stops. Nothing notable happened, and nothing notable was to be found in the carriage. No powder, bottle, paper or tinfoil. Nothing. It was a simple, everyday ride. A whole night wasted for nothing. What about you?'

'Have you eaten breakfast?' Sévère asked.

'Let me think… No, not yet. I had a baked potato around midnight, I believe.'

He stood, called for Netty, and told her to bring a tray with food and tea for his wife.

'And coffee, please,' Olivia called over her shoulder, a yawn making her voice hollow.

Sévère took his seat. 'Dr Barry isn't convinced that Johnston was poisoned. He knows of no case similar to what I and Drs Tailor and James, who performed the postmortems, described. Strychnine, arsenic, and cyanide can be excluded with certainty. In a few more days Dr Barry might be able to give us the preliminary results of his extractions. Assuming he's able to extract anything of interest from the organ samples.'

For a few moments, Sévère gazed at the cigar that smouldered in the ashtray, and wished his mind were faster, sharper. But exhaustion was taking its toll. He pressed the heels of his palms against his eyes, and said, 'I have to hold two inquests tomorrow and I don't feel suffi-ciently prepared for either.'

She did not answer. He looked across the desk.

Olivia's eyes were shut, and her chest rose and fell slowly.

He stood, stubbed out the cigar, and quietly let Netty

know that breakfast would have to wait, and that they were not to be disturbed. He picked up a blanket from his footstool and gazed at Olivia's face. The strand of black hair that had come undone, and that now rested on her cheek. The pale bruise around her left eye. The small cut on her upper lip.

He spread the blanket over her and got back to work.

## CHEMISTRY

The two inquests Sévère had held today left him unusually tired. Despite the luxury of a few hours of undisturbed sleep. Despite his leg feeling better, the pain being less pronounced than on previous days. But the fatigue that was tugging at his every limb…

He tried to recall his boyhood, when paralysis had first struck him down. Had tiredness been one of the symptoms? He couldn't say. He'd spent most of his time in bed. There'd been no opportunity to be tired of anything much but boredom, pain, loneliness, and the bedpan.

The clock on the mantlepiece told him it was twenty minutes past two. Time was flying, and work was piling up faster than he and Olivia could get it done. His stomach grumbled, and he put his hand there, wondering if he'd had breakfast. He couldn't recall that, either.

With effort, he stood and reached for the bell rope. Netty arrived a moment later, took his order for "whatever cook has simmering on the stove," and delivered it swiftly.

As he ate, he went through notes on recent cases, ignoring the stack of papers on Johnston's death. If he touched that case now, he wouldn't be able to put it aside for the remainder of the day. And that, he couldn't afford.

Four inquests were scheduled for the following week, and several witness statements were incomplete. The jury for two inquests had not been fully appointed. He made a list of tasks for himself and Stripling, and pulled out the postmortem reports. He swallowed. Johnston had performed them.

A knock startled him.

'Enter,' he said gruffly, but Olivia had already opened the door. She carried a sandwich in one hand, a bowl in the other, and a notebook clamped under her arm. She sat down across from him, and began to shovel food into her mouth.

'That smells delicious. What is it?' he asked.

'Goulash.' She held a spoonful across his desk. He closed his mouth around the offering, and was struck by the familiarity between them. Had this grown, or had it suddenly happened? Had she allowed it, or had he?

'All I got was broth.' He glanced into the now empty plate. 'No one mentioned goulash to me.'

'Cook lets me taste dinner before it's served. All you need to do is go down to the kitchen, say *ohhh!* and *ahhh!* and then you ask what smells so delicious, and if you might have a taste.' She shrugged and tipped the last puddle of goulash into her mouth. 'So,' she said and plopped the bowl onto the desk. 'I went to every single chemist in a two-mile radius around Johnston's home. Which reminds me…'

She bent down and unlaced her shoes, pulled them off and massaged her feet. 'Thank goddess. My toes were suffering a slow death.'

She wiggled her feet, curled her toes, and sat up straight, then snapped open her notebook and leafed though the first pages. 'I'll begin with the negatives. None of Johnston's servants are known to have purchased toxic substances from chemists in the area. Except for a bottle of cough syrup. But Johnston wasn't killed with opium, so that's irrelevant. I even enquired at the fashion boutique across from Johnston's home. They employ a dye chemist who regularly works with thousands of grains of arsenic. But that's irrelevant to us, because arsenic wasn't what killed Johnston.'

She tapped her index finger against paper. 'And then there's Mrs Baker — the char woman who is the only servant not living with the Johnstons, and who comes to their house once a week. She has not purchased anything suspicious. Not at the chemists in the area, nor at any of the chemists in East End, where she resides. However,' Olivia paused to take a bite of her sandwich and brush the crumbs off her notes. 'Mrs Frank was purchasing medicine for her weak heart, medicine that can be used to poison people at high-enough dosages.'

'Digitalis,' Sévère said.

'Yes. Mrs Frank has been taking it for the past eight or nine years, as prescribed by Dr Johnston. He told her to take three drops, three times a day. Their chemist told me that twenty to thirty drops taken at once are lethal. The bottle of digitalis tincture you found on her night stand was almost full. I measured how much fit in the dropper — thirty drops. Then, judging from the loss of volume when taking out one full dropper, I estimated how much might have been taken from the bottle before you confiscated it. Assuming the bottle was full to the brim, one and a half droppers full of digitalis tincture are missing. More than enough to kill Johnston.'

Sévère nodded and picked at his notes. 'Mrs Appleton had the opportunity and the means to poison Johnston. But did she have a motive?' He cocked his head.

Olivia waited.

After a moment of consideration, Sévère continued, 'I am certain that no chemist would know if Molly Johnston was in the possession of poison. She would not be stupid enough to purchase it if she wished to kill her husband. She would simply take it from him.' He frowned and reached toward a cigar stump, struck a match and lit it.

'We may further assume that an intelligent murderer would not purchase a poison near his home.'

'He might not even purchase the whole dose at once,' Olivia mused. 'Sales of arsenic to individuals are limited. A chemist isn't allowed to sell more than a grain to any customer without special authority.'

'Which leaves us with half of London as suspects. Let us focus on the persons who had access to Johnston on the night in question — Molly Johnston and her servants, as well as Mr Frank and his servants. And me. Not to forget Netty.'

'Let's exclude you, shall we?' Olivia said. 'Let's exclude Netty and anyone from the Johnston household as well. For now. What I find remarkable about Mr Frank is that he seemed ill. His wife was ill, he was ill, and Johnston was ill too. Until he died. Mrs Appleton — the house-keeper — was not ill. The maid and the cook weren't ill either, and they had already retired to their rooms, according to Mr Frank and Mrs Appleton. You had their statements confirmed by the servants. Now I wonder...'

'I sent samples of the Franks' dinner leftovers to Dr Barry. And of the Johnstons' dinner.'

'Oh,' Olivia waved a hand at Sévère, 'I'm sure you did. What I find unusual is that Mrs Frank's illness did not prevent her from dressing in her finery. Why is that?'

'Isn't that what women *do*? Dress fashionably, even though it makes them quite uncomfortable?'

'In the middle of the night? When they feel deathly ill? Are you jesting?'

He shrugged. 'It must have been before your time, so perhaps you don't realise that ladies once wore ball dresses that help up to a thousand grains of arsenic, knowing full well that the fashionable green dye was killing them.'

Olivia sucked air through her teeth. She'd read about the killing dresses. And she had to admit that Sévère had a point.

'Nevertheless, you are correct, Olivia. It *is* odd and worth investigating. I talked to Dr Barry this morning and he said that it might be possible for Johnston to have ingested vegetable alkaloids. Digitalis, for example. John-ston's last words were, "You are hurting my arm." I was supporting his left arm with my right. Pain in the left arm is a common symptom of heart failure.'

'When is his burial?' Olivia asked softly.

'In two days.' Sévère pushed the case notes aside and extinguished the cigar. 'Now to our special case. I agree with you that we should not use a young girl to bait Frost. We will, instead, bribe a seductress.' His eyes flickered.

Exhaling, Olivia leant back. 'You are thinking of Mrs Gretchen.'

'Do you know where she lives?'

She shook her head. 'After she abducted me, she kept me for a few months, and then sold me. That's more than six years ago. I believe she is moving from boarding house to boarding house, to minimise the risk of being discovered. But I do know who—'

The door was pushed open and Netty stepped through, Inspector Height and two more policemen entering directly behind her.

Sévère stood. 'Gentlemen, may I ask why you burst into my office without the common courtesy of announcing yourselves?'

'Coroner Sévère,' Height began, 'the case has been fully considered. You were heard to have had an argument with Dr Johnston, upon which he cried, "You are hurting me." Only moments later, he was thrown down the stairs by you. Preliminary results of the toxicological analysis indicate the use of a vegetable alkaloid. Furthermore, we have found proof that you purchased aconite — a highly toxic vegetable alkaloid. The amount of aconite you purchased was sufficient to poison the victim ten times over.

Coroner Sévère, it has been decided to charge you with causing the death of Dr Peter Johnston, in your own home, on July the second, 1881. You are required to hand over all aconite in your possession, so that Dr Barry can compare it with the poison found in Dr Johnston's organs. I will now take you into custody.'

Sévère sank back onto his chair. 'An unexpected turn of events.' He looked up at Height. 'Inspector, I do hope you know what you are doing.'

'I do, Coroner. The Home Secretary will be notified and a replacement for your office will be assigned.' Height unclipped a pair of manacles from his belt.

'Those won't be necessary,' Sévère said. 'But I will require my crutch, my pain medication, and my cane. Will I be sent to the House of Detention?'

'No. Given your position, I believe it unwise to put you up in a cell with men who might want to do you harm. You will be transferred to a solitary cell at Newgate.'

Sévère shut his eyes for a moment and nodded. 'May I have a word with my wife before we leave?'

'Of course,' Height answered. 'You have as much time as I should need to search your house and confiscate further evidence.'

Unspeaking, Sévère rose and approached Olivia. He pulled her aside and spoke softly into her ear, 'Contact your barrister. You'll want someone who's familiar with certain facts. Ask Mr Gladstone and Mr Robson if they are willing to assist Mr Bicker in my defence.' Seeing the faint tremble in her shoulders, he took her hand in his.

'Whatever should unfold, your future will be taken care of.'

'You have such a charming way of offending me, Coroner.' She straightened, squeezed his hand in return, and subtly nodded toward the police. 'I'll have to be faster than they, I suppose.'

## STONE WALLS

*lick.*

Sévère's gaze followed a spider scuttling across the arched ceiling of his cell until it disappeared into one of the many cracks in the mortar. For lack of a pillow, he'd folded an arm under his head. His legs were stretched out. At least there was a blanket. He'd wrapped it around his left leg, and covered it with his jacket. Cold crept into that limb faster than any other.

He caught himself counting the whitewashed bricks, wondering if the mortar might be soft enough to carve himself a window to the outside world. Or an escape route. The chuckle that rolled up his throat sounded hollow.

*Click.*

He tried to direct his mind back to the case, to analyse the limited evidence he and Olivia had collected, and line up the events that had led to his arrest. But worry muddled his thoughts. What if... He pinched the bridge of his nose, forcing his mind to focus.

*Click.*

Growling, he sat up and searched for the source of the clicking noise. In the semi-darkness it took him a while to locate a small puddle on the floor, and high above it, a white bump. A minuscule stalactite. Probably lime, he thought. Not that it mattered.

He pulled off a sock — his right one — and placed it on the puddle. The next drop hit with a dull *fop*.

Satisfied, Sévère covered up his weak leg again, and lay back down. If Olivia were able to find Bicker in his office and talk to him, the barrister should be arriving soon. Sévère needed to get a better grasp on himself. His time with Bicker would be limited. An hour or two at the most. He'd best make use of it.

He tried to understand how precisely he had ended up in Newgate. The evidence against him was weak and circumstantial...although, to be honest, Inspector Height had shown decent detective skills. Sévère had to admit he would have seen himself as one of the main suspects had he considered the small bottle of aconitia powder and the jar of unguent. But there was nothing that could have been done differently. And there was no turning back time.

Sévère put the matter aside.

The hasty arrest was certainly due to a series of unfavourable circumstances: The dislike police and coroners cultivated against one another. The increasing demands of public and press for swift apprehensions, convictions, and sentencing. It was the fashion for policemen to quickly arrest whomever fit the bill of might-have-done-it. Which usually was the person who found the body, reported the crime, or was married to the victim.

In this case it happened to be Sévère.

To make matters worse, he was married to a former prostitute whose former regular was the Chief Magistrate — the man who had signed the warrant to take him into custody.

He should have to navigate carefully around this topic when he spoke with Bicker.

Sévère sucked in a breath. Inspector Height, too, knew Olivia's background. Should she ever be called onto the witness stand, Height and Frost would make public what she'd been. Or still was. In the eyes of society, a whore was always a whore. And no jury would believe a word she said.

Even if she never had to give her statement, Frost would not let slip this opportunity to further discredit Sévère. Most likely, some newspaperman would get an anonymous tip to check the true identity of the Coroner's wife. And that would cause a scandal of such proportions as London had rarely seen. All Sévère's and Olivia's missteps and misfortunes would be paraded in court, and expatiated in all major newspapers across the city. Most likely across Britain. Their private lives would be dragged out into the open and run through the sewers.

'Goddammit!' he cried, and slammed a fist against the wall. The sharp pain didn't calm his nerves in the least.

As he sucked the blood from his knuckles, he came to realise that he would have to stay in gaol for weeks while Olivia was being deeply humiliated. And he wouldn't be able to do anything about it.

They were both already ruined.

---

OLIVIA STEPPED ONTO THE PAVEMENT. She shut her eyes and filled her lungs. The attorneys Mr Gladstone and Mr Robinson had both agreed to take on Sévère's case and assist Mr Bicker. Bicker was an agreeable man, she thought. He made a solidly professional impression, and had departed at once to see Sévère at Newgate.

Her next task wouldn't be as straightforward.

She looked up and pushed through the bustle of afternoon shoppers, searching the busy street for an available cab. Several hansoms wove through the press of carts, omnibuses, bicycles, and hurried pedestrians. None of the carriages were empty.

She walked down the street until she spotted a waiting cab, but quickly doused the reflex to summon it, wondering if she really needed to involve William. She felt an aversion to stirring up her past. William had been a regular client for more than two years. He had always been a perfect gentleman, but he certainly wouldn't be happy when she showed up on his doorstep. There was a good chance he would be appalled.

Her eyes followed the trajectory of a small, green

ribbon as it was blown across the street by a summer breeze, then caught by the wheel of an omnibus, and slammed into horse dung.

Smiling, she recalled William's offer when they'd parted half a year ago. "If your husband causes you any trouble, let me know and I'll turn him to pulp." She lifted her arm and cried, 'Cabbie!'

'MR BURROUGHS CAN SEE YOU NOW,' said the clerk who had admitted Olivia a few moments earlier. He showed her down a short corridor to William's office.

She stepped into the room and found herself facing an expansive behind in pinstripe trousers. 'Did you drop something?' she asked softly and shut the door.

He wheeled around, his wrist knocking against a coffee pot that sat on a large desk. He just managed to catch the vessel before it vomited its contents over a disorderly stack of papers.

'Damnation!' burst through his formidable moustache. William cleared his throat, and looked up. Flustered, he blinked, and then his mouth split to a grin. 'Such a pleasant surprise!'

He approached her, grabbed her outstretched hand with both of his, and lifted her knuckles to his lips. 'You look splendid, Olivia.' He indicated a chair. 'Please, sit, and pray tell me what brings you here.'

She sat, dropped her bonnet on his desk, and pulled off her lace gloves, finger by finger. 'I expect you've already heard it.'

Mischievously, he waggled his eyebrows. 'If your

husband is involved in a scandal, then, no, I haven't…' His expression fell. 'Clearly, something is worrying you! What is it? How can I help?'

'Sévère was arrested this afternoon. Murder charges have been brought up against him.'

William blew though his moustache. 'Bloody hell. Did he do it, do you know?'

'He is innocent. His friend died under suspicious circumstances in our house. We've been investigating it, and now…' She clamped her mouth shut and frowned.

William waited for her to continue. When she did not say more, he asked, 'May I ask if you require a lawyer or a friend?'

She inhaled deeply. 'I believe I need both.'

'Well, then.' He leant back, and pushed a hand between two buttons of his waistcoat to scratch his portly stomach. 'Allow me to offer you both.'

Faintly, she smiled and gave him a little nod. 'This case has taken on…proportions which are rather disturbing.'

'Here, have a drop. You seem to be in need of it.' He poured coffee into a small cup, and pushed it over to her.

She drank, cleared her throat, and folded her hands on William's desk. 'The case against Sévère is fabricated. Chief Magistrate Frost signed the warrant.'

'Frost signing the warrant does not indicate a fabrication—'

'In this case, it does. Frost is a former client of mine. Among…certain individuals, he's well known to have a taste for underage girls. Sévère and I were collecting evidence against him, and I believe he is behind this arrest because he knows we are investigating him.'

William had grown still. His gaze lost focus, then flicked to the door and back at Olivia. He signalled to her to check the door. She rose without making a sound, tiptoed to the door and yanked it open. The corridor was empty.

She shut the door and looked questioningly at William.

'One of my clerks is a chronic eavesdropper. It has it's uses...at times,' he explained. 'Come. Let's sit over there.' He indicated the chaise at the far side of the room. 'And tell me everything from the beginning.'

THE WARDEN WALKED Olivia to the galleries. A glass ceiling admitted the late afternoon sun, staining the golden rays a muddy yellow. Dust rained through the beams of light, creating an impression that the odours of stale urine, sweat, faeces — and the starchy smell reminiscent of the cheap establishments where she'd worked when she was very young — were a sticky substance that was destined to remain in her lungs forever.

She clenched her teeth and followed the warden up the first flight of stairs, the second, third, and fourth. The metal steps echoed their footfalls. At each storey, prisoners pressed their faces up against the high, barred windows of their cell doors to see who was being brought in. Upon glimpsing Olivia, they hollered obscenities and made crude gestures.

She wondered what Sévère had been obliged to endure when he was brought here. Surely, the news that the

Coroner of Eastern Middlesex himself had been arrested on murder charges had spread like fire. Had anyone helped him climb the many stairs? Was he in fear for his life, or would the wardens be keeping him safe from the other prisoners?

They came to a halt in front of a cell. She curled her trembling fingers to fists.

---

SÉVÈRE ROSE as the warden locked the door behind Olivia's back. As the man's steps faded, her eyes touched on the whitewashed brick walls, the decrepit water tank in the far corner, the basin beneath it, and the bucket that served as privy. The bedding Sévère had risen from. His crutch. Next to the door, a table provided just enough space for one plate and one mug. A small stool that seemed to have been fashioned for a child. She blinked, and Sévère had the impression she was trying to will a window into the walls.

He watched her turn and look at the small opening in the cell door — the only opening that let in light. She turned back and finally gazed at him. Her chest was heaving and her mouth a thin line.

He sat back down on the bedding and bade her join him.

'How are you doing?' she asked, her voice brittle.

'I am well, thank you.' He inhaled and continued in a whisper. 'Olivia, you must leave London.'

He found no surprise in her expression.

'I thought about it and decided against it,' she answered quietly.

'Olivia,' he growled, 'as soon as your past becomes known — and believe me, it will — every man will treat you as fair game. Especially Frost. I remember how that man looked at you. It still chills me. He is…an aberration, and yet, not the only man with such…tastes. If you could hear men talk amongst themselves, you'd know that—'

'Don't you think I know this?'

His expression darkened, a dangerous flicker in his eyes. 'You probably know this much better than most women.'

Stretching his legs, he gazed up at the ceiling. Then he shook his head. 'You *must* leave London in any case. Frost will make certain your past becomes known. The man wants you for himself. He probably believes that I'll divorce you as soon as he spills the dirty details. Or he simply wants to discredit us. Whatever his motivations, as long as I'm in gaol, you are unprotected.'

Olivia laughed, then made to speak. A nearby noise in the corridor stopped her. She scooted closer to Sévère and said softly, 'Frost won't dare reveal a thing.'

Sévère lifted an eyebrow.

She shrugged, but said no more.

'If you believe he'll refrain from doing so because he was your client and exhibited tastes the Bible doesn't condone, you are mistaken. It's always the woman who lures a man into immoral actions. Men can't help themselves.' His voice was thick with sarcasm.

'Oh, that's not it.' She waved a dismissive hand. 'I know

I'll lose credibility the moment it becomes known I was a whore. But I once *had* credibility. It was Frost who took it from me.'

Sévère froze. His stomach roiled. He swallowed, and spoke with considerable effort. 'He was your first.'

'Yes. He was the man who paid Mrs Gretchen to abduct me.'

'Why the deuce did you never tell me?' His hand came down on his mouth. 'And, by god, how could I have been so blind?'

'I did not mention it because I found it insignificant.'

'Insignificant? *Insignificant?* Woman, I can't believe what I'm hearing.' He rubbed his scalp with vigour, then regarded her sharply and whispered, 'I will kill this swine for you.'

She smiled at him, then shook her head once. 'We need Frost to make sure that no one mentions my past during the proceedings. And I'm certain he doesn't want it mentioned, because he doesn't want to take the risk of being implicated.'

She sighed. 'It will already be difficult enough for you to gain back your office as Coroner. You don't need everyone knowing what I am. Or was. Now, let us focus on the case. Oh, but how is your leg doing? It's awfully chill in here.'

He grumbled at that. 'The warden took the unguent from me.'

'I will kill this swine for you,' she said with a twinkle in her eye. Sévère snorted and poked a finger at her stomach.

'Who's your chemist?' she asked.

'Mr Walker.'

'The one at Whitechapel Road?'

'The very one.'

'Was Bicker of any help today? Could he say anything as to the bail?'

'There is no bail for murder suspects. And yes, he's been very helpful already. He secured a second visitation, else the warden wouldn't have allowed you to see me. It's an exception. Only one visitor per day is permitted, one hour, at noon. It is best if Bicker and you visit on alternate days. In the meantime, write down all the questions you have and all the developments in our case. Bicker can bring your letter to me, so I can read it the day before you come here. Under the given circumstances, this is the most effective way to communicate.'

'At least you have a very positive way of describing it,' she said dryly.

He took her hand in his, but dropped it after a short moment. 'I am sorry you have to do this alone while I sit here and…take a holiday.'

'Well, now I finally have the opportunity to prove my worth.'

'You don't need to prove anything to me, Olivia.'

'Then I'll prove to everyone else that a woman can solve a crime. Newspaper men are drooling over this case. The whole of London will read about Mrs Sévère saving her husband from the gallows.' She clapped a hand to her mouth, all colour draining from her cheeks. 'I am so sorry. That was tasteless and cruel.'

Sévère's jaw set. 'I fail to see how the reward of fame

and glory could possibly be worth me sitting in a windowless cell in Newgate.'

She dropped her gaze. 'Gavriel,' she said softly, 'if it were possible, I would trade places with you.'

'It is a waste of time to speculate—'

'I'm not speculating,' she cut across him. 'I'm simply saying that I would take your place. It would make more sense. I'm well practiced in being held captive, and you are well practiced in investigating murder cases.'

'And now our roles and expertise are reversed.' He dropped his head in his hands and laughed. 'Well, dammit to hell and back!'

'I'm scared.' She grabbed his arm, her fingers digging into it.

He glanced down at her hand. 'I am not. The bill of indictment will be rejected by the Grand Jury within a week. The evidence against me is too weak. I'll never be brought to trial.' He looked up at her then. 'I'm convinced of that.'

She cocked her head. 'You are lying. I can see that you are worried.'

'A little. This place isn't exactly…pleasant.'

Both froze as the clanking of keys and heavy footfalls announced the approaching warden.

'I'll get you out of here.' She grinned and whispered, 'Right after I kill that warden for you.'

He covered her hand with his. 'Whatever you do, Olivia, finding Johnston's murderer is your first priority. Don't let the trail go cold. Forget Frost for the time being, and focus on Johnston.'

The sound of a key turning in a lock sent her to her

feet. She straightened her skirts and gave Sévère a curt nod. 'I'll be the finest detective you've ever known.'

He watched her leave, wondering what kind of man would ask his wife to hunt down a killer alone.

One who was truly desperate, or utterly out of his mind.

# THIRD ACT

*Run my dear,*
*from anything*
*that may not strengthen*
*your precious budding wings.*

Khwāja Shamsu ud-Dīn Muhammad Hāfez-e Shīrāzī

## MESSENGERS & RUFFIANS

*H*iggins stood by the mulberry hedge, one hand pinching a cigarette, the other scraping something off the sole of his boot with a stick. Olivia acknowledged him with a nod and entered her home.

She came to an abrupt halt, gazed at the flickering lamp on the wall to her right, and stepped back out of the house. She shut the door and rang the bell.

Netty opened the door, and her expression of busy professionalism was at once replaced by puzzlement. She patted her apron as though creases there needed smoothing.

'Good evening, Netty. Please pretend I'm Dr Johnston,' Olivia said. 'And do precisely what you did when he visited. Take your time. I want you to remember every detail.'

Netty's hands shot up to the frills of her white cap, then slid lower to check her severe hairdo — a bun pulled so tight that her scalp shone through her greying strands. Her eyelids fluttered.

'If you don't mind,' Olivia added.

Netty sucked her lower lip between her teeth.

'It's all right, Netty. Just…shut your eyes and try to remember the night of the second of July. If you would, please,' she said, infusing her voice with enough impatience to let the housekeeper know she'd had enough of the fidgeting.

Netty squeezed her eyes shut, a blush colouring her cheeks.

'What am I wearing?' Olivia began softly. 'A bowler…'

'Damp at the inside of the brim,' Netty continued, eyes firmly closed. 'White shirt, black waistcoat, black tie. He… tucked his watch back into his pocket and bade me to take the bag and the hat. I brushed off his hat and placed it on the hatstand.'

Netty opened her eyes and cleared her throat. 'I was thinking he must be ill.'

'Why?'

She opened her mouth, shuffled her feet, and finally said, 'Perhaps… Well, he… He was pale and sweating, wasn't he?'

'Where's the bag?' Olivia asked.

'By the hatstand, as he wished it. He walked past me as I placed the bag down. Went up the stairs. To the smoking room.' She accompanied every sentence with a nod. 'Would you like to take your supper now, missus?'

'Not quite yet.' Olivia gazed toward the stairs and back at the hatstand. 'Stand over there and watch me climb the stairs,' she said and walked away. 'What was different that night?' she called over her shoulder. 'Take your time.'

She reached the first floor and then walked back down, watching Netty gnaw on the inside of her cheek and blink nervously.

'Well?'

Netty produced something between a shrug and a curtsy. 'Begging your pardon, but... I don't know how the fashion of Dr Johnston climbing the stairs might be in any way...suspicious.'

'Did he stumble? Did he sway? Did he stop and turn to look at you, or did he walk up the stairs as he always did, with a little spring in his step like a man of twenty?'

Netty dropped her gaze, and produced a shrug. 'I couldn't tell.'

Olivia took in the stiff set of Netty's back and jaw, her tittering lashes. 'Thank you,' she finally said. 'I'll be taking supper in the smoking room. And I may be needing your assistance again a little later.' With that, Olivia turned and stared up the staircase toward the first floor. She waited for Netty to shuffle to the kitchen, then directed her gaze down to the bottom of the stairs, recalling the position of Johnston as he lay there, Sévère's hand on his throat.

'Not yet,' she muttered, and went up to the smoking room.

SHE SAT in Sévère's armchair and eyed the closed door. No, that was wrong. She rose and opened the door, then sat back down. She found a cigar in a box on the desk, stuck it between her lips, lit a match, and sucked fire into compacted tobacco.

'Gah! What a vile concoction!' Coughing, she placed the cigar onto the rim of the ashtray, then leant back and slowly took in the room.

A door made of dark wood, panelled, about three-quarters open. Its knob reflecting dim light from the corridor.

The walls. Panelled below throat level, painted light green above that. She wondered if the paint had been made with arsenic. But Johnston wouldn't visit Sévère to lick poison off the walls.

Her gaze strayed up to the lamp suspended from the ceiling. She shut her eyes and tried to recall odours. Cigar smoke, yes. But gas, no. Had there been a leak, Sévère would have been affected as well. Both men would have noticed the gas before anyone could have died. And Johnston's lungs would have smelled of it.

She opened her eyes.

The fireplace. Cold now. And Sévère wasn't here to warm his leg.

She inhaled a sigh and her gaze slid to the window sill, the ebony elephant with it's small ivory tusks glinting in the light. The tall brass lamp. The chess board on a side table. Some nights, Johnston and Sévère played chess and discussed a case.

Had played.

Nothing seemed out of place here, except Sévère and Johnston were missing. And the bottle of brandy. Height had taken it.

Her mind went back to what Sévère had told her about

Johnston's evening. He'd attended to a patient. The patient had died. Johnston gave the certificate of death, then took a cab.

He'd mentioned the bottle with tincture of digitalis. Did he touch it before he left? Did he sniff it to make sure it was correctly labelled?

Olivia sat up straight. Sévère had confiscated the bottle and sent it to Dr Barry for analysis. She'd soon know precisely what that bottle contained.

Her eyes flicked to the door. Johnston had appeared ill when he arrived. He said he'd been thinking about the brandy ever since his patient died. He drank quickly, tugged at his collar. Sévère had observed that Johnston seemed to swallow rather often, as though his throat felt swollen or his mouth dry. Thirsty. Johnston said he believed he had caught influenza. His pallor had worsened quickly. He'd wiped his brow frequently and...gazed at his hands and rubbed them on his trousers? Why would he do that? Sweat, perhaps.

She'd had influenza once and recalled the aching of her skin and bones. But those were just her own symptoms. She didn't quite know what was common and what was unusual. She'd have to research influenza symptoms. Perhaps they were similar to symptoms of poisoning, and with any luck, she might be able to pinpoint the substance faster than Dr Barry.

Or perhaps not.

Sévère said that Johnston had seemed to grow disoriented. He'd blinked as though his vision were impaired. Then he'd almost fallen over when he'd risen from the chair. Sévère had helped him down the corridor, and

Johnston had complained about pain in his arm. *You are hurting my arm.*

Something niggled at the back of Olivia's mind. She scratched her neck and jerked up in her chair. Owing to his weak leg, Sévère had to support his left side with a cane or crutch. So when offering his arm to someone, it would have been his right.

Johnston had complained about pain in his left arm, the one Sévère must have been holding. Pain in the left arm was a symptom of heart failure, wasn't it?

Ah, no, it couldn't have been his heart. They'd already discussed it, and the postmortems had excluded a weakness of Johnston's heart.

'Focus, woman,' she grumbled and rubbed her burning eyes.

But if he'd been poisoned with digitalis, would his heart look any different? Would such a poisoning be visible in a postmortem examination?

The maid, Marion, chose this moment to step into the room. 'Netty said you wish to take your supper here.'

Olivia lifted an eyebrow. Had Netty offered Marion the use of her first name, or was the maid being disparaging? She realised that she knew little of the goings-on between the household members. How very unwifely.

She waved at the desk, and Marion put down a bowl, a plate, cutlery, and a glass of wine.

Olivia neither looked at the food nor did she notice the maid leave. Her mind was elsewhere.

The brandy. That was the only substance Johnston had ingested during his visit. He had stayed in the smoking room for about ten, fifteen minutes, during which he had deteriorated quickly.

That Johnston was given an aggressive poison seemed extremely likely. But who had wanted him dead?

Olivia stood and strode to the door. Had Johnston grabbed the frame for support? She scanned the wood and sniffed it. It smelled lightly of beeswax and dust. She found no smudges on door, knob, or frame.

She stepped into the corridor.

It had been late, later than it was now. But the conditions were similar: Two lamps provided light. Then, no one was about the corridor, as the servants were soon to retire. Slowly, she made for the stairs, checking the rug for scuff marks, stains, smudges, or anything that seemed out of place.

She reached the stairs finding nothing remarkable. Groaning, she sat and put her chin in her hand.

Sévère had said that Johnston's knees gave way and then abruptly straightened. It was as if he meant to dive from a cliff into the sea. Sévère couldn't hold on to him. The moment his fingers slipped from Johnston's arm, Sévère realised something terrible was about to happen. Witnessing his friend pitching into the abyss must have been…impossible for him to forget.

Yet, when Sévère had recounted the series of events, he'd appeared entirely detached. A list of occurrences. First A, then B, then C. That simple.

Still, in their short time together she'd learnt how to interpret the twitch of his pupils and the subtle flattening of his lips. The stretching of skin around his eyes.

Sévère said he wasn't certain whether Johnston was

already dead when he hit the landing. It had taken him a moment to remember to press his finger to Johnston's neck. And when he did, he'd found no pulse.

She recalled the moments before she glimpsed Johnston and Sévère at the bottom of the stairs. The agitated voices. Rose braiding her hair. Sévère's hand at Johnston's throat.

The postmortem showed that Johnston hadn't been throttled.

According to Sévère, Johnston's heart had stopped beating six minutes before she reached the bottom of the stairs. All the servants had been alerted and were present, except Alf, who returned later that night. He'd stated that he'd had gone on a stroll. She guessed he'd spent coin in a brothel.

She made a mental note to interrogate the boy.

Ah, interrogations! Dammit. Olivia pressed her knuckles against her eyes, wondering how long she could use Sévère's warrant. He'd issued it for her to take witness statements in the Johnston case. As of ten o'clock tomorrow morning, the office of Coroner of Eastern Middlesex would be held by a Mr Baxter. News would spread quickly, and people would soon realise that the warrant she was waving at their noses wasn't worth a fly's fart.

But there was nothing to be done about that now.

She wondered what time it was. Nine? Ten? Her stomach felt hollow. Dimly, she remembered the food on Sévère's desk, but she didn't think she could eat anything.

Her first instinct was to wait for the next day. It wasn't

an appropriate time to call on people. But then…perhaps it was the appropriate time to get answers.

She stood and went to her room, found Rose reading in her bed, and told her she would be home late, and that if Rose was hungry, she might eat the supper left in the smoking room. The girl was eating like a dust bin these days.

Olivia picked up her bonnet and heard a knock. Netty stepped in and held out an envelope on a silver platter. 'You received a message, Mrs Sévère.'

Olivia frowned. A note from William, perhaps? She ripped open the letter and found a small, typed note. The hairs on her neck rose.


*You are alone.*


There was no signature.

Her head snapped up. 'When was this delivered?'

'A few minutes ago. By a boy.' Netty's eyes flicked to the note in Olivia's hand, then up to her mistress' face.

'I didn't hear the bell. Describe him.'

'He…I…'

'Spit it out, Netty!'

'Higgins received the note, not I!'

Olivia whipped her skirts around, rushed from the room and down the stairs. 'Higgins!' she called, and abruptly sucked in a breath when she spotted a dark figure standing by the entrance door.

'You accepted this?' She held up the envelope.

'Yes.'

She gazed up at his shuttered expression. There was

something in his eyes she couldn't quite identify. A darkness that reminded her of the men who frequented the cheapest of bawdy houses. And yet, something essential was missing. As if… As if he were a predator that was blind to its prey.

She wondered once again what life the man had led before he'd been offered this post. Or how her husband had found him. At times she toyed with the thought that Higgins had spent time in gaol, and that it was there that Sévère had met him.

She brushed the thought away. 'I need you to describe the boy to me.'

His gaze did not slide down to the envelope in her hand, but instead held hers calmly. 'Dirty face, dirty clothes. A street arab, the sort you can find by the hundreds in East End or Whitechapel. Dark hair, dark eyes. Perhaps ten or twelve years old. I might be able to recognise him should I see him again. But I doubt he'd loiter in this area.'

Olivia felt her shoulders deflate.

'You might wish to send Alf to tail the next one,' he added.

She narrowed her eyes at him.

'…if there's a next one. It seems as if…you might be expecting it.'

'I honestly don't know. I don't even know who sent this.' She had an inkling, though — the same man who had killed Johnston. 'Thank you. You are dismissed,' she said.

'Mrs Sévère, may I have a moment?' He took off his bowler and clamped it between his fingers.

'Of course.' Olivia suspected that he was worried about

his situation, and might have already received an offer elsewhere. Despite his ruffian-like looks, Higgins was reliable and lacked any tendency to gossip or drink. He would easily find a new master.

'Now that Mr Sévère is in gaol, and you are investigating this case without him, I was thinking…' He smoothed his rumpled hair and placed his bowler back on his head. 'I see you are about to leave…' He paused, eyeing her. 'You'll be needing a driver. And perhaps you can find use for a man who is able to…rough up people if the need arises.'

She opened her mouth, but nothing appropriate came out, so she shut it.

'The horses are ready,' Higgins added with a twitch of his mouth.

## WITNESSES

Olivia pulled out the warrant and flattened it, careful not to smudge Sévère's signature with her damp gloves. A violent shower had come down the moment she'd alighted from the brougham and hastened to Mr Frank's lodgings.

Higgins kept watch from his perch on the other side of the street. Hoping he wouldn't fall asleep, Olivia knocked.

A somewhat disgruntled Mrs Appleton admitted her and helped rub down Olivia's dress with a towel, before showing her to the parlour, and taking her bonnet down to the kitchen to dry by the hearth.

The clock on the mantelpiece struck eleven. It *was* late. She tapped her fingers against the windowsill, fingered the curtains and pulled them aside a fraction. A lamp spilled yellow light through the downpour and onto Higgins, haloing his hunched form.

Olivia directed her attention back into the room. She pricked her ears. The ticking of the clock. Rain tapping against the windowpanes. But no creaking of stairs or floorboards, no footfalls or muttered conversations.

Mrs Appleton hadn't mentioned when Mr Frank would see her, if perhaps he'd already retired and now needed a few moments to dress and come down to the parlour. In fact, Mrs Appleton hadn't even asked the reason for Olivia's late visit.

How queer.

Olivia turned and made for the door.

'Mrs Appleton?' she called. There was no answer. Olivia made her way to the kitchen.

Copper and iron pans dangled over a well-polished stove. A cupboard with cans of salt, sugar, and flour. Bundles of herbs hung from a beam. Next to them, soup ladles, whisks, and other tools. Her bonnet was perched on the back rest of a chair, dripping water onto bare floorboards.

A clanking noise drew her back through the door and farther down a narrow corridor. Mrs. Appleton was moving something into a corner of the laundry room. When she turned and spotted Olivia in the doorway, she jumped. Her hand went to her bosom. 'Christ!'

'Good evening. Again. You wouldn't know where Mr Frank has got to, would you?'

The housekeeper smoothed her apron. 'Has he not come down yet?' Her eyes darted to a pile of dirty laundry on a table in the centre of the room. She moved toward it and Olivia glimpsed the item Mrs Appleton had pushed about: a bucket with towels, adorned with a pile of…what was it? Crumpled waxed paper, perhaps?

Mrs Appleton caught Olivia's gaze, picked a sheet

picked from the pile of laundry, and began to smooth it. Smoothed it some more. Folded it.

'Is he feeling better?' Olivia asked.

'Who?'

'Mr Frank. He was ill last time I spoke to him.'

Mrs Appleton stopped stroking the sheet. 'Thank you for asking. Yes, he's doing much better. Perhaps we should go up and find him.' She shuffled past Olivia and into the corridor.

'Mrs Appleton, would you please remind me what Dr Johnston did when he entered your house?'

Mrs Appleton almost bumped into the doorframe to the kitchen. She patted her bun, and sucked in a breath with an unmistakable air of have-you-already-forgotten-it-you-goose. 'As I said the other day, I fetched Dr Johnston, told him everything I knew about Mrs Frank's ailment. He knew this already, but I thought it would do no harm reminding him. Then I led him into the house and up to the bedroom where Mrs Frank lay on the bed. And then—'

'Did he look ill?'

'Mr Frank?'

'No, Dr Johnston.'

'Oh! Ah, no. I believe not.' A frown from Mrs Appleton was followed by an encouraging nod from Olivia. 'Well, and then… Dr Johnston asked me to open the windows, which I did at once. He talked to my mistress, but she could not reply for she had lost her senses already.' Mrs Appleton sniffed. 'And then he undressed her.'

'Why was she dressed in her finery?'

'Because of the anniversary, of course!'

'The Frank's wedding anniversary?'

'Yes.'

'Did they plan to go out? To the opera? Or an eating house?'

'No, they planned to stay at home, for Mr Frank didn't feel well.'

'Mr Frank, not his wife?'

A nod.

'But they dressed up nonetheless?' Olivia asked.

Mrs Appleton twitched her shoulders. 'As I said, it was their anniversary.'

'I see. So you are saying that Mr Frank was unwell, but Mrs Frank was feeling perfectly fine until later that evening. When precisely did she begin to feel ill?'

Mrs Appleton's gaze drifted away, then focused back on Olivia. 'About an hour before I called the doctor.'

'I see. And what happened then? After Dr Johnston had undressed your mistress?'

Mrs Appleton blushed. 'He touched her all over.'

'He palpitated her,' Olivia provided.

'I guess that's what he did.'

'Was she completely naked?'

Mrs Appleton's hands contracted. 'What? No! He'd taken off her dress and unstrung her corset, no more!'

'So she still wore her stockings, drawers, chemise, and what else?'

'I believe that...that is all she wore, yes. And then...he instructed Mr Frank to rub the mistress' legs, and then Dr Johnston lifted her and hit her on her back.'

'Hmm...' Olivia frowned. 'You wouldn't know if he used a stethoscope, would you?' She knew the answer.

They had found Johnston's stethoscope under Mrs Frank's bed. He must have pulled it out of his bag, perhaps used it, and then dropped it.

'He put his ear to her bosom and her back. Then he pronounced her dead.' Mrs Appleton rubbed her left eye.

'And she died because of her weak heart,' Olivia said softly.

'Yes. She did.'

'Did Dr Johnston touch the bottle with tincture of digitalis?'

Mrs Appleton frowned, then shook her head. 'Not that I know.'

'Hmm,' said Olivia again, and chewed on the inside of her cheek. Mrs Appleton began to fidget with her apron.

'Was this the only medicine Mrs Frank took?'

Mrs Appleton's jaw twitched. 'She was in the habit of taking several tinctures for health. I have cleaned her rooms and poured them all out.'

Olivia cursed herself. She should have searched the whole house and taken anything suspicious to Dr Barry.


A FEW MINUTES LATER, Mr Frank joined Olivia in the parlour. He looked even more worn than the last time she'd seen him.

'It is not precisely an acceptable time to pay visits,' he muttered.

'My sincere apologies. Had I known you had retired, I would have waited until tomorrow morning.' She flashed a smile and clapped her hands together. 'Shall we?'

'Shall we what?'

'Begin. I am investigating the murder of Dr Johnston, and I need to ask you a few more questions.'

Mr Frank wobbled. He locked his knees and caught the back of a chair, eased himself into it, but didn't seem to find a comfortable position. 'Murder!' he huffed, eyes as round and dark as chestnuts.

'Unfortunately, yes. Would you mind recounting the events that led to the death of Dr Johnston?'

His head snapped up. 'Why would you believe I know which events led to Dr Johnston's death?'

'You were here, weren't you?'

'I… Yes, I was.'

'It is known that Dr Johnston died from a *very* aggressive poison, which must have been given to him less than an hour prior to his death. He wasn't given anything in my home. Nothing but a glass of brandy, that is. My husband drank it too, and felt no ill effects.'

Mr Frank stared at her, as if waiting for something

Olivia inhaled. 'Dr Johnston must have been poisoned in your home, Mr Frank.' She kept her friendly facade, hoping that her half-knowledge disguised as solid fact would sufficiently scare Mr Frank into confessing. Whatever it was that needed confessing.

She wondered, briefly, if it was normal procedure to treat witnesses and suspects alike.

Mr Frank's face derailed. His mouth sagged, his chin pulled tight into small dimples, the skin around his eyes turned a snowy white. She'd never seen a man's expression change so rapidly, except of course when the man had just spent himself. But that usually resulted in a very different change of mood.

Mr Frank muttered something she didn't understand. 'Excuse me?'

He cleared his throat. 'Do I need an attorney?'

'Not thus far. My warrant only permits questioning.' She leant back against the windowsill and relaxed her posture. 'To be honest with you, Mr Frank, I doubt you did it.'

His gaze flickered.

'My husband and I have met numerous murderers and there is something in their eyes that is...' she waved a hand at her own face and trailed off, allowing his imagination to fill the gap.

He nodded. Yes. Don't we all know how murderers look. Haven't we all seen those damned creatures in the Illustrated Police News.

'But the police think differently,' she added softly. 'Inspector Height...' Again, she trailed off, hoping for help from Mr Frank's fear-infused imagination.

His shoulders snapped back. 'I am innocent!'

'Oh, I do know that, believe me. I just came to tell you to be careful. To let you know that the police will come looking. So you can be...prepared. That is why I didn't wish to wait for tomorrow morning.'

'They'll come? Tomorrow morning?'

She lifted a shoulder, innocence filling her eyes.

Mr Frank dropped his gaze to his hands, investigated the lines on his palms. A hangnail seemed of particular interest all of a sudden.

She approached him and asked, 'Was there anything you found...peculiar about Dr Johnston's behaviour?'

He wiped his brow and shook his head.

'Was he disoriented? Flushed? Did he say he was thirsty or hurting? Feeling unwell?'

Mr Frank gazed toward the window. Drops of rain glinted yellow against the black night. 'No, he didn't.'

'Well then,' she said cheerfully. 'I need to get going.'

His gaze was back on her. 'Going? Where to?'

'Home, of course. It is close to midnight.' She yawned and pushed away from the window.

Mr Frank jumped from his chair. 'And what am I to do now?'

'Go to bed, sleep well, and when the police come to interrogate you, tell them the truth. What you told me and my husband. You did tell the truth, didn't you?'

'Of… Of course I did!'

She watched him.

His eyes darted to the door and back at her. He nodded. 'Yes, I'll tell them what I told you. What else is there to do?' It wasn't intended to be a question. It was more like the waving of a white flag.


'I'LL BE DAMNED if he isn't hiding something,' Olivia muttered as she stalked across the street. The rim of her damp bonnet hung limply into her face. She wished she could wear a bowler instead.

'Anything to report?' she called up to Higgins.

'Lights were switched off about half an hour ago. Do you wish to go home?'

'Are you cold?'

'I'm all right.' He flashed a grin at her that wasn't entirely respectful.

'I'll be right back. Please do keep an eye on the house of Mr Frank.'

He tapped two fingers to his hat and nodded once.


'GOOD EVENING, MRS SÉVÈRE.' Mrs Johnston opened the door the moment Olivia rapped knocker against wood. 'I hope your coachman won't catch a cold.' She stepped aside to admit her late guest.

'You expected me.'

'The brougham has been standing there for about an hour. One couldn't miss the implications. Anything useful to be gained from Mr Frank or his housekeeper?' Mrs Johnston had yet to invite Olivia into the parlour. Olivia suspected that tonight she'd have to make do with the entrance hall.

'I hope I didn't keep you up.'

Mrs Johnston's eyebrows rose.

'The police have arrested a suspect,' Olivia said softly.

'They found the murderer?'

'They did not. They arrested my husband.'

Something clattered to the floor. Olivia's eyes caught the gleam of brass and mother of pearl as Mrs Johnston picked up the item. An opera glass.

'How would you describe the relationship between the Franks?'

Mrs Johnston blew air through her nose. 'Normal.'

'Please elaborate.'

'I find it a bit late for elaborating, but if you insist. The Franks had an utterly unremarkable marriage. Which means they mostly ignored one another.' The way she eyed Olivia made clear she believed the Sévères practiced that same kind of relationship.

Olivia ignored the jab. 'Any affairs?'

'How would I know?'

Olivia's gaze slid to the opera glass in Mrs Johnston's hand. 'I expect you do know enough.'

'Are you sure your husband is innocent?'

'A swift change of subject? Very well, then. Which vegetable alkaloids do you keep in your house?'

'I was wondering why neither of you attended his funeral. But your husband's arrest appears to be a sufficient explanation.'

Olivia clapped a hand to her mouth. She had completely forgotten Johnston's funeral. 'Where is he buried?'

'Mrs Sévère, I must ask you to leave now.' Arms went across her chest. The lapels of her robe parted, revealing a black nightgown. Mrs Johnston wore mourning attire even in bed.

'Where can I find his grave?' Olivia asked.

Mrs Johnston's eyes grew cold.

'I beg you. Your husband was a friend.'

'Duke's,' Mrs Johnston said in a flat voice.

Olivia dipped her chin. 'Thank you. And thank you for receiving me despite the late hour. I wish you a good night.'

---

OLIVIA WOKE TO A RUMBLING NOISE. At first, she thought she was still sitting across from Mrs Johnston, who was hammering on a table with overlarge fists. No, that had been a dream. The meeting with Mrs Johnston hadn't gone well, but the woman had definitely *not* morphed into a rock-fisted creature who was insisting Sévère had killed her husband.

Olivia shivered.

There was a knock on her door. Perhaps that was what woke her.

'What is it?' she called.

'A telegram,' Netty said.

'Come in.'

Olivia took the slip of paper, unfolded it, and almost dropped it.

*Bill of indictment accepted. Meet me in my office at noon.*
*Bicker.*

She gazed at the clock on the mantelpiece. Almost ten in the morning.

'Why did no one wake me?'

'Rose tried, but she said you were sleeping like a stone. Then Marion woke you, and you said you'd take breakfast in a few moments. That was at seven.'

'Oh. Really?' Olivia rubbed her eyes. She'd been exhausted last night. Ashamed, she sat up, touched her brow and her neck. Her skin felt a bit hot.

And then the full weight of the message hit her: Sévère would be led to trial for murder or manslaughter.

How could the Grand Jury have accepted the bill so swiftly?

Something was foul.

Olivia grew cold. Of course they could do it if someone asked them to give priority to the case.

She felt an overpowering urge to throttle Frost, to chop off his balls, and hammer them into his ugly mouth with a mallet.

She tamped down her rage when she heard the doorbell ring. Marion's voice in the hallway. And that of Inspector Height.

## THE NEW CORONER

'The police have confiscated our case notes.'
Olivia caught herself wringing her hands. She dropped them to her lap and wiped her palms on her dress. Inspector Height and his lackeys had dug through Sévère's office, and then proceeded to upturn the rest of the house. They asked the same stupid questions they'd asked the first time they interrogated her. She'd barely made it to Bicker's office on time.

'Knuckle-brained meaters,' she muttered at the carpet, before telling herself that none of it mattered. She didn't need Sévère's notes. Every detail was firmly lodged in her mind.

Bicker coughed.

Olivia looked up at him. 'Don't you think it suspicious that the Grand Jury accepted the bill in less than twenty-four hours?'

Frowning, he dabbed at his whiskers.

She blurted out, 'It's Frost. He wishes—' She clapped her mouth shut and dropped her gaze. 'He has an agenda.'

'I greatly doubt that. But given the circumstances, it's not surprising that you are so…upset.'

Olivia leant back in her seat, regretting her outburst. Bicker didn't know that she and Frost shared a past, had no idea why she'd come to such a conclusion. And yet… She pinned the attorney with her gaze, wondering how quickly *he* would lose his nerve should his wife face murder charges for killing her best friend. How well would he hold up with her life on the line?

Nausea swept through her. Olivia touched her neck. Too hot. She'd been running a fever since rain had soaked her to the bone the night before. She groaned and tried to take her mind off all the seemingly unsolvable problems by counting the buttons on Bicker's waistcoat. There were only six, and her anger flared up. Anger toward Bicker, who knew too little to be of any help.

She folded her hands in her lap, smiling mildly. 'Mr Bicker, I suggest you discuss Chief Magistrate Frost with my husband. He will know how much information can be dispensed to you.'

Bicker frowned. 'If it is relevant for the case, I must know about it at once.'

Olivia said nothing.

'Very well. I shall talk to your husband. As to the swiftness of the Grand Jury's decision — an official of the Crown is accused of an unlawful killing. As such, the Grand Jury requires that justice be served swiftly in order to keep face and appease the public.'

Bicker shifted in his armchair, fingering his thick

whiskers. 'Mrs Sévère, the press will pick up this case before this day is over. I suggest… My wife swears on needlepoint for calming the nerves.'

At her stare, he dropped his gaze.

She huffed and said, 'Given the impatience of your juridical machinery, may we expect the trial to be opened soon?'

'Yes,' he said. 'In fact, the date is already set.' His eyes slid up to her face. 'In five days.'

Her stomach dropped. 'So soon? The results of Dr Barry's analysis won't even be ready!'

'They will be.'

She watched Bicker squirm in his chair. His waistcoat bulged over his portly stomach. Two ruddy spots formed on his furry cheeks, like red beets riding a wooly mammoth. She almost laughed.

Bicker shut his eyes and cracked his knuckles.

She ripped off her lace gloves. It had grown unbearably hot in the room. Or perhaps it was her. Hot and cold. It would stay thus until the fever burnt itself out. Damn this impeccable timing! Damn time altogether. 'How in all that is holy will I catch a murderer in five days? How the bloody hell will you have enough time to prepare a defence?' Abruptly, she stood. 'I need to speak with my husband at once.'

Bicker dropped his palms to his desk with a meaty thud. 'That, Mrs Sévère, is impossible.'

'What?'

'Your husband is awaiting trial and is not allowed to receive visits from members of his family.'

For a moment, she was dumbstruck. Then it dawned

on her. 'I am not the assistant of the Coroner anymore. I'm merely a prisoner's wife.'

'Indeed.'

She rubbed her face and counted her options. There weren't many. In fact, there was only one: she had to find the person who had poisoned Johnston.

She took in Bicker, wondering if he believed that Sévère could… No, she wouldn't allow herself to think about that. 'The police have collected evidence against my husband. Except for the two of us, no one seems to consider him innocent. Mr Bicker, it is of utmost importance that I be permitted to speak with him. If I have to solve this case without the benefit of his acumen, he'll be…' She set her shoulders. 'I cannot simply sit at home and hope the jury will deem the evidence too weak to find him guilty. I *cannot* wait it out. You have to help me get into Sévère's cell.'

Bicker stared at her. The church bells struck one o'clock. His gaze grew glassy, his lids slid to half-mast. Pushing a fist under his chin, he said, 'Hum.'

He stood and strode to the window. He ran a finger around the rim of a large vase, plucked the petal of a pink rose and crushed it in his fist. 'My apologies for the needlepoint suggestion. I know how much he values your insights. But it will be…nearly impossible to help you with…'

Olivia watched his stance, how it gradually shifted from slightly clenched to upright.

'Hum,' he said again and turned to her. 'I believe this might work.'

'HELLO, Sévère. I am here on official business,' Olivia announced, stepping past the warden. The man still eyed the folder she was holding like a shield to her bosom. The papers had already been searched — by him, two turnkeys, and the officer who'd led her into the main hall, but it appeared as though the warden wanted to look through them again.

Irritated, she patted the warden's elbow and said, 'That will be all.'

With grunt, the man left, wrenching the key in the lock with more force than was absolutely necessary.

Olivia's eyes fell on Sévère. He was sitting on the bedding, his left leg wrapped in a blanket, the right pulled to his chest. His attention was on the noise the warden was making as he dawdled in the corridor, perhaps eavesdropping on their conversation. Or did the man expect him to take his pleasure with his wife, here in Newgate prison?

'The new coroner is Wynne Edwin Baxter. Have you heard of him?'

He looked up at Olivia. 'Coroner for Sussex. He was all over the papers only a month ago. Murder of Frederick Gold on the train from London Bridge to Brighton. He handled the case quite remarkably. An excellent replacement.'

Exhaustion fell heavy onto her shoulders. She sank to the bedding and whispered, 'Have you given up?'

He snorted. 'I couldn't care less about my career when my life is at stake.'

She grabbed his hand, but he pulled it away. 'We don't have much time,' he said. 'Tell me about the raid.'

'You heard about it?'

'Bicker sent me a note, letting me know the police had taken all my notes on Johnston's death. Is it true?'

She nodded faintly.

He motioned to her folders. 'And what, pray tell, are those?'

'*My* case notes. I wrote them up before I came here.'

Sévère's eyebrows rose. He bent closer to his wife and said softly, 'So Mr Bicker's letter to the Magistrate, begging for a concession to be made so that you could help me transfer all my open cases to the new coroner is a ruse that no one noticed as they rifled through your papers?'

She twitched a shoulder, a smile tugging at the corners of her mouth. 'Well, I did bring *some* notes on your open cases.'

Sévère grinned, shook his head, and touched his fingers to her knee. 'It doesn't matter now. Our time is limited. Let us go through this case. Step by step. And tell me about all new developments.'

She was staring at the spot Sévère had touched. Her leg prickled. Shaking off the feeling of — What was it? Discomfort? Weakness? — she opened the folder for his reference, and began recounting events from the moment Johnston left his home up until he was pronounced dead and was cut open in their laundry room. And she told him about her visits to Mr Frank and Mrs Johnston.

Sévère's gaze darkened. 'No news, then.'

'No.'

His lips were pressed to a thin line, brows drawn low. After a moment he cocked his head at her. 'Have you ever asked yourself why? Why Johnston had to die?'

'Of course. That's what we already asked his wife, and she said there was no one who hated him or bore him a grudge. I thought of talking to his colleagues. But it makes no sense. He died from an aggressive vegetable alkaloid that must have been given to him half an hour to three hours before he died. During that time, only his wife, his servants, the Franks and their servants, you, and Netty had access to him. These are the only people who could have given him the poison.' She tapped the papers before them. 'I'm certain their dinners weren't poisoned. — the servants fed the leftovers to alley cats that are still very much alive.'

Sévère nodded. 'Dr Barry's analysis will likely corroborate that. But you seem to believe Johnston's wife might be involved. The way you spoke about her...'

Olivia shook her head. 'She grieves. She doesn't want me to poke around in her life. I believe that's why she's so...cold.'

'Hmm.' He unwrapped his leg and began massaging it, his breath shallow.

'It's growing worse in here, isn't it?'

One sharp nod.

'Oh! I brought you a present.' She stood, and almost lost her balance in the process.

'What is it?' he asked, flinging out an arm to steady her.

She took a step back and said, 'Nothing.' She hoisted

up her skirts and searched for something between her legs.

Sévère cleared his throat.

'Almost...there,' she muttered. 'Dammit.' She bent farther down, cursed once more and finally extracted a small jar from her stockings. She held it up triumphantly.

His gaze was trapped by her exposed ankles. Straightening her skirts, she cleared her throat. Then she offered the jar to him. His fingers touched hers as he took it. She felt as though lightning had struck her, saw how gingerly he held the jar in his palm, how his finger brushed its smooth surface to feel the heat of her body lingering within it. She saw his gaze flicker, his Adam's apple bob once, his cheeks redden.

Her knees felt strangely too soft. She sat down on the bedding.

With his free hand, Sévère brushed the hem of her dress. A few burrs were stuck to the fabric. Thistle seeds hitching a ride. The soft tug of Sévère's fingers plucking the burrs, his expression of...of...

Shocked, she rose and took a step away from him.

He looked up and said softly. 'Thank you, sweet wife.' Hastily, he added, 'Thank you for the unguent. For being a friend.'

Ice dropped to her stomach. 'You misunderstand, Sévère. All I am is a person who knows how to treat others with consideration and respect. I am not your friend, I am your *assistant.*'

'I... What?'

Stiffly, she made for the door. 'Warden, I wish to leave.'

'Is it because I offered you money to bed you?'

'Excuse me?' She turned to face him.

'Is it because I was once your client?'

The warden approached, the clank of his keys echoing sharply in the corridor.

She stepped closer to Sévère, lowered her face to his, and whispered, 'It is because you found it only natural to bend a woman to your will. I remember that night *very well.* You planned to rape me. Don't play the hero while condemning Frost for his actions, because there is no reason for you to believe you are a better man.'

His jaw dropped. His gaze turned murderous. 'That night, *you* violated *me*. It might be all right for you to violate a man you tie to your bed under false pretences, but it isn't all right with me. Yet despite the pain and humiliation you subjected me to, I decided against taking revenge. I have never forced a woman. *Not once.* And yet, here you are, looking down upon me, calling me a rapist, and telling me I am just like the man who raped you when you were a girl of only nine years. A man who abused you, again and again, for seven long years.'

Silence roared in her ears.

'If this is what you see in me,' Sévère continued, 'you should leave now. Leave this cell, leave my house. And don't you ever return.'

A key slipped into the lock. The door creaked opened. 'Mrs Sévère?'

'My wife wishes to leave,' Sévère snapped at the warden.

# FROST

*O*livia leant against the fence, her hands grappling for support, her heart hammering. Oh gods! Sévère was nearly crippled, locked in a cell, accused of a crime he didn't commit, and she had thrown even more accusations at him. Why the deuce had she chosen such an unfortunate moment?

Her knees nearly buckled. It was too late to explain herself, to make her words less terrible. Comparing him to Frost wasn't at all what she'd meant to say. What she meant was…was…

Fighting the urge to scream at someone, anyone, she gritted her teeth, pushed away from the tall metal fence of Newgate prison, and crossed the pavement to her waiting coach.

'Back home?' Higgins asked softly.

She merely nodded and climbed inside. The door shut behind her. The brougham sagged as Higgins jumped up onto the driver's seat.

The setting sun flickered in and out the carriage window, stabbing into her eyes and her brain. Groaning, she pulled the curtains shut and pressed her brow against the wooden frame, praying that her strength and wits would not leave her.

They reached the Sévères' lodgings, and the brougham came to a halt. Netty opened the door. The letter in her hand didn't need an explanation.

Olivia ripped open the envelope. A note was tucked into it. Her chest contracted.

Briefly, she considered burning it. If it weren't for her curiosity…

She unfolded the note and read:

*I can make you scream. Would you like me to do that for you, my sweet?*

---

SÉVÈRE TRIED TO STAND, but his damn leg wouldn't let him. As soon as he put his weight on it and tried to straighten himself, pain lanced through his knee. Sweat itched on his brow as he grabbed the crutch harder and managed to pull himself halfway up. His bad leg wobbled, and finally caved in. Sévère collapsed back onto the mattress — the filthy, stinky thing a hundred men had abused before him.

With a bellow, he flung the crutch against the wall. It bounced off and hit his ankle. He slammed his fist against the floor. A curse remained stuck in his throat.

The whooping and cackling that followed was all too

familiar. The cell to his left. A man who had murdered a family of six. He called himself, "Gentleman." His real name was less grand: Tom Cobb.

Sévère remembered him well. The way Cobb had slouched in the prisoner's dock at first, but when it became clear at the Coroner's Inquest that he would be found guilty, he began boasting of his deeds. Now, Cobb relished whispering *endearments* to Sévère. How well he knew one of the wardens. How he would make Sévère regret having been born. That all it was going to take was a small bribe, and then Gentleman would bring the long nail he'd worked out of a piece of furniture. And Sévère's trousers would serve as a gag.

This — or one of the many variants of the same tiresome theme — Cobb whispered down the deserted corridor every night.

Sévère was certain the wardens were receptive to bribery. Especially in his case. That he had been assigned a cell on the top floor was no coincidence. He knew that the bottom floor was the least crowded. He had made for great entertainment when he'd been brought up the many flights of stairs. *Cripple coming up!*

Soon, he would be doing this twice every day. Until his acquittal. He huffed. As it looked now, a death sentence was just as likely. He wondered how, though. It was doubtful his leg would allow him to stand for a hanging.

The clanking of the warden's keychain approached. Sévère laid back.

The door opened. 'What happened here?'

'I fell,' Sévère said without taking his eyes off the ceiling. He heard the warden step closer, then lightly kick his crutch.

'It's broken,' the warden said.

'Spoken like a true detective.' Sévère looked at the man now. He was bony. Perhaps a head shorter than Sévère himself. He thought the warden neither evil nor good in character, just…malleable. He would go with the flow, whatever direction the flow might take. If enough men felt motivated to make the life of the former coroner a little harder, the warden would do precisely that, and more. But if no one acted against him, the warden wouldn't, either.

Sévère wondered briefly if exposing his own weakness to the man would pull him over to his side. He wouldn't bet on it. Should he wait for the next shift? No, that man didn't even talk to him.

'I need a physician,' Sévère said.

The warden crossed his arms over his chest. 'Do you, now?'

'The leg has grown weaker.'

No reaction.

'I can't stand up anymore. The consequences should be obvious, I expect.' Sévère threw a quick glance at the bucket that served as a privy.

The warden's eyebrows shot up.

'I'm certain a brace would solve this issue at once. So if you'd please summon a physician before I'm forced to foul the bedding?'

A lazy nod, and the man slunk out the door.

Sévère put a hand over his face, trying to swallow an overwhelming sense of inadequacy and helplessness.

------

METHODICALLY, Olivia folded the note and stuck it back into the envelope. She wanted to burn the damn thing, turn it into black ash and never lay eyes on it again. But maybe one day she could use it as evidence.

At least she now had a good idea who was writing these *love letters*. Frost.

He had a penchant for sensing a person's weakness, and acting on it for his own pleasure. The urge to murder the man made Olivia's flesh ripple.

Netty cleared her throat. Still holding open the brougham's door, gaze firmly plastered to the pavement, she said, 'Higgins ran off to catch Alf.'

'This message was just delivered?'

'Mere moments ago. Would you like a cup of tea, Mistress?'

Olivia sucked in a breath. 'Yes. Hot. With honey.' She heaved herself out of the carriage and made for the house. Her joints were aching.


THE FIRE BURNT HIGH. Olivia sat close to the heat, a blanket wrapped around her shoulders, a cup of tea in her hand. She stared at the flames, furious at herself, her own shortcomings. None of her theories were leading anywhere. They weren't even worth mentioning. If only she weren't ill…

She jerked as an idea hit her. She threw off the blanket, set the tea aside and went to enquire after Higgins.

MRS APPLETON'S expression remained carefully neutral as she opened the door. 'Mrs Sévère. Good evening. I'm not sure Mr Frank can see you.'

'Is he home?'

'He is about to leave.'

'Excellent. I would take only a minute of his time.' Olivia took a step forward, but Mrs Appleton held her ground.

'What will the neighbours think if a woman is seen loitering on your doorstep so soon after the mistress has died?' Olivia mused.

Narrowing her eyes, Mrs Appleton took a step back and admitted her. 'If you will wait here, please,' she said, patting the back of a chair in the hallway. 'Mr Frank will be with you in a few minutes.' With that, she left.

Olivia's gaze followed the housekeeper until she disappeared. Her footfalls trailed off toward the kitchen. There was no sign of Mr Frank. Olivia walked softly toward the parlour, glanced up the staircase, pricked her ears. A door shut. Quickly, she retreated back to the chair in the hallway, dropped her bonnet and rubbed her cheeks, pinched them. Mr Frank took a final step off the stairs, and came into view.

'Good evening,' Olivia said.

'Why… Oh. Mrs Sévère!' He looked over her shoulder as though expecting someone else. 'I see that your husband did not accompany you. He seems to be making a habit of it. Is the coroner unwell?'

'Indeed he is. Mr Frank, what is it about your home that makes people fall ill?'

'Excuse me?' He paused before putting on his top hat.

'You and your wife were both ill. Dr Johnston attended to her, then fell violently ill, too. He and your wife died the same night.' Holding Mr Frank's gaze, Olivia added, 'And you didn't.'

His nostrils flared, he slammed the tip of his cane onto the floorboards with a loud *crack*. 'Are you insinuating I killed my wife and Dr Johnston?'

'I'm not in the habit of insinuating when evidence does it for me.'

Mr Frank stood frozen for a moment, then shook himself, and said, 'You will excuse me now.' He turned and took long strides to the door.

'My husband is accused of killing his friend, Dr Peter Johnston. He's been taken to a cell in Newgate prison. His health is failing him, crippling him. He suffers for someone else's deed. I won't accept that and will do *everything* to find the murderer.'

Mr Frank stopped with his hand on the doorknob. His shoulders set. He faced the door when he replied, 'I cannot help you.' And then he left.

'What is it with this household that a guest is never attended to?' Olivia muttered, turned on her heel and strode to the kitchen.

'Mrs Appleton!' she called out. 'Mr Frank said you are to answer my questions because he has no time to assist me.'

The housekeeper's head popped around a doorframe. She adjusted her cap and clasped her hands in front of her apron.

Olivia heard a softly muttered, 'Did he, now.'

'What illness befell Mr Frank the night his wife died?'

ANNELIE WENDEBERG

'I am no doctor,' Mrs Appleton answered.

Olivia's gaze flicked to the large soup ladles that hung over the hearth. She wanted to snatch one and rap it against the housekeeper's forehead. 'Describe the symptoms, if you please.'

Mrs Appleton turned her gaze to the ceiling. Her chest lifted once, twice, then she narrowed her eyes at Olivia. 'It was merely his nerves, I believe. Their twentieth wedding anniversary. They'd been chatting about it for weeks. In hushed voices. Endlessly. I don't know what they'd planned, where they wanted to go, but it was most certainly something grand.'

Mrs Appleton's expression drifted toward something that seemed almost dreamy. 'I thought it romantic. Unfortunately, it ended…unromantic.'

'Unromantic? Is that what you think of the death of your mistress?'

'Och, romance. That's not for folk such as myself.' She shook her head, almost amused now.

'I know what you mean.' Olivia produced a conspiratorial twitch of her mouth.

'Do you, now?'

'What else was…uncommon that night?'

'Don't you think it uncommon enough that Mrs Frank died?'

'I do. Forgive me.' Olivia lowered her gaze and took a small step back, as though she were considering to take her leave.

'He didn't kill her, you know,' Mrs Appleton said.

'Did *you?*'

'Mrs Sévère!'

'Well, *someone* must have. And there aren't all that many suspects available. May I see the laundry room?'

'What for?' Mrs Appleton pushed her feet slightly apart, her hands propped on her hips. Ready for battle, if need be.

'Because it appeared to make you particularly nervous last night.'

Mrs Appleton harrumphed. 'Of course it did. I'm not in the habit of exhibiting my dirty laundry to strangers.'

Olivia laughed softly and wiped her brow. 'My apologies, Mrs Appleton. It's just that… I don't know. Why is it that everyone seems so untouched by all these horrible deaths?'

'Really, Mrs Sévère! You must be half blind if you don't see how much Mr Frank is suffering!'

'He seemed quite happy just now.'

'He was merely looking forward to visiting his wife's grave. That's all he has left.'

'Late in the evening? He looked like he was going to the opera,' Olivia said.

Mrs Appleton wiped the argument away with a sweeping gesture. 'They always dress their best when they go out.'

'Might I speak with Mrs Frank's personal maid? She employed one, didn't she?'

'Oh, *her*. She's long gone. Was relieved of her duties about…what was it…eight, nine months ago.'

'Why?'

'Mrs Frank couldn't stand being touched by her. She was a bit—'

'Eccentric?'

'Yes. Well, different. Unusual. Mr Frank helped Mrs Frank with her dresses after they sent the maid away.'

'And he was all right with that?'

'Of course. Why wouldn't he be?'

Olivia shrugged, a thought niggling at the back of her mind. 'But you washed her body.'

'Oh, well, I…' Mrs Appleton cleared her throat. 'He insisted on washing her.'

'But—'

'Yes, when you and the coroner visited, I was washing her body. She'd been dead for hours, and I thought… I thought that she had begun…smelling a tad. He wasn't up to it, so I washed her the second time.'

'So he washed her the first time, and you washed her again a few hours later, is that correct?'

'Yes.'

'Did it help? Against the smell?'

'Ah, no. Not quite.'

'And what happened after my husband and I left?' Olivia pressed on.

'Mr Frank took to bed again. He instructed me not to disturb him for the remainder of the day, and to arrange for her body to be prepared for burial.'

'Hmm,' Olivia said, nodding slowly. 'What was the waxed paper for? It lay crumpled on top of a pile of towels.'

'The… Oh.' Mrs Appleton turned her face away. 'I don't know what is was for. Mr Frank put it in the laundry room, instructing me not to touch it.'

'Queer, don't you think?' Olivia asked.

Mrs Appleton shrugged.

'And did you touch it?'

'Of course I didn't. He was quite insistent.'

'Hmm.' Olivia nodded, although she didn't know what to make of it all. 'May I see it?'

'The towels and waxed paper are all gone now. He burnt them last night.' Mrs Appleton scratched her scalp just below her white cotton cap. 'Just after you left.'

'Burnt, you say? Why?'

'I assume he didn't wish to be reminded of the day he had to wash his wife's dead body.'

'That makes...sense. May I take a sample of the ashes?'

The housekeeper picked at her apron, and mumbled, 'I guess Mr Frank wouldn't mind.'

Olivia borrowed a jar from her and shovelled bits of scorched fabric and flakes of black ash from the hearth into it.

Then she stood and said, 'You wouldn't know if there should be a life insurance in Mrs Frank's name?'

'I'm the housekeeper, Mrs Sévère. I do not know of such things.'

'Of course you don't. Well, I guess I should be leaving.'


SHE MET Higgins not far from Mrs Johnston's lodgings. He leant against a lamp post, cigarette in the corner of his mouth, whiskers twitching as she approached.

'Dammit!' Olivia huffed. She felt out of breath, her head was pounding. 'Mr Frank has left the house. I suppose you haven't seen him?'

'If I had, I would be following him now. When did he leave?'

'About ten, fifteen minutes ago. You won't catch him anymore. Did you find out anything interesting from the neighbours?'

'Maybe. Very few urchins in this area. But one or the other proved rather attentive. Talkative, even.' He pointed his chin up the street and began to walk. 'We have the usual: milk is delivered daily, meat every Wednesday and Saturday, and so on. There were a few visits by the dye chemist from the shop down the street, who's said to be a friend of Mr Frank. No one seemed to consider the Johnstons' and Franks' marriages as noteworthy, except that the Johnstons never fought. Or did it so quietly that the neighbours couldn't eavesdrop. The Franks, however, entertained themselves with regular shouting matches. Not in the days or weeks her heart was giving her troubles, mind. But the interesting bit is that a rich fella was seen at the Frank's about a month ago. He visited several times, and left with a smile.'

'Who told you that?'

'About the rich fella? The kitchen boy who works at the Doughty household that's two houses down from the Johnstons.'

'Did he know who the man was?'

'No. But I'll keep asking around.' Higgins lit another cigarette, paused, and glanced at Olivia. 'Would you like a smoke?'

Olivia regarded him. Was it so obvious she wasn't a lady? 'No, thank you,' she said. 'Mr Higgins, do you have family here in London?'

'I don't. Why are you asking?'

'Because I'm wondering about your wages. Your

responsibilities are...' She stopped and frowned. 'They exceed those of a coachman. What does my husband pay you?'

'Fifty pounds per annum.'

'Would it suffice for now if I raised it to seventy?'

Higgins gave a single nod, but didn't speak.

'May I ask you something, Mr Higgins?'

'I believe that's what you've been doing the entire evening.' A grin flashed across his face.

'Did you work as a coachman before you came into my husband's employ?'

'I did not.'

'What did you do before entering the employ of my husband?'

He flicked a sideways glance at her, sucked on his cigarette, and said, 'Baked bread.'

'You are a baker?'

Higgins dropped the butt of his smoke onto the flag-stones and methodically ground it under his boot. 'Mrs Sévère, let us make an agreement.'

She frowned at him.

'You don't ask me about my past, and I won't ask you about yours.'

Aghast, she took a step back. 'Higgins, you are forgetting yourself!'

'Believe me, Mrs Sévère, it takes more than a little prodding to make me forget myself. I will not answer questions about my private life, or my past. Accept this, or send me away.' He looked at her sharply. 'What will it be?'

'Did he tell you where...I come from?'

'Everyone knows you grew up in an orphanage.' He twitched his shoulders.

Olivia nodded once. People ate up the orphanage lie particularly well. She tried to imagine the uproar if they learnt she'd earned a living as a whore.

'I apologise,' she said to Higgins. 'I know what it means to have a...difficult past. I won't ask you about yours again.'

---

DIM LIGHT from the street lamp seeped through the curtains. Rose's warm body was pressed to her back, but still Olivia shivered.

She longed to discuss her thoughts with Sévère, but that was impossible now. Investigating Johnston's murder was like rolling a boulder up a mountain. Not only did she have to catch a murderer without Sévère's help, she had to do it without his warrants, and without the aid and protection of his title.

She sighed. And coughed. Coughed, and couldn't stop.

Rose stirred, reached over to place her small hand onto Olivia's brow. She rubbed her eyes. 'Want tea with honey? I can fetch it. Cook keeps it warm for you on the stove.'

'Thank you,' Olivia said hoarsely and sat up. 'Tea would be nice.'

Rose slipped from the bed, snatched a robe and went down to the kitchen. A few moments later, she returned with a teapot, a small pot of honey, and a candle on a tray.

She bumped the door closed with her heel, and sat back down on the bed.

'You look sad,' she said.

Olivia stirred honey into the hot tea and answered, 'I don't know how to fix this.'

Rose tipped her head at the teacup. 'Fix what?'

'Sévère's in gaol, the new coroner may not be willing to talk to me, and I don't have a warrant that gives me the right to question witnesses and suspects. I don't even *have* a suspect.'

'You aren't a detective anymore?'

'No.'

'Oh.' Rose dropped her head, but before Olivia could pat the girl's hand to comfort her, she squeaked, 'Then we can be pirates!'

Rose scrambled over Olivia and began hopping on the bed. 'On our pirate ship!'

'I'd rather be a pirate detective,' Olivia said dryly, and placed the cup on the night stand to avoid a life-threatening, honeyed-tea flood.

Rose jumped even higher at that. 'Pirate detectives Mistresses Sévère and Rousseau, at your service, Your Highness!'

Olivia couldn't help but chuckle. Until... She grabbed the girl's ankle. 'Rose, you are brilliant!'

Rose plopped down and sat cross-legged, beaming like a Christmas tree.

'My dearest First Mate,' Olivia said, 'I so adore your sharp mind.'

'You do?'

'Yes. As it so happens, Sévère won't be needing his

office for a few weeks. We might as well use it for our private detective agency,' Olivia said with a grin, balled her hand to a fist and bumped her First Mate's bony shoulder. 'I'll register the business tomorrow morning.'

'Pirate detective agency?' Rose's eyes glittered in the candle light. Her hair stood up, forming a frizzly halo around her head.

'Officially, it's a *private* detective agency, First Mate. The Londoner's wouldn't approve of pirates investigating crimes. You must swear to keep it secret.'

Rose placed her hand to her chest, and nodded solemnly. 'I swear upon cook's fresh breakfast muffins.'


LONG AFTER OLIVIA had emptied the tea pot, she stared at Rose's curled up and softly snoring form, and wondered if Johnston's death might have been accidental. Perhaps Mrs Frank had been the intended victim, and Johnston had simply been in the wrong place at the wrong time.

Her thoughts drifted to Sévère and the harsh words they had exchanged. She would have to undo the damage.

She rose and lit a candle, set out paper and pen, and began to write.

## PIRATE DETECTIVES

*T*he stone floor of his cell was littered with case notes in Olivia's hand — script that didn't roll or slant, but stood upright, the *f*s and *g*s cutting sharply into the words below. Had he not known his wife's hand, he would have thought a man had penned the notes. They were precise, defined. Not a single annotation, not one word crossed out. She'd thought about this thoroughly before writing it down for him.

One page contained all the questions she intended to answer before the trial began. Why had Mr Frank burnt towels and waxed paper in the dead of night? Why had he insisted on washing his dead wife, and later couldn't be bothered when Mrs Appleton thought the body needed to be washed once more? Who was the mysterious rich man, and what did the dye chemist know about the marriage of the Franks, the Johnstons, and the two sudden deaths? What had Mrs Johnston seen when she watched the house from the other side of the street with her opera glass?

Sévère heard the clanking of metal bowls and soup ladles from the storey below his own. Lunch time. By now, Olivia would have talked to Dr Barry and presented him with the new samples she'd collected from the hearth of the Franks' household. If Barry turned her down, she would have to talk to Bicker, who then would have to talk to the magistrate to obtain a warrant, and then she would finally have to convey the samples back to Dr Barry.

Sévère dearly hoped that Olivia wasn't made to run back and forth through half of London.

There was so little time left.

He sighed. His gaze fell to the page that was giving him heart ache. It was a letter to him, disguised as a case note. She had even used her old name — Miss Mary.

He brushed his fingers over one of the edges, picked it up, and read it again.

*On the other case we recently discussed:*
*I talked to Miss M, the woman who was sold into prostitution as a young girl. I'm not sure if her statement is relevant to this particular case, but I believe you should know about it anyway. In her own words:*
*"Many men told me they loved me. And I hated it. I could predict with some accuracy when they would say those words. Their gaze, their expression would soften. They would look at me as if I were their princess, their saviour, the only woman who understood all their needs. Because it was always their needs they saw, their urges, their body, their wishes. They hid their egoism behind their countless mutterings of "I love you so, my sweet," because most weren't dumb or blind enough to completely ignore that they were using a child — and later a*

*young woman — for their own pleasure, without ever asking what she needed or wished for herself. Or what she didn't want. When I saw that expression on my husband's face — that softening — everything inside me went dead. I felt like a tree that had suddenly lost all its leaves to an autumn gust. And then, everything revolted. Rarely have I been so angry at the wrong man.*

*I never wish to hear those words again, never wish to see that softening. Please understand that I am not sorry. I have been made to be this way. And I don't have more in me."*

*As to her former client, Mr F: I strongly believe that he is connected to another case we are currently investigating, specifically in a way that might influence evidence to make an innocent appear guilty. I will investigate this further and let you know about all new developments, but I would greatly appreciate your thoughts on this matter as well.*

*Yours,*
*Olivia.*

*PS: Your offices will temporarily be turned into the offices of Sévère & Sévère, Private Detective Agency. Hire me, Gavriel! Bicker is not doing any field work for you.*

*PPS: I increased the annual allowance of your coachman to £70 and made him my assistant investigator. He is surprisingly helpful.*

Gently, Sévère placed the letter back on the mattress, and began tightening the straps of his temporary brace.

He began at the top of his thigh and worked down to his ankle, then pulled his bad leg in with his hands, grabbed the crutch, and stood. The brace was sufficient to help him stand, but the buckles were made of a cheap leather that cut into his flesh, the joints creaked, and the wood threatened to splinter. In two or three days, the physician had told him, he would receive a new brace that would comfortably stabilise his ankle and knee. He would walk upright into the court room, not crawl on all fours.

He limped over to the bucket and relieved himself, one hand clawing the wall.

Back on his bed, he loosened the buckles, and gazed again at Olivia's letter.

*I don't have more in me.*

He thought back to their wedding night. Why the deuce had she insisted on the consummation if she felt this way? Could she have truly made herself do that for legal reasons? He barked a bitter laugh. She'd made herself bed men for years.

He racked his brain, trying to recall a moment, a word, a flicker in her eyes that would indicate she hated what she was allowing him to do. He had felt her body moving with his, had seen the blush rising to her face, her eyes darkening to deepest black.

But lust and love were two entirely different creatures. And he'd never liked the complications of the latter.

*I don't have more in me.*

He shook his head. She loved Rose, of that he was absolutely certain. The way those two stuck their heads together, how they play acted, and invented silly contraptions they baptised *pirate ships* made it obvious they were friends. But Olivia was so protective of Rose, she must have maternal feelings for the girl as well.

*I don't have more in me.*

But then it hadn't been little girls who had hurt her. It had been men like himself.

Six, seven months ago he wouldn't have thought twice about visiting a prostitute. Bloody hell! The day of a release from gaol would have found him tangled in sheets with at least two pretty and willing women. But knowing what he now knew…

*I have been made to be that way.*

He had never considered taking a maiden for his pleasure. Men who did so disgusted him. Even so, many of the *willing* women who had invited him into their beds in exchange for coin did so of necessity. He had never bothered to ask what they wished for themselves.

A sick and heavy feeling settled in Sévère's stomach. Before marrying Olivia, he'd never even considered asking a woman what she wanted.

*I don't have more in me.*

His gaze kept going back to these words, and he felt an urge to undo them, to undo…everything.

With an impatient growl, he pushed the letter aside.

Then he gathered the scattered case notes and stacked them to a neat pile, leaving Olivia's letter at its very bottom. Methodically, he went through every witness statement, every piece of evidence, every question his wife had brought up, and added his own thoughts. He didn't have the luxury of considering anything but his case.

'THE TRIAL IS IN TWO DAYS,' Olivia glanced at every face in the room. Alf scooted around on his chair as if he were sitting on a nest of bumblebees. He pulled on one over-large ear, and then on the other. Rose sat ramrod straight, cheeks red as though someone had slapped her, eyes glistening with excitement. William slipped one of the biscuits Netty had placed on the desk into his mouth, and wiped his crumbly palms on his trousers. Higgins stood by the door, still wearing his bowler, looking like he didn't quite belong.

Olivia flattened her hands on the notes before her. Then she began, 'Correspondence with Sévère is agonisingly slow, and this problem needs to be solved right away. Hence, I have registered a private detective agency as my new business. Higgins is my assistant, Alf and Rose are…' she glanced at the girl and smirked, '…my spies. And Mr Burroughs…' she gave William a nod, '…will make sure that we do not get ourselves arrested.'

'At least not before you've got your husband out of gaol,' William said through a mouthful of crumbles.

'Precisely. Now, as Mr Burroughs has explained to me, Sévère is allowed to hire a private detective to assist his case. Acting as Sévère's private investigator permits me to meet him in his cell to discuss evidence, strategy, and the like. The second advantage is that I can collect said evidence as official business.'

'Given anyone takes a lady detective serious,' William muttered.

Higgins glued his gaze onto William.

Olivia looked up at the coachman. 'This is where Mr Higgins comes into play.'

He answered with a small nod, and pushed his bowler off his brow with a lazy flick of his fingers. 'The lady will be taken serious, have no doubt.'

'Thank you, Mr Higgins. As to—'

'But what about me?' Rose piped up. Alf pulled harder on his ear.

'You, my impatient pirate, will put on trousers, hide your hair beneath a cap, and rub soot on your cheeks. I assume you know perfectly how to do that?'

Rose had the decency to look a little ashamed. She had months of experience sneaking away in disguise, believing no one knew.

Olivia gave a satisfied nod, and turned to Alf. 'You, young man, will be a perfect gentleman. I'm not planning to send you into dangerous situations, but you will look out for Rose. Is that clear?'

Alf dropped his gaze, and nodded once.

'And you.' She narrowed her eyes back at the girl. 'Show him some respect. You two will be working together. I have no need for two assistants that keep pulling each other's hair.'

'She punched me!' Alf provided.

'You pinched me first!' Rose stamped her foot. 'And you put tadpoles into my soup!'

'Quiet,' Higgins said in a voice so low that silence fell at once.

Until a loud slurping noise pulled everyone's attention to William. He emptied his teacup and placed it with a soft *clink* on its saucer. 'Excellent. Now that I have your attention,' he said, and smacked his lips, '…and the children have ceased their bickering, may I recommend we hurry up and address the list your husband has sent you?'

Olivia cleared her throat. 'Rose, Alf, whenever your school and work duties permit, you will mingle with the local urchins, talk to costermongers, crawlers, anyone who might be able to provide information on the Johnstons and the Franks. But don't be too obvious about it. And be careful.'

Alf rolled his eyes and was promptly thwacked by Rose.

Olivia dismissed the two, and addressed Higgins and Williams. 'Sévère asked me to cast a wider net. To talk to all shopkeepers in the area of the Franks' and the Johnstons' homes, tail all household members. Learn about all friends, enemies, neighbours, colleagues. Find out about life insurances and bank accounts, and if there have been notable withdrawals, cheques that have not been honoured, and so on.'

'The police might have already looked into those last,' William said.

Olivia's eyebrows rose. 'Mr Frank is a witness, not a suspect.'

'Well then, we make him one.'

'How?'

'Do you have your cards?'

'They'll be ready by tomorrow, the printer assured me.'

William scratched his chin. 'Hum.'

When he didn't continue, Olivia said, 'There's not much hope Dr Barry will find anything in the samples I brought him today.'

William looked up. 'Samples?'

'Oh, did I forget to tell you? Well, last night…' She told him about the scorched remnants of the towels and waxed paper she'd collected from the hearth at the Franks' residence, and that she'd brought them to Dr Barry to have them analysed for poison. And that Barry had expressed sincere doubt that the fabric, even if it had been in contact with a poison prior to burning, would have any trace of it left on its remains.

'Olivia, you *must* understand that you are not acting on behalf of an official of the crown anymore.' William rubbed his scalp and shook his head. 'You are the prisoner's wife. You cannot confiscate evidence, and hope to have it hold up in court.'

Olivia shoulders slumped. 'So even if he does find poison, it can't be used as evidence?'

'Bet on it.'

'But what if *you* confiscate it, Mr Burroughs?' Higgins asked.

'An entirely different matter. As long as you don't hire me as your attorney, that is. And that is why you'll need me—'

'What did you mean with making Mr Frank a suspect?' Olivia cut across William.

He tilted his head to one side, eyeing Higgins and Olivia. Then he smiled meekly. '*Suspect* is such a harsh word. Let us simply say that shedding a new light on the man might come in useful. And not to forget Mrs Johnston! In the court room, they'll both be treated like victims. They've lost their spouses and are in mourning. No attorney in his right mind would touch them with anything less than kid gloves. However, if we can make the police believe that Mr Frank and Mrs Johnston might not be as innocent as they appear, Inspector Height might aid us in our investigation.'

Higgins left his spot by the door, sauntered across the room, and took a seat next to Olivia. William narrowed his gaze at the man, an expression of calculation flickering across his face. 'Is Mr Higgins the tail?'

Higgins lowered his head in acknowledgement. 'That is one of my responsibilities.'

'Excellent. Now, we want to be extremely careful. Olivia, you will need to be established as a private investigator. It has to be official. Public, even. Hum… Best announced by the judge himself, and spread by every newspaper in town.'

Olivia spit out her tea. 'Excuse me?'

William grinned and slipped another biscuit into his mouth. 'A good attorney at law is much like a warlord. He must know his enemy's every next step. Should it give him an advantage, he allows himself to appear weak when in truth he is strong. He must hit his adversaries when least they expect it.'

'Sounds to me much like being a—' She clamped her mouth shut, her teeth clacking together.

She'd almost said "whore."

## EVIDENCE

*O*livia waited for Higgins to shut the door. Then she pushed the tray with the last biscuit over to William, leant back in her chair, and rubbed her burning eyes. She dearly hoped Higgins would find the mysterious stranger who had visited the Franks shortly before the death of Mrs Frank.

She stretched her neck until it crackled. Her bones felt brittle, her muscles ached. She longed for a hot bath and several hours of uninterrupted sleep. 'Frost is sending me love letters.'

William coughed. His belly hopped beneath his waistcoat and the buttons threatened to pop off. 'Love letters?'

'I'm being sarcastic. He's threatening me. He knows that I'm alone, now that Sévère is in prison. What precisely his goal is, I don't know, but...' She curled her fingers to a fist and watched how the blood drained from her knuckles. 'I *know* that he's using this mess to his advantage. He would love to see me fall, and so...he's now...'

'Giving you a shove,' William completed her sentence.

She huffed.

'But why?' he asked.

'He needs to win. At any cost. Whenever I was unable to receive him — and this happened only a handful of times in all those years — he would punish me afterwards. And now I'm eluding him for good. He can't live with that. He *must* own me, yet he can't. So he seeks revenge.'

'And you believe he arranged the evidence so that your husband appears guilty instead of...whom? Frost himself?'

Olivia frowned. 'I wish I knew. I doubt Frost did it. At least I can't see why he would...' She groaned and pressed her knuckles to her eyes. 'There's so much to do and so little time! But I know... I just *know* that I have to find evidence of Frost's crimes. He has to be made responsible. If only I could prove that he assaults young girls... They would be rid of him. And I would be rid of him. And he couldn't...' impatiently, she waved her hands in the air, '... manipulate evidence, and whatever else he's doing. By the Queen's arse! This is utterly frustrating!'

'It won't help you,' William said softly. 'I've been frequenting bawdy houses for years. You know that.'

Indeed she did. She'd been one of the women he visited.

'And I've known about these "seductions" for just as long. I've tried to help. I've interviewed several girls. Perhaps fifteen, twenty. None of them were willing to prosecute. None of them knew their assailant's name. Most said they had not even seen the assailant's face, or wouldn't recognise him if they saw him again. A few said they might recognise his voice.'

Olivia swallowed. She hadn't recognised Frost when he had come to her the second time, a few days after his first assault. Until she saw the backs of his hands, heard his voice, his groans.

She turned her face away as William continued, 'They did not wish to prosecute because they know that no one believes a girl who cries rape. A woman who has lost her chastity is a discredited witness. The fact that she was in a brothel would be seen as evidence of her consent, even though she had been abducted and drugged. The madam and all who work there would always swear she'd been a consenting party. And the girl would be condemned as an adventuress.'

Silence settled in the room. Olivia heard the tireless struggle of a fly as it bounced up and down a window pane. The clattering of hooves down on the street. One man shouting at another.

'And this will go on as long as men have money and power, and women are forbidden both,' she said.

'And instead of protecting them, parents keep their daughters in the dark about all of this. A girl who knows what a man is capable of doesn't appear innocent enough to potential suitors, making it harder to marry her off,' William added sourly.

'The meat market must thrive.' Olivia inhaled deeply, pushed out a breath, and forced herself to not throw Sévère's ashtray at William's head. None of this was William's fault.

'As to building a case against Frost — theories of moral

contamination are shifting. The law is growing more aware of rape and abuse. However, the legislation for prosecuting child abuse is extraordinarily complicated. You will find that a perpetrator might be charged with rape in one district, with a misdemeanour in another, and not at all in yet another. Successful prosecution depends not only on reliable witnesses — whom you don't have — but also on the experience of the magistrate, the police, and the attorneys, as well as on the attitudes of the jurymen.'

'Are you saying I will have to catch him in the act of raping a child?'

'No, because he will claim that she told him she was of age and had offered herself to him. Furthermore, he'll claim that you are accusing him to distract the jury, to influence your husband's trial.'

Olivia gazed out the window. She clenched her jaw until her teeth screeched.

'I am sorry, Olivia. I truly am,' William said softly.

She shook her head and blinked the burning from her eyes. After a moment, she asked, 'Can he influence the outcome of Sévère's trial?'

'Officially, he can't. Unofficially, he can steer your ship against a cliff. He can make evidence appear and disappear. He need only be careful about it. No one would think anything amiss. No one would ever suspect him.'

Olivia gazed at her hands, and nodded. Of course. He is the Chief Magistrate. He can do as he wishes.

THE BELL RANG as she entered the chemist's shop. She caught a whiff of something bitter. The scent disappeared the moment she sniffed again. At the counter, a man was bent over a note a customer had just given him. 'I am not quite sure what it says here.' A hairy finger pointed at crooked script.

'Might want to ask Mr Walker to help you read it,' the customer said gruffly. 'It says "quinine," by the by.'

The man squinted at the note. Olivia guessed him to be a rather new addition to the flock of assistants Mr Walker kept in employ.

'Twenty grain?'

The customer — a bespectacled man in his seventies, pulled off his hat and pinched the bridge of his nose. He cleared his throat and said, 'Indeed. Twenty grains.'

'Humpf.' The assistant frowned at the note.

'My dear man, my presence is required elsewhere. So if you would please weigh twenty grains of quinine at your earliest convenience?'

Olivia's gaze swept the room, the hundreds of small brown bottles, larger white bottles, dark wooden drawers and boxes. She folded her hands behind her back, and watched the assistant systematically weigh small amounts of white powder onto a piece of tinfoil, remove excess quinine, add a tiny bit more when he saw that the weight wasn't quite correct, and again scoop off what he had put on too much.

Pulling in a slow breath, she begged for a patience she didn't have.

The assistant folded the tinfoil to a neat square, then chose a small paper envelope, wrote his name, the chemist's name and address, the contents, date, and time onto it, then slipped the tinfoil packet inside. The customer reached for it, but the assistant held up his hand and said, 'I have to enter the amount and your name into our poison register.'

'Quinine is a poison?' the customer said, gripping the front of his waistcoat.

'Indeed it is.' With that, the assistant whipped out a fat volume and slowly wrote the date, his name, the type and amount of poison, then looked up expectantly. 'Your name, sir.'

'Walter Clifton.'

'Thank you.'

Money was exchanged for drug, and Mr Clifton left the shop. Olivia stared after him, thinking.

'Miss?'

She turned and smiled. 'Does the law require you to ask the name of a customer who wishes to purchase a poison from you?'

'Of course it does. Do you wish to purchase a poison, Miss…?'

'Mary Andrews. I need a small jar of *Unguent aconitia*.'

---

OLIVIA HELD out her hand and the horse nuzzled her palm in the darkness. Long, soft hairs tickled her skin. Warm scents of horse dung and straw, of barley and fresh hay soothed her. She leant her brow again the chestnut's forehead. The horse snorted and pulled away.

'You are making her nervous. Place your hand on her neck instead.'

Olivia jumped. She had not heard Higgins enter the stable.

'So you do in fact know something about horses,' she said, lifting her fingers and brushing them down the horse's neck. The animal blinked its large, dark eyes and huffed.

'I know how to listen.'

'And did you learn anything new?'

He leant against the stable wall. 'Other than you not being able to sleep, I've not learnt much. No one came or left. Mrs Johnston was watching the street and the houses across from hers until just after midnight. Two urchins are now keeping an eye on our subjects. I will catch a bit of sleep and relieve them before dawn. I doubt much will happen between now and then. What time is it, anyway?'

'Half past one.'

'Well then, I'd better make it quick,' he said and rolled up in the straw.

'You are sleeping in the stable?'

'Harrumph,' was the only answer.

Olivia fidgeted with a strand of the horse's mane. 'Mr Higgins, I have a favour to ask.'

He grunted and clapped one eye open.

'You may…chose to not aid me in my…in that particular… Well, dammit. I need a revolver. You wouldn't know how I could come by one, would you?'

# FOURTH ACT

*Stars,*
*hide your fires,*
*Let not light*
*see*
*my black and deep*
*desires.*

William Shakespeare

TRIAL

ay one

THE COURT ROOM was packed to suffocation long before the opening hour of the trial. The corridors were crowded, as was the domed marble hall, and even the stairs to the entrance. Ladies had donned their most fashionable garments and fanciest hats, as if this spectacle were not a murder trial, but a garden party.

The whole of London wanted to see the Coroner of Eastern Middlesex in the prisoner's dock. Who would have thought the man a murderer? Who would have thought a respectable man so cold-blooded?

At quarter to eleven the judicial procession strode into the court room. Justice Sir Charles Hawkins was an imposing figure, robed in scarlet and ermine. He was immediately followed by two aldermen, the recorder, the sheriffs and under-sheriffs, and several Middlesex magistrates, among them Linton Frost. The man was like a knife slipped through Olivia's armour.

The bench bowed to the court, the court returned the salutation, and everyone sat down.

Olivia's stomach was in knots. She wanted to swipe the stupid flower bouquets and the small heaps of dried herbs off the desks that stood alongside the bench. She wanted to snatch the black cap from the judge, rip it to shreds and burn it. That black cap would press heavy on her every minute Sévère spent in the prisoner's dock. It was a constant reminder that this trial was a matter of life and death.

All eyes turned to a small door in the back. It opened, and Sévère was led in. A man walked on Sévère's right, while his left side leant heavily on a crutch. He appeared composed, almost detached, but Olivia saw the tension in his shoulders and jaw.

He faced the bench and managed an awkward half-bow.

The judge waited for Sévère to take a seat in the prisoner's dock, then he began to read the indictment, 'The jurors of our Lady, the Queen, upon their oath present that Gavriel Sévère, former Coroner of Eastern Middlesex, on the second day of July, in the year of our Lord, one thousand eight hundred and eighty one, feloniously, wilfully, and with malice aforethought, did kill one Doctor Peter Johnston, house surgeon of Guy's Hospital, against the peace of our Lady, the Queen, her Crown, and dignity. How does the prisoner plead?'

'Not guilty,' Sévère said.

A small part of Olivia's mind expected all men to rise, bow to Sévère, and release him right then. And that small part couldn't grasp why a jury was empanelled and sworn, why everyone in the room looked sombre, why the trial continued undisturbed. Hadn't they heard what Sévère said? A mad chuckle threatened to escape her. She pressed a palm to her mouth until her teeth cut the soft flesh of her upper lip.

The solicitor-general rose and began to outline the case. The man's voice was without pitch, without passion, as he recounted what had occurred. Logic. Observation. And yes, such cases rested almost entirely on circumstantial evidence. One could not watch a killer do the deed. But the evidence was so complete, it would satisfy the jury beyond a shadow of a doubt that the prisoner committed the heinous crime of which he stood charged.

After one hour and twenty minutes, the solicitor-general straightened the hems of his robe with a snap, drank from a cup of tea, and called the first witness.

One Mr Walker, chemist at Whitechapel Road, stated that he had always found the prisoner to be a kind-hearted and amiable man.

Sévère arched an eyebrow. Olivia ground her teeth, wishing he wouldn't appear so arrogant.

The chemist couldn't say how long the prisoner had been suffering from joint pains, but he had been his customer for three months now, and was making up his own ointments for which he would buy the drugs. He would purchase small jars of white lard, aconitine powder, and arsenic. The chemist couldn't say where the prisoner kept the drugs. Early in May, the prisoner came to the office as usual, and purchased fifty grains of aconitine and three small jars of white lard. He did not purchase arsenic as he usually did. The prisoner had shown no trace of uneasiness, and his appearance was not worried. There was no trace of abruptness. He was as kind as ever.

The solicitor-general stood, his expression that of utter astonishment, and asked the chemist if he had heard correctly. Did Coroner Sévère buy fifty grains — an eighth of an ounce — of aconitine at his office?

'Yes, he did.'

'And you did not find this amount alarming?'

'Of course I did not. He is the Coroner.'

'But don't you know the law, Mr Walker? Dispensing chemists are not allowed to weigh more than a grain of aconitine.'

'I do know the law, sir, but this was the Coroner who bought it from me. He is duly qualified. I did not expect...'

'What did you not expect, Mr Walker?'

'I did not expect that Mr Sévère might be planning something...unlawful.'

The chemist went on to explain the kind of aconitia he was keeping, which was Morson's, and what he had read in the papers about Sévère, at which point Justice Hawkins shut the man up with a glance that made the entire jury flinch.

The cross-examination by Bicker was short. Was Walker sure that Sévère had bought the fifty grains, and not five or even less. Yes, he was quite certain.

'Quite?'

'Yes, quite certain.'

Bicker nodded, deep in thought. 'You are in the habit of entering all sales of poisons into the poisons register, is that correct?'

'Yes, we do.'

'So of course you know precisely how much aconitia the prisoner has purchased.'

Mr Walker paused. 'Sales to medical men are not entered into the poisons register.'

'Did the prisoner pretend to be a medical man?'

'Well... No, he did not.'

'Mr Walker, I am puzzled. Aconitia and its preparations are under the Poisons Act. If a purchaser is not a medical man, you are legally obliged to enter the name of the purchaser, the quantity of the purchased poison, and the date of purchase into the register, and then you are to take the signatures. Yet you did none of these things. You do, however, recall clearly and with precision how much aconitia — aconitia, and not any other poison — the prisoner bought that day and what mood he was in. Would you mind telling me what else you sold that same day, and to whom, and would you mind describing the moods of every one of these customers?'

Walken's face went blank. After some throat clearing he stated that he could, in fact, not name a single client. He was released from the witness stand, and the judge announced that the trial was adjourned for the day.

Before the jury was dismissed, Bicker stood, his knuckles rapping against the desk, his voice clear as a bell. 'I would like to take your Lordship's opinion on a pressing issue.'

The shuffling of feet on floorboards and backsides on

chairs ceased at once. The judge gazed at Bicker as though he were pigeon shit fouling his scarlet and ermine lapels.

'The prisoner — a man who is entirely unable to walk without a full leg brace and a crutch — is being made to climb four steep flights of stairs to reach his cell which is located on the top floor, although several cells on the ground floor are unoccupied. He has received threats to his life from fellow prisoners — murderers whom he helped convict while faithfully serving the Crown. Yet no action has been taken against those men. Furthermore, he was not allowed to see his private detective, who is probably the only person left bothering to identify the real perpetrator after the Grand Jury was in such a hurry to accept a bill of indictment. Were I not as familiar with our judicial system as I am, I believe I would assume that it is desired the prisoner not attend his own trial upright and alive.'

'Mr Bicker!' The gavel hit the dais with force, and all newspaper reporters scribbled away frantically. 'Are you insinuating that justice is not being served? In my own court room?' the judge thundered, his cheeks a deep raspberry-red.

'On the contrary, my Lord. Justice doesn't seem to be served as soon as the prisoner *leaves* your court room.'

The judge's head snapped to the magistrates. His jaw muscles were rippling, his moustache stood on end. He narrowed his gaze back at Bicker and growled, 'The prisoner is to be moved to a cell on the ground floor. At once! A warden is to be placed at his door at all times, and every man who has dared threaten the prisoner's life is to be punished.'

The gavel clonked against wood.

Bicker raised an eyebrow and cleared his throat.

'As to the private detective,' the judge added sharply. 'What is his name?'

'Olivia Sévère,' Bicker answered calmly.

The newspaper reporters froze with their pencils mid-air, their eyes darting between the attorney for the defence and Justice Hawkins, and upon a seemingly invisible sign, they all resumed scribbling like whirlwinds.

'Are you jesting?' The judge's face grew a shade darker.

'I am not. Mrs Olivia Sévère assisted the Coroner of Eastern Middlesex for months, until he was arrested. She has experience in interrogating witnesses, seeking evidence, and building a case. She has now established a registered detective agency, and is perfectly able to investigate this case. In fact, she is already doing so. Quite capably, I should add.'

The judge puffed up his cheeks, narrowed his gaze on Olivia, and grunted, 'And this is the prisoner's wish?'

'It is,' Sévère said.

Olivia couldn't command her mouth to operate.

'The prisoner is permitted to see his private detective, Mrs Olivia Sévère, in his cell.' A *clonk,* and the judge left the dais.

---

Rose unwrapped a candy. Alf had just sneaked away to *wring his snake* as he dubbed it. It was probably a maggot he wrung. Or a pimple.

She wondered if the candy would be raspberry or

strawberry? It was red, so it could be either. Or maybe blackberry? She popped it into her mouth. Sour and sweet. Rhubarb, then.

She spotted Alf slouching by a corner shop. He was approached by a stranger, and they began to talk. Alf pushed his hands into his trouser pockets, chin high, cap askew. Pursing his lips, he shook his head at the young man who now stepped closer, crowding him with his height and bulk. The stranger lifted a fist and sniffed it theatrically, then said something that made Alf extract his own fists from his pockets and clench them at his side.

Rose sauntered over to them and said in a low voice, 'I wouldn't do that if I were you.'

'Shut ya trap,' the young man said, and looked her up and down — her filthy torn shirt, the countless patches on her trousers, her dirt-rimmed nails and wrists — and added, 'Bum raisin.'

Then he turned his attention back to Alf. 'Ya owe me a shilling. I get me money now, or I take a tooth. What is it?'

'You get a shilling when I get a name, that was the deal,' Alf said.

The fist moved closer to his right eye.

'I really wouldn't get so close to him what with the diseases and all,' Rose provided cheerfully.

Now it was Alf who turned to her and said, 'Shut your trap, bum raisin.'

'And since when is my name bum raisin, pimple prick?'

'Pimple prick?' Alf blinked. 'PIMPLE PRICK?' Then he pounced. And missed her by an inch.

Giggling, Rose sprinted down the road, turned a

corner and into an alley, another alley and yet another. She heard Alf right behind her. The second and heavier set of footfalls was fading. And fading.

When she was convinced they'd lost their tail, she stopped and positioned herself behind a lamppost in case Alf wanted to punch her. He definitely looked it when he skidded to a halt merely two steps from her. 'Why is it always prick words? Cauliflower prick. Pimple prick. You haven't even *seen* it.'

'Are you complaining?'

Alf shut his mouth, and his gaze zeroed in on her face. 'Is that candy you are eating?'

'Yes it is.' She broadened her shoulders, working her jaws for emphasis. 'And it's *not* honourable to steal candy from someone who just saved your life.'

Alf snorted — probably to hide his embarrassment — and turned away. 'We have work to do.'

Just as they turned onto Sillwood Street, Mrs Johnston stepped off the stairs to her house. Alf turned Rose around, so that he was facing the street and she was facing him. They pretended to discuss a topic of great importance, while Mrs Johnston manoeuvred around cabs and pedestrians to reach Mr Frank's residence.

'Oho!' Alf said under his breath. 'Mrs Johnston is visiting Mr Frank. I wonder what this is about.'

Rose groaned and shook her head. Alf was a lost cause when it came to spy language. He kept forgetting that Mrs Johnston was *the finch*, Mrs Appleton was *the donkey*, and Mr Frank was—

A sharp jab rang through her ribcage. 'Ow!' Glaring at Alf, she massaged her side.

'I didn't elbow you *that* hard,' Alf grumbled. Then he nodded toward Mr Frank's house. 'Two windows are open. We should try to eavesdrop.'

Casually, they walked over to the white-washed house and leant against the metal fence, hands in pockets, eyes trailing over passers-by, ears pricked. But the clopping of horseshoes, the rattling of wheels, and chattering of people made it impossible to hear what Mrs Johnston was saying to Mr Frank, or if she said anything at all.

So they waited.

A costermonger's cart approached slowly, pulled by a tired mule. The animal held its head low, froth was oozing from the bit.

'Ice cream,' Rose whispered. 'He has ice cream.'

Alf shushed her. A short moment later, his stomach yowled, and Rose smiled at him with triumph in her face. 'What will you give me if I buy you a scoop?'

Alf ground his teeth and looked up at the dark blue sky.

'You can have one if you swear you will never again put anything in my food. No tadpoles, no earth worms, no—'

'Turds?' he said with a smirk.

'What?' she squeaked and instantly felt sick. 'Disgusting, horrible pig!' she hissed.

'What? No prick word?'

She pushed off the fence, approached the costermonger, and paid for a scoop of ice cream on a waffle. Grinning, she turned to face Alf, stuck out her tongue and lavishly ran it across her treasure. She grunted with satisfaction and slowly walked back to him.

He ignored her as she leant against the fence, saying, 'Hmmmm,' and 'Ohhhh,' and ate her ice cream with utmost focus.

And then he reached out and mashed the entire thing into her face.

Stunned into silence, she picked waffle shrapnel off her cheeks, and used her whole hand to scrape all the ice cream off her face and into her mouth. But much had already dripped to the pavement. 'I hope your prick rots off. *And* your balls.'

He shot her a warning glare.

From behind them, sounds rose. The opening of a door and a shuffling of feet. And then, Mr Frank's voice. 'Have a nice evening, Mrs Johnston.' He sounded a bit stiff to Rose's ear, but then most adults spoke as if they had a fork shoved up their bum.

'We will see,' was Mrs Johnston's icy reply.

There was brief moment of silence before Mr Frank called out, 'Get away from my fence, you two!'

# GRAVEYARD

*O*livia presented her papers to the officer who received her at the gates of Newgate prison. The man nodded and walked her through a lodge, then headed in the wrong direction.

'Excuse me,' she said, motioning the other way. 'But I'm to visit Mr Gavriel Sévère.'

He spat on the walkway and muttered, 'Prisoner had been moved.'

How efficient, she thought.

They turned into a yard and stopped at a thick iron gate. A turnkey admitted them, and they went deep into a maze of corridors guarded by armed men, gates, gratings, and more iron-banded doors. When they reached yet another ward, cold sweat began to trickle down Olivia's spine.

The officer opened the door for her and said with a smile that didn't touch his eyes, 'The condemned ward.'

Olivia's jaw felt as though it had come off its hinges.

'Newgate has a capacity for nearly two hundred prisoners, and my husband was put in the *condemned* ward?' Her voice sounded too shrill in her ears.

The officer merely shrugged. 'Far as I know, he asked for it.' Then he jerked his head, motioning her to step through.

She entered the damp corridor. Her ribcage grew tighter with every gulp of foul air she sucked into her lungs. Several oil lamps vomited unsteady light onto the flagstones, turning the slime inhabiting the cracks into a living, writhing thing. At the far end loomed a narrow staircase. Everyone knew it led to the Graveyard — a place of utter desolation where hanged murderers were buried beneath thick slabs of stone.

An armed guard stood in front of each of the twenty-four cells — mere holes in the walls, secured with gratings, locks, and iron bands. The pitiful homes of men whose only future lay in meeting their maker at the end of a rope.

'For the coroner,' the officer said to no one in particular, then stepped back through the door and shut it with a loud clank. The noise bounced off the walls.

Olivia knew hell. She'd lived it. But this — *this* was hell and bottomless despair, decay, and death all at once. She rolled her tongue around in her dry mouth, trying to swallow.

A guard asked for her papers, and she held them out to him. He read them twice, turning them over, and over again. And finally, he unlocked a cell.

Bracing herself, she entered. The door closed behind her — a sharp, unforgiving noise. Like a gunshot.

'Welcome to my new lodgings, dear wife,' Sévère said. 'Please excuse that I remain seated.'

Her eyes adjusted to the gloom, but the rest of her body didn't. Her breath came in short bursts, her knees clacked together. 'Why… Why *here?*'

'I needed better protection and this place certainly has it. Courtesy of the Chief Magistrate.'

Sévère sat awkwardly in a small hammock that was fastened to iron rings on both sides of the cell. The floor, the walls, all was wet and grimy.

'It's so cold,' was all she managed to say.

'Nothing we can do about that now. Tell me news about our case.'

She blinked, motioning at his canvas bed. 'Can you even sleep on this contraption? And is the unguent helping at all?'

'The unguent was confiscated when they moved me down here.' Sévère made a half-hearted wave at his small, windowless enclosure. 'And I'm quite happy with the hammock. The alternative would be to sleep in a puddle of…well, whatever it is that has trickled all the way down here.'

She bit her tongue, yanked up her skirts, slipped her fingers into her stockings, and pulled out the jar she'd purchased the previous day. 'I had an inkling you might be needing more of this.'

Sévère stared at her outstretched hand and said, 'You are an angel.'

He scooted to the edge of the hammock, unstrapped his brace, took it off, and placed it next to him. His fingers stopped at his trouser buttons, his gaze flicked to Olivia.

She turned around to give him privacy. Her eyes followed a drop of water as it crawled down the wall, whitish grease in its wake. She heard the rustling of fabric, the soft clink of the jar being uncapped, and a small, happy grunt as Sévère rubbed the unguent onto his bad leg.

'You can turn around now,' he said a little later.

As he strapped his brace back on, Olivia bent forward, dipped her finger into the unguent, and spread it onto her palm. 'So this is the murder weapon.'

'Apparently.'

'It tingles,' she observed.

'In a few moments it will begin to prickle and burn.'

'How odd.' She gazed at her hand for a moment, wondering how much of the unguent one needed to swallow in order to die. 'I purchased the unguent yesterday under a false name from an assistant at Walker's. He didn't ask for my papers. Whoever bought this poison to kill Johnston probably hasn't used his real name. Or hers. It's easy.'

He didn't answer, so she looked up from her palm.

'Olivia,' he began. 'I apologise. And I promise I will try my best to behave.'

'What are you talking about?'

'Your letter.'

'Oh.' She dropped her gaze to her exposed ankles. Hastily, she arranged the hems of her skirts. 'I apologise for my harsh reaction. It was unjustified.'

'It was entirely justified.'

'It… Let us not talk about it now,' she said, and looked up. 'There's so much to do.'

He nodded once. 'And too little time. But I need to tell you that… The night I visited you and my behaviour… I despise the man I was.'

Olivia swallowed. 'Sévère—'

'Let me finish, please. I entered your room expecting to get… I paid a prostitute for her services and she was to give them to me, that's what I expected. After all, I gave her my money. A guinea!' A harsh, rueful laugh erupted from him.

Olivia's stomach roiled. Blood roared in her ears. 'Sévère—'

'I have not ever questioned what is considered normal. I have not for a moment wondered if a soul might be worth infinitely more than a gold coin. I wish I could undo everything.'

Darkness descended on her. The stone walls. Sévère's presence. All collapsed onto her chest. She pressed her hands to her ears, squeezed her eyes shut, and chanted, 'Be quiet. Be quiet. Be quiet.'

When her forehead hurt from pressing it too hard against the stone wall, when her lungs ached from strained breathing, she straightened up, wiped her face, and cleared her throat. 'Alf and Rose mingle with the urchins around Sillwood Street. They witnessed Mrs Johnston paying Mr Frank a visit earlier this evening. There must have been an argument, because they bade farewell in a rather…icy manner.'

Only then did she look at Sévère. He was utterly pale.

He opened his mouth, considered, and said in a hoarse voice, 'I see.'

She brushed wrinkles from her skirts and continued,

'Alf and Rose heard how Mr Frank bade Mrs Johnston a good evening. Alf said his voice was flat. She answered with, "We will see." Which is a little odd, but nothing... nothing that should cause concern. Probably irrelevant. But Alf might have learned more about the mysterious man who visited the Franks. The wealthy-looking one. One of the street urchins says he heard the man tell another that he's from London Joint Stock Bank. No name, though. William will try to find out more tomorrow as soon as the bank opens.'

'Anything else?'

'No. I'm sorry.'

He rubbed his face, then his scalp, and murmured, 'What if Johnston's death was an accident?'

'I had the same thought a few days ago.'

'You did?'

'Yes. And then I...forgot about it.' She twisted her fingers in her lap, a deep frown carving her brow.

Sévère made to touch her hand, but she stepped out of his reach. 'Leave your fingers attached please,' he said. 'How else will you write case notes for me?'

A small snort erupted from her, and even Sévère's mouth twitched.

'That leaves us with only one question,' he said. 'If Johnston wasn't supposed to die, who was?'

'The Franks? Mrs Johnston?'

'Hum.'

---

DAY TWO

Sévère watched with a puzzling degree of detachment as the prosecution called in witnesses to describe his character and outline the events leading up to Johnston's death. A tiresome lineup of servants, neighbours, and his officer, Stripling — or rather, his *former* officer. Sévère observed the jury grow heavy-lidded while the audience up in the galleries gradually thinned.

When Netty stated that she had overheard Johnston complaining about Sévère hurting his arm, and that the two men had been arguing — about what precisely she wasn't sure — the jury seemed to come awake. Bicker then questioned Netty to establish that Johnston had arrived at the prisoner's home looking ill, that he was pale and sweating before he even entered the house.

Straight-backed, the jurymen listened to the statement of Inspector Height and two of his deputies. Again, Sévère's character was outlined. This time, the solicitor-general demonstrated how driven Sévère was, how great his interest was in all medical matters related to deaths by violence, poison, and neglect. Yes, the coroner was known for insisting that the doctor who was to perform a post-mortem wait for him. Yes, he had attended many post-mortems. Unusual for a coroner. Quite unheard of, in fact. And yes, one can be certain that he knew everything about aconitia, given the unguent he was using and his medical knowledge.

Sévère found the entire thing fascinating — a novelty to experience the system from such a unique angle. On the other hand, it shocked him utterly just how little power he had.

He caught himself wondering who might be doing this

to him. Who wanted to kill him in such a torturous manner? His gaze kept straying to Linton Frost. The man looked through him. As though the prisoner weren't worth the Chief Magistrate's attention.

Sévère found nothing surprising in how the case was laid out against him. The previous day, as the solicitor-general described all events to jury and judge, Sévère relived Johnston's final hours. He could almost see himself applying poison in a mysterious fashion that the prosecution would be revealing during the course of the trial. As it stood, he would probably be found guilty. He must have done it: there seemed no other conclusion. With each piece of evidence, each witness statement, the tightening around Sévère's throat grew worse.

His gaze drifted to Olivia who sat by the jury box. The tension in her shoulders. The whiteness of her knuckles. Would she come up to the dock and talk to him in a hushed voice? Words seemed to be burning in her mouth. She would probably tell him that the prosecution had thus far failed to provide a motive. As though this would in any way change the bleakness of his prospects.

The glances she kept throwing at Frost seemed to contain more than the usual cold contempt she cultivated for the man.

He wondered how long she could endure the pressure. A shudder crept over his neck as he thought about the previous day. What had caused her violent reaction? Twice now she had… How could he even put it into words? Folded in on herself and exploded at the same time?

But why, precisely?

He laughed. Just once, quietly. The solicitor-general threw him an irritated glance. Justice Hawkins' fingers moved toward the gavel. Sévère answered with an apologetic smile.

His gaze went back to Olivia. How young she looked. How...breakable. A woman who had been owned since the age of nine.

She could have filed for a divorce the moment he lost his position as Coroner of Eastern Middlesex. Their contracts were void. Why hadn't she?

Perhaps he should ask her about it.

Or better yet, he would present her with divorce papers. She would be free at last.

---

As OLIVIA HURRIED from the Old Bailey to catch a cab to Sillwood Street, she desperately wished there were two or three copies of her. Sitting through Sévère's trial, she couldn't aid William in trying to find information on the mysterious visitor; when trying to find clues on who'd poisoned Johnston, she couldn't discuss the case with Sévère; and while visiting Sévère, she couldn't ask Higgins, Rose, and Alf what they'd found out.

Her teeth were hurting from so much grinding. And her aching neck and shoulders robbed her of what little sleep she allowed herself to catch.

OLIVIA RUSHED into the fashion boutique not far from Johnston's home, and was hit by wall of rose water and lavender scents, by the chattering of excited customers, and the patient answers of those who attended them. She pushed herself to the front desk, cleared her throat, and said, 'May I speak with your dye chemist?'

One of the men attending the bustling ladies turned to Olivia, inserted a needle into the small cushion that was strapped to his wrist, and said, 'Ahem. It is a bit early…' He trailed off and narrowed his eyes. 'You are not picking up an order, are you?'

'Not today. But I was hoping he might be able to help me with new colours I have in mind for an elaborate ball gown.'

The man tipped his head to the side, then shook it. 'My apologies. You did look familiar for a moment.'

'People tell me that all the time.' She smiled, whipped out her fan and fluttered fresh air into her face. In fact, she'd met the man in passing when she'd questioned the owner — a Mr Hall — on the death of Dr Johnston.

Suddenly, the tailor's head snapped up, his eyes latched onto someone behind Olivia. 'Mr Perkin! There's a lady who wishes to see you.'

She turned and found a man by the door, a curse on his lips — swallowed before anyone might see it. She thanked the tailor, and approached the dye chemist. 'I see that you were about to leave. I have but a few questions, and promise I won't bother you for long.' Then she showed him her card.

His brows rose.

'So far they believe I'm a client,' she said, and cocked her head in the direction of the tailor, who was still watching. 'I need your help with something. Shall we walk, Mr Perkin?'

'I was about to take an early dinner. I forgot to eat lunch.' For emphasis, he patted his stomach. It seemed almost concave beneath his waistcoat.

She snapped her fan shut and pocketed it. 'I haven't eaten anything since…probably…breakfast.'

'There's an eating house up the street,' he suggested.

She gazed at him fully then. He had large, dark-brown eyes, long lashes. Bushy black eyebrows and a thin, almost girlish nose. She guessed him to be in his late thirties, although there was something fresh and boyish in his eyes. Her gaze snagged on the scar on his upper lip. A harelip, somewhat crudely corrected when he must have been a small child.

Upon her scrutiny, he didn't lower his face, didn't turn it away the slightest. Instead he smiled broadly, intensifying the asymmetry of his mouth.

Olivia liked him at once. She smiled back, and said, 'Splendid! I'm perishing.'


As they walked, Olivia asked, 'How long have you known the Franks?'

He frowned at her. 'Long.'

'You are a friend of the family?'

'One could say.'

'Could you describe Mr Frank's relationship to the housekeeper, Mrs Appleton?'

Mr Perkin stubbed his toe on a cobblestone. 'An odd question. I don't know what to answer.'

'Well, you could, for example, tell me whether or not their relationship extended beyond what is considered normal?'

'How would you specify *normal?*'

They reached the eating house and entered. Fresh sawdust covered raw floor planks. The scents of salt pork and oatmeal made a puddle on Olivia's tongue. They sat on rickety chairs and placed their orders. Then she said in a voice low enough to not be overheard by other clientele, 'I was wondering if they occasionally or habitually shared a bed.'

Mr Perkin didn't even flinch. 'I doubt it. But I do find it rather alarming that a stranger is poking about the Franks' private affairs. You can't possibly expect me or anyone else to answer your questions truthfully.'

'I'm a private investigator,' she reminded him, but he only shrugged.

The matron appeared, her arms as thick and reddened as her neck, her footfall making the planks shudder and whine. She placed a crock of apple butter, a loaf of fresh bread, and a block of hard cheese on the table, and disappeared with a grunt.

Olivia shoved a piece of bread into her mouth, wondering how to best pry him open. 'Until eight or nine months ago, Mrs Frank employed a personal maid. I forgot to ask Mrs Appleton about the maid's name and her whereabouts. You wouldn't know, would you?'

'Addie Shepherd. She was offered a position at Mrs Muir of Vernon Street. Just across from the Baptist Chapel.'

'How do you know where she works now?'

'I gave her a character for Mrs Muir. Or rather…Mrs Frank did. I wrote it for her and she signed it. She wasn't very good with words.'

'I see. Hum…' Olivia dipped a piece of bread into the butter on her plate, orbited it around, once, twice. 'Have you ever accidentally poisoned yourself or others, Mr Perkin?'

He laughed at that. 'I'm an accomplished dye chemist. I don't accidentally poison anyone.'

'And intentionally?'

He chuckled again. 'Your interrogation methods are rather queer, Mrs Severe.'

'It's Sévère. French intonation rather than English.'

'My apologies. How long have you been a private detective, if you don't mind my asking?'

'A few days.' She smiled at him.

'Ah. Well… I see.' He continued eating, his gaze stuck to his plate.

'For how long have you known the Franks, Mr Perkin?'

He took his time chewing, then answered, 'I've known Minnie since I was a babe.'

Olivia placed her fork aside, folded her hands below her chin, and asked Perkin to continue.

'It's not a secret that I'm her bastard brother. Our late father was… Well, I guess one could call him a ladies' man. Minnie and I sometimes wondered how many siblings we really had.'

'Why didn't he keep you a secret?'

'Because my mother was the lady's maid. It was hard

to deny that she carried his child. She and Minnie's mother were good friends at that time.'

'And now they are not.'

'It's not what you are thinking. My mother died from a fever a few days after I was born.'

'I am sorry. I know how it is to…' She cut herself off. What was she thinking to talk to a stranger thus?

She inhaled, straightened her spine, and said, 'They raised you as their son?'

'No, as the kitchen boy. But they paid for my education and kept me fed and clothed.'

'Did Mrs Frank always have problems with her heart?'

Mr Perkin chewed on his scarred lip, his brow in creases. He pulled in a slow breath. 'It began, I believe, after her first miscarriage. For a month, she didn't want to see anyone. Not even me or her husband. She looked like a wraith when I was finally permitted to visit her. After that, she complained about a weakness of the heart.'

He rubbed his ribs just below his heart. His gaze was unfocused. 'They never spoke of it, but I believe she had several miscarriages. She didn't ever show, but from how…how her nerves grew utterly fragile from one day to another, I believe it could only have been because she'd had been with child, but lost it early on.' He shrugged apologetically.

'Had you ever met Dr Johnston?'

Perkins looked up. 'I heard he died.'

'Yes. The same night Minnie Frank died.'

'What a queer coincidence, isn't it?'

'I don't believe in coincidence.' Olivia rested her gaze

on Mr Perkin. 'Who, in your opinion, wanted Minnie Frank and Peter Johnston dead?'

Perkins sank against the back rest of his chair. A light creak of old wood. As if his bones were protesting the movement.

# ay three

OLIVIA SETTLED into her accustomed seat by the jury box, and looked straight at the Chief Magistrate as he walked in. She kept her eyes on him all through Mr Frank's witness statement. When Mrs Appleton was brought in, Frost's gaze flickered to Olivia.

She gifted him a smile. One of those sweet and innocent smiles she'd given him every time he was tucking himself back into his trousers.

Frost's chin jerked, his eyes darting away from her.

Olivia's hand strayed to her sleeve, the tingling there, and the note she'd tucked into it.

*Soon, my sweet, you will feel me again.*

She hadn't dared enter the court room armed, so she'd left her revolver in the brougham. Higgins had shown her how to use it. Her aim was poor, but she wasn't concerned. At close range, with Frost pressing himself against her, she would *not* miss.

She forced her attention to the witnesses that were brought in, but neither Mr Frank nor Mrs Appleton had anything to add to what Olivia already knew, nothing she hadn't heard or read at least twice.

Her stomach clenched when Mrs Johnston was called onto the witness stand. Had she ever told her how sorry she was that her husband had died there, in Olivia's own home, when neither she nor Sévère had been able to stop it?

She probably had. Several times. She'd lost track of time these past weeks. Or rather, time had lost track of her, was racing ahead of her, running away from her.

'Mrs Johnston, would you please recount the evening of the second of July for us?' the solicitor-general asked.

Olivia knew that evening by heart. She could have spoken the words for her.

When Molly Johnston was cross-examined, and Bicker asked her to describe the relationship between the prisoner and the deceased, Molly spoke of the friendship as though it were a thing of a time long past. Cold crept over Olivia's arms. She willed Bicker to stop. But he asked the next question without so much as a mild smile toward the jury.

'Mrs Johnston, did your husband appear in any way fearful of the prisoner? Or rather, had he looked forward to spending the evening at the prisoner's house?'

Molly Johnston inhaled a sharp breath, gazed at her fingers steepled in her lap, and squeezed her eyes shut.

'Mrs Johnston?'

She looked up, her face pale. 'I cannot be certain.'

The silence that followed was perfect.

Eventually, the judge broke it. 'Are you not certain whether or not your husband feared the prisoner, or are you not certain whether or not he looked forward to spending the evening with a friend?'

'I am certain he looked forward to it. He always did. But…' Molly's gaze latched onto Sévère. 'But there was something. Something had occurred between them. It was a few days before my husband…died. Perhaps two weeks before. Mr and Mrs Sévère visited late at night. She needed my husband's assistance. Her face…' Molly Johnston touched her eyebrow. 'Peter said someone attacked her. He attended to her injuries. They were minor. But something transpired that night that disturbed him greatly.'

'What transpired that night?' the judge asked, ignoring Bicker's raised eyebrows.

'He did not tell me. But I know my husband. He wasn't easily rattled by anything. He was a surgeon for many years, and had strong nerves.'

The judge signalled to Bicker to continue.

'Mrs Johnston, you stated that you are certain your husband was looking forward to meeting his friend, the prisoner. If he was looking forward to it, how could he possibly be afraid of it at the same time?'

She gifted him a smile such as one offers a child. 'You see, Mr Bicker, he looked forward to seeing his friend, but he was dreading that a specific issue might be raised that evening. Does that make sense to you?'

Someone up in the galleries chuckled. Justice Hawkins called for order.

From a corner of her vision, Olivia saw Frost dip his chin ever so lightly. The solicitor-general answered with a curl of his lips.

'When you say he dreaded a specific topic, would you know what it might have been?'

'I do not.'

'So you are merely speculating.'

'I am using the limited information available to me and making an assertion, as I was asked to.'

'Thank you, Mrs Johnston. I have no further questions for the witness.'

Before the judge could release her, the solicitor-general stood and announced that he had one more question for the witness, but that the topic was so delicate, he did not wish it to leave the court room.

A feeling of sickness spread in Olivia's chest.

The galleries were cleared, and the newspaper men were asked to leave as well.

Sévère shot a glance at Olivia and shook his head once. *Do not say or do anything.*

'Mrs Johnston, you said your husband had strong nerves because that is what is required of a surgeon. You also said,' and here the solicitor-general consulted his notes, '...that he was not easily rattled. What *did* rattle your husband, Mrs Johnston?'

She blinked, uncertain as to where this question might

lead. 'He… Ignorance disturbed him. Stupidity. Arrogance.'

'Can you think of anything else?'

The judge leant forward. 'I do not see where this is going and neither does the witness, it appears. If you would clearly state what it is you wish to know, this trial might move forward.'

'I apologise, my Lord. I merely wished to be considerate.' Turning to the witness he said, 'What transpired that night, the information that disturbed your husband so deeply, was a well-kept secret: the true identity of the prisoner's wife.'

Olivia fought not to cry out, not to bury her head in her hands, or run away. All was lost. Sévère would never recover from this blow.

Never.

A short moment later, the whole truth sank in: the one thing that put this case on wobbly legs was that the prosecution had not presented a motive for the murder.

But now they would.

And it couldn't be any more compromising.

'What do you mean by that?' thundered the judge. Molly Johnston flinched.

'Dr Peter Johnston confided in a colleague. I present here a letter that was sent to me this morning.'

The judge received the paper, read it slowly, and returned it to the solicitor-general. 'You received this only this morning?'

'Yes, My Lord.'

'And this relates to the case in which way precisely?'

'It shows the motive of the prisoner to murder the deceased Dr Peter Johnston in cold blood.'

'Go ahead and read it aloud, Mr Hanbury.'

'Thank you, My Lord.' He turned to face the jury, and began. 'Dr Johnston and I have been working together for more than ten years. On occasion, we talked of private matters, such as on the fifteenth of June, when Dr Johnston asked me for advice. He told me that a friend — he did not give the name — had married a prostitute, and that he didn't know whether he should allow himself to be seen with this man again. After reading about the murder of my dear colleague, and learning that Coroner Sévère — who is known to be a good friend of Dr Johnston, and who is also known to have a wife of unknown parentage — I drew my own conclusions. I will not divulge my name, but am well aware that you might need a sworn witness who can corroborate these accusations. If in fact I understood Dr Johnston correctly, Inspector Height will be able to do that. Respectfully, Dr X.'

With that, the solicitor-general walked up to the jury, handed the letter to the foreman, and turned back to face a pale Mrs Johnston.

'Mrs Johnston, has your husband ever mentioned Mrs Sévère's past to you?'

'No.'

'Did the prisoner or his wife ever mention that Mrs Sévère was a prostitute?'

She huffed. 'They most certainly did not.'

'A betrayal of friendship,' the solicitor-general muttered, and before the defence could protest, he announced that he had no further questions for the witness.

Bicker stood, straightened his robe, and walked up to the witness stand, but then turned to face the jurymen. 'My dear colleague wishes you to believe that mere speculations are hard facts.'

Behind him, the judge rapped his gavel. Bicker lowered his head a fraction, and addressed the witness. 'Mrs Johnston, did your husband occasionally offer medical treatment for the unfortunate?'

'He regularly did so.'

'And were prostitutes among his patients?'

'Of course. He wouldn't turn away a man or woman in need of medical attention.'

'And on such occasions, when he treated prostitutes, did he seem upset or — to use your own word — *rattled?*'

'No, why would he?'

'Why, indeed. Thank you, Mrs Johnston. The defence has no more questions for the witness.'

Molly Johnston was released, and the prosecution asked to re-examine Inspector Height.

Olivia kept her chin high. Inside, she wilted.

'Inspector Height, pray tell us how you came to know the wife of the prisoner, Mrs Olivia Sévère, née Kovalchuk?'

Height kept his body turned toward the jury as he said, 'I came to know Mrs Sévère about seven months ago when Mr Sévère and I arrested her.'

'You arrested her?' The solicitor-general feigned surprise.

'Yes.'

'Would you please explain to the jury the circumstances of the arrest.'

'She was suspected of having concealed the death of one Mr Alexander Easy and of having unlawfully disposed of his body. The man died of a heart attack and was thrown into the Thames soon after his death. She was soon released, for we could not give sufficient evidence to keep her on remand.'

'How did you make the connection between Mr Alexander Easy and Mrs Sévère? Surely, a respectable woman wouldn't have disposed of a body?'

Height nodded once. 'During the postmortem, a card was found on the body of Mr Alexander Easy, which led us to an…establishment, where we met the woman who is now the prisoner's wife.'

The solicitor-general paused for a moment, then continued with a low voice, 'What kind of establishment?'

'A house of ill repute.'

'A brothel?'

'Yes.'

Olivia's eyes slid shut. Her teeth hurt from clenching her jaw too long, too hard. A faint screeching of enamel, pain beneath her shoulder blades, the urge to scream. She held her breath and counted to ten. Then she opened her eyes and met Sévère's calm gaze.

'What did Mrs Sévère do there?'

'She worked and lived in a room on the first floor.'

'She worked as a prostitute?'

'Yes.'

'Under which name?'

Height inhaled, paused, and said, 'Miss Mary.'

The solicitor-general walked up to his desk and picked up a brochure that lay hidden beneath several folders. 'Miss Mary, you say? Might it be *the* Miss Mary from an establishment known as Madame Rousseau's?'

'Yes.'

'According to this night life guide she is one of the most sought-after ladies of her trade. Is that correct?'

'I wouldn't know.'

'Hum.' The solicitor-general replaced the brochure and announced that he had no more questions for the witness.

The judge asked the defence if they had questions for the witness. Mr Bicker pushed off his desk, hummed and nodded, then said, 'Inspector Height, you stated that you have known of Mrs Sévère's past for about seven months now, is that correct?'

'Yes.'

'And Mr Sévère was aware of your knowledge?'

'Very much so.'

'Has he ever threatened your life?'

A smile flickered across Height's face. 'No.'

'Has he tried to blackmail you?'

'No.'

'Did Mr Sévère ever put you under duress so that you wouldn't speak about his wife's past?'

'No, he did not.'

'Are you friends with the prisoner?'

'Work brings us together on occasion, but I can't say that we are friends.' He glanced at Sévère as if to make sure he hadn't offended him.

'Please correct me if I'm mistaken: You have

known about the prisoner's wife's past for seven months, and not once did the prisoner attempt to murder you?'

Several jurymen chuckled, Height lowered his head to hide a grin, and the judge cleared his throat.

'No, Mr Sévère has neither threatened me nor tried to kill me.'

'One last question: would you please tell us why Mr Sévère married Olivia Kovalchuk?'

Puzzled, Height shook his head. 'I...can only speculate.'

'Precisely.' Bicker snapped the lapels of his robe straight, and sat.

After a moment of silence, the judge cleared his throat and asked Bicker if the defence's plan was to disrespect the court. Bicker looked up from his papers, blinked innocently, and said, 'Of course not, my Lord. I was merely pondering the rather unusual, if not to say queer, behaviour of the prisoner.'

'Mr Bicker, I am about to lose my patience.'

'My apologies. I shall ask the witness one last question.'

'And here I am, believing that you'd done that already,' muttered the judge, straightening his wig.

Bicker stood again and pursued his lips. 'Inspector Height, would you please tell the jury who asked — or I should say, *demanded* — that organ samples of the deceased be taken and sent to Dr Barry to be analysed for poisons?'

'Coroner...' Height cleared his throat. 'Mr Sévère asked Dr Taylor who performed the first postmortem to take samples of Johnston's organs and send them to Dr Barry.'

'Why?'

Height huffed a laugh. 'Mr Sévère is well known for his methods. When his instincts tell him something is amiss, he's like a bulldog.' Height threw a glance at Sévère. 'My apologies,' he muttered, and continued, 'As written in Dr Taylor's postmortem report, no evidence was found for death by poison. However, Mr Sévère still insisted on organ samples being taken and analysed for poison. He even scheduled an inquest. He witnessed Dr Johnston's death and he concluded Dr Johnston was poisoned.'

'In the years you've worked as a policeman, how often has it occurred that a murderer has insisted that evidence be gathered against him? Evidence no one would have found if not for his insistence? Evidence that would find him guilty and condemn him to the gallows?'

'Not once.'

'Thank you, Inspector Height. The defence has no more questions.'

The trial was adjourned for lunch and the court room emptied, save for two ushers, the attorney for the defence, Olivia, and Sévère, who was flanked by two wardens and moved from the prisoner's dock to a more comfortable seat where he could stretch his aching leg.

Unspeaking, Olivia leant against the desk opposite Sévère. The wardens gave them more privacy, and Sévère reached out and took Olivia's hand in his.

'You are shaking,' he said.

She pulled her hand away and wrapped her arms around her ribcage.

Bicker moved closer to them and said in a low voice, 'You should have told me.'

'You did well enough,' Sévère replied.

'Johnston would never have said those things to anyone. Besides, we never told him that Inspector Height knew about me,' Olivia whispered to Sévère.

Bicker brought his head down, and said quietly, 'Would someone please explain all this to me?'

Sévère held Olivia's gaze. Both were ignoring Bicker's request. She slipped her fingers into her sleeve and pulled out the note. Sévère unfolded it and flinched. He opened his mouth to speak, but an usher arrived with a bowl of slop and a cup of hot water.

Bicker straightened up. Olivia leant back. The usher placed Sévère's lunch on the desk, and retreated.

'How many have you received?' Sévère asked.

'This is the fourth. It arrived this morning.'

'And when had you planned to tell me?'

'Only after your release,' she said softly. 'But given the…new developments, I thought you should know now.'

He laughed, rubbed his face. 'God, I wish you would trust me.'

'I didn't wish to bother you. Higgins is helping me collect evidence. He and Alf track the boys who deliver the messages. But so far…nothing.'

'Perhaps you should find a new attorney,' Bicker said abruptly.

Sévère's head snapped up.

'I am trying to save your life, Mr Sévère, yet you and your wife deign not to let me in on a secret — *several* secrets it appears — that are crucial for your defence.'

'I need to protect my wife,' Sévère said matter-of-factly. 'We'll discuss this when the trial is closed for today. And there's another matter I wish to address.'

Then he began to shovel slop into his mouth. Not because he was hungry, but because he didn't want to talk to anyone.

He needed to think.

DR TAYLOR GAVE his statement on the postmortem he had conducted, much to the delight of the newspaper men. After all, gore was selling well.

Next, Dr Barry was brought onto the witness stand, and with every word of his introduction, Olivia saw the jury shed any doubt they might have had on his credibility. Doctor of Medicine, fellow of the Royal College of Physicians. Fellow of the Council and Institute of Chemistry, lecturer on medical jurisprudence and chemistry at Guy's Hospital. Examiner in the newest branch of medical sciences — forensic medicine, at the London University. Expert in analytical chemistry with a focus on toxicology. Employed by the Home Office for the past nine years to make analyses in cases of suspected poisoning. Whatever the man would say in the course of his statement would be considered the truth and nothing but the truth. Even if he merely hypothesised.

Barry listed the samples that had been duly handed to him by the colleague who'd performed the postmortem on the deceased. Bottle A, secured and sealed, labelled liver, spleen, and kidney. Bottle B, secured and sealed, labelled duodenum, colon. Bottle C, secured and sealed…

Olivia pinched the bridge of her nose. There was a dull ache behind her eyes. She glanced to the prisoner's dock. Sévère's attention was fully on the witness. Once in a while he wrote in his notebook — as when Barry mentioned the bottle of brandy and the small jar with unguent that had been taken from the prisoner's home, and when he outlined how each of the samples had been subjected to a lengthy process of extraction, as to how an alkaloid had been obtained, and how, upon Barry's placing a small portion of it upon his tongue, it had produced the effect of aconitine: a peculiar burning sensation, extending toward the stomach.

'Did you experience this with every sample you analysed?'

'I did experience these symptoms in all the organ samples. However, I found no aconitine in the bottle of brandy the police confiscated from the prisoner, nor in the food samples the prisoner confiscated from the Franks and the Johnstons. I analysed Mrs Frank's heart medicine, which was a tincture of digitalis, and did not find aconitine there, either.'

The solicitor-general nodded solemnly. 'But you found aconitin in all organ samples, including the stomach contents and the urine of the deceased?'

'Yes, I did.'

'How can you be certain that it was aconitine and not another poison, such as digitalin — a vegetable alkaloid found in great quantities in the tincture you just mentioned. A tincture Dr Johnston regularly prescribed to the patient he saw shortly before he died?'

'I am absolutely certain that it was aconitine and no other vegetable alkaloid. I have eighty vegetable preparations in my possession and have tasted all of them. In this particular case the sensation on the tongue lasted for four hours. I made an experiment with the alkaloid extract. I used the quantity corresponding to two ounces of urine and two ounces of the stomach content of the deceased and injected it beneath the skin of a mouse. First symptoms appeared after two minutes. The animal died after thirty minutes. I used a small amount of the unguent confiscated from the prisoner, an amount corresponding to the size of a pea, and extracted it in the same manner. Its effect upon the mice was undistinguishable from the effect produced by the extracts from organ and liquid samples of the deceased. A solvent which was a solution of tartaric acid was used on a mouse as well, and found to be quite inoperative.'

Olivia found no emotion on Sévère's face other than curiosity. He looked to be simply sitting through an intriguing trial, trying to figure out the guilt or innocence of the man in the prisoner's dock. When Dr Barry said that he had examined Johnston's stomach contents microscopically but could not find anything corresponding to the root of aconite, Sévère tapped the graphite point of his pencil against paper, lost in thought.

Barry was asked as to the severity of symptoms observed for each analysed sample, and while he was stating that the weakest were urine and stomach contents, and the strongest were liver, kidneys, and unguent, Sévère leant back and turned his head so that the attorneys for the defence could see his face. Sévère gave a small nod as Bicker met his gaze. One of the attorney's two assistants — Mr Gladstone — rose, and took a note from Sévère.

When the judge told the defence that the witness was now theirs, Bicker called for a thirty minute break, for the defence to consult with the accused on an issue that had just arisen.

As the court room was emptied, Bicker indicated to Olivia that she was needed.

'Dr Barry has just stated the obvious,' Sévère said.

'That Johnston was poisoned?' Bicker must have meant it as a joke, but no one laughed.

'That Johnston did not take the poison orally. According to the postmortem, it wasn't injected, either. And honestly, wouldn't Johnston have noticed if someone had pricked him with a needle?' Sévère paused and hefted his gaze on Olivia. 'Just before he died he said two things to me, and I didn't pay much attention to the crucial one. *God, how my hands burn*, and *you are hurting my arm.* Whatever it was that contained the poison, Johnston touched it. His hands burned. I know from personal experience that aconitine is absorbed by the skin and that it causes a prickling, slightly burning sensation. What I do not know is whether the poison at a high-enough dosage can kill by contact, and if that dosage causes a painful burning sensation. And this, Mr Bicker, is what you will have to establish today.'

Bicker rubbed his chin. 'And you have come up with this while the prosecution was trying to get you hanged?'

ONCE DR BARRY had taken his place on the witness stand, Bicker put on a confused expression. 'Dr Barry, excuse my ignorance, but if the weakest effect was observed in the contents of the stomach, how likely is it that the deceased took the poison orally?'

'It is…unlikely,' Barry answered, frowning.

'Unlikely or impossible?'

Barry thought about that for a moment, then answered, 'Quite impossible.'

'How, in your opinion, did the poison enter the body of the deceased?'

'Well, as there were no needle marks found on his body, injections can be excluded. As his stomach content contained only trace amounts of aconitine, oral application can be excluded as well. I have never heard of anyone inhaling a powder of aconitine, and I don't believe that possible. You see, the substance is highly irritating. It would cause a severe burning sensation in the airways. I can only imagine that a person inhaling it would choke, rather than die of poisoning.'

'So you can't think of any way the poison might have been administered?'

'N-no,' Barry said.

'How much aconitin is required to kill a grown man?'

'There has been only one fatal case that I know of. The quantity that proved fatal was known to be not less than one-twentieth part of a grain, and not more than one-thirteenth of a grain.'

'How much, in your opinion, was present in the deceased?'

'In my judgement, the stomach contents and the urine

contained less than the fatal dose. Approximately one-seventieth to one-fiftieth of a grain. The liver and kidneys, however, contained considerably more. It was not less than one-tenth of a grain, and not more than one-sixth.'

'What precisely does that mean?'

'It means the poison had been absorbed by the body, but had not yet been excreted into the urine and faeces.'

'Did you find any poison in the brandy?'

'I did not.'

'If not given orally or via injection, could the poison have entered Dr Johnston's body via absorption through the skin?'

Dr Barry squeezed his eyes shut, uttered a single, 'Hum,' nodded slowly, and said, 'It is possible.'

'Did you analyse skin samples?'

'No. We did not receive skin samples.'

'And you did not ask for them after it became clear that the poison could not have been given orally or through a needle?'

'I had not considered the possibility of the poison having entered through the skin. Not until you brought it up.'

'I see. You found the highest concentration of aconitine in the unguent?'

'Yes.'

'Do you believe the prisoner could have rubbed a fatal amount of the unguent onto Dr Johnston's skin without the latter noticing it?'

'I... No, I do not.'

Giggling burst from the audience and quickly spread

through the court room. The judge called for order and addressed the witness. 'I should like to know whether or not the tests you performed are specific for aconitine.'

Barry nodded solemnly, his tongue searching his mouth for saliva to wet his dry throat. 'The tests I conducted are general chemical tests for alkaloids. When I discovered an alkaloid, I performed physiological tests. Those of taste and of the effect upon the tongue and neighbouring parts, and then the other physiological test, whether it would kill after a defined course of symptoms.'

'And there is not the least doubt that aconitine was present in all samples?'

'Not the least doubt, my Lord.'

Bicker stroked his lapel, harrumphed, and said, 'You are the leading expert in forensic toxicology?'

'In Great Britain, I am, yes.'

'Is it correct to say that there is no specific chemical test for aconitine?'

'Yes, that is correct.'

'And yet you insist that there is no doubt, not the least, that it is aconitine that killed Dr Johnston?'

'I do insist.'

'Do you know that *Unguent aconitia* is mentioned in the British Pharmacopoeia and that it contains aconite?'

'Yes.'

'Are you aware that this unguent is used to relieve pain?

'Yes. It is applied in cases of neuralgia, joint and muscle pain.'

Bicker picked up a copy of the British Pharmacopoeia. 'Do you agree with this: "A piece of ointment the size of a bean or nut should be applied with friction, which enhances its efficacy."'

'Yes, this is correct.'

'A piece the size of a bean or nut of the unguent found in the prisoner's possession would contain a grain of aconitine, would it not?'

'I believe it would contain barely half a grain.'

'An amount sufficient to cut short pain, such as that of a person suffering from paralysis?'

'Yes.'

'An amount sufficient, according to your statement, to kill a man?'

'Yes.'

'As you can see, the prisoner is alive and well.' Ignoring the amusement spreading through the room, Bicker continued, 'In your statement you wrote that dilated pupils are a symptom of death by poison, and you there-fore concluded Dr Peter Johnston was poisoned. Is that correct?'

'Yes, it is.'

'You mean to say that, in your opinion, dilated pupils invariably point to death by poison?'

'I did not say that—'

'Isn't it so that pupils of a dead person are invariably dilated three days after death?'

'Yes. Yes, they are.'

'So they are not a distinctive symptom of aconite poisoning?'

'No, they are not.'

'According to the statement of the prisoner, the deceased complained about a burning feeling of his hands. Could the man have touched a substance that contained aconitine in such a high concentration that he accidentally poisoned himself?'

'I object!' an attorney of the prosecution called. 'The defence is asking the witness to speculate.'

'I merely ask an expert in the field of forensic toxicology if it is generally possible to accidentally poison oneself by applying large amounts of aconitine onto one's skin.'

'Granted,' the judge said, and nodded at the witness to go on.

'I have never heard of such a case, but I believe it would be possible.'

'Thank you, Dr Barry.' Bicker turned to the judge. 'My Lord, I respectfully ask for an adjournment of three weeks, so the defence may be allowed time to exhume the remains of Dr Johnston, to procure skin samples and let them be analysed for aconitine.'

'To what aim precisely, Mr Bicker?'

'My learned colleague here,' he waved at the solicitor-general, '...wants us to believe that the prisoner murdered Dr Johnston by poisoning him with aconitine. Yet, how the poison was administered is entirely unknown. It is furthermore unclear if Dr Johnston did indeed die of an aconitine poisoning event, or if he had simply used an unguent similar or identical to the one the prisoner was using, which resulted in elevated aconitine concentrations in his bodily fluids. The postmortem showed that the poison wasn't given orally or via injection. How, then, did it enter the body? If Dr Johnston touched an object or a substance that contained a sufficient amount of aconitine to kill him, we need to know what it was, how it came into his hands, and with what — if any at all — intent. A life is at risk.' His gaze slid to the black cap that lay limp and harmless near the judge's elbow.

'Very well. The trial is adjourned for three weeks.'

As the court room emptied, Sévère motioned to Bicker and handed him a note. 'I need you to contact this barrister for me.'

Bicker paled. 'What I said earlier was in…in the heat of the moment. Really, I cannot recommend changing your defence attorney in the middle of the—'

'I don't want him to defend me. I want him to help me modify my will.'

# EXHUMATION

Olivia felt a soft tap on her elbow. She looked to her left, where Inspector Height stood, and lifted her eyebrows.

'Are you quite all right?' he asked.

'Why wouldn't I be?

'Well…' he cocked his head toward the hole. Ropes creaked, and pale-brown soil shifted off engraved wood. Four men perspired in the sweltering sun, their calloused hands strangely clean, their corded arms tanned. Another five men stood nearby, their heads bare, necks bowed, eyes on the casket.

She gave Height a curt nod, about to tell him that his concern was unnecessary, when a peacock butterfly landed on his chest. The insect prodded a yellow waist-coat button with its curly trunk, its wings snapping open and closed.

He huffed softly as it took off toward a summer lilac. 'Doesn't seem to approve of my taste in fashion.'

With a low, scraping noise the earthly remains of Dr Peter Johnston were revealed. A cloud of sharp and somewhat sweetish chemical odours rose. The casket lid was placed aside, and the four diggers stepped back.

If not for the smell and the waxy sheen of Johnston's face, one might have believed him sleeping.

'Will there be enough poison left to analyse after days in the ground?' Olivia asked.

Dr Barry adjusted his hat. He had looked pale on the witness stand, but now his face and neck were suffering a sunburn.

'I would hope so,' he said and threw a glance at Dr Taylor and his two assistants, who had brought their instruments in two large black suitcases, and — for lack of a suitable table — the entrance door of a nearby pub. 'Although,' he added, 'I fear the embalmment fluids may interfere with my analysis.'

'In what way precisely?' Olivia asked.

'They are highly toxic and produce a sharp, stingy sensation on the tongue, followed by numbness. It might be impossible to identify a comparatively small quantity of aconitine among a much higher quantity of embalmment fluids.'

'And if you injected it into a mouse? As you did earlier?'

'The mouse might die from being embalmed alive before exhibiting any symptoms of aconitine poisoning.'

With a small, 'Oh,' Olivia fell silent. Her stomach sank.

Johnston's body was lifted from the casket and placed upon the door that lay in the grass. Dr Taylor took a step forward. His Adams apple bobbed. 'Mrs Sévère?'

'Dr Taylor?' Olivia replied, somewhat puzzled. Hadn't he paid attention when he examined Dr Johnston's body? Hadn't he seen her then, and noticed that she had not passed out?

His assistants fumbled with their suitcases, the clasps seemingly too complicated to operate. Dr Taylor produced a small cough. Then he knelt on the sun-burnt lawn and began to unbutton Johnston's jacket, waistcoat, and shirt. His fingers hovered over the trouser buttons for a moment before he undid those, too.

And that was when she understood. Everything had changed. They all knew what she was. Did they wonder if she had lusty thoughts whenever she beheld a naked male? Did they believe she would throw herself upon the corpse?

Perhaps it was much simpler: They didn't wish to be seen in the presence of a whore.

Olivia's throat clenched. She swallowed hard.

'Mrs Sévère?' Height whispered. 'Would you like me to—'

She shut him up with a brisk shake of her head, and kept her eyes on the body. Johnston appeared unchanged. The salt and pepper hair covering his chest. The seams — coarse black thread pinching flaps of white and bluish skin together in a regular, winding pattern.

'Knife,' Dr Taylor said and held out a hand to his assistants. The handle was placed onto his palm, and he began slicing through the sutures. Once Johnston was opened, Taylor picked up the internal organs that were wrapped in pieces of cloth, placed them next to the body, and instructed his assistants to unpack each of them and take a sample for Dr Barry.

'Are there any doubts as to the results of your first analyses?' Olivia asked.

'None whatever. But I'll need these for comparison. One cannot treat one sample this way and another sample another way and hope to be able to compare the two. The symptoms the embalmed samples might cause are likely to differ from symptoms caused by fresh samples. Analysing all organs once more will allow me to better understand the effects of embalming fluids on the overall effects of aconitine on the tongue.'

Olivia nodded. She'd felt strangely detached from the procedure up until several small squares of skin were cut from Johnston's palms. For some reason, it hurt to watch them do it.

The samples were bottled, the bottles sealed and packed away. When they made to lay Johnston back into the casket, Inspector Height interrupted, 'Gentlemen, the Judge wishes to keep the body available for further analyses.'

Dr Taylor wiped his hands on a kerchief, and said, 'He'll keep fresh down there. Cooler than the morgue, for sure. If we have further need of him, we know where to find him.' Then he nodded at the diggers to lower Johnston into his casket and back into the ground.

---

OLIVIA FOUND Higgins smoking idly on the stairs to the house. 'Walton Winspear,' he said and flipped his cigarette butt into a nearby shrub. 'It was Mr Burroughs who identified the man. Mr Winspear manages investments at London Joint Stock Bank. Mr Burroughs said the man wasn't willing to share information on his client, Mr Frank.'

'Did Mr Burroughs say what he plans to do next?'

'*Employ special methods*, whatever he means by that. He'll inform us as soon as he learns why Mr Frank needs Mr Winspear's services.' Higgins sucked air through his teeth and glanced at his fingertips, yellowed from tobacco.

She kicked dirt off her shoes. 'Where are Rose and Alf?'

'Haven't seen a trace of them today.' Higgins shrugged.

Frowning, Olivia made for the door. She strode through the hall and called for Netty, who arrived in a heartbeat. The housekeeper's hair was in disarray and she was kneading her apron as if her life depended on it. 'Mrs Sévère! A package has arrived!'

Olivia's stomach dropped to her toes.

'Alf wasn't here and Higgins was...well, he wasn't here either, was he? Cook was busy, and Marion can't do *anything* with speed, and so I... I followed the boy.'

'You did what?'

'I followed the boy. He was very fast. Going left and right like a rabbit. And then...I lost him.' Netty heaved in a breath, took off her cap and smoothed back her hair. Her fingers fluttered over her head, making sure nothing was out of order. Then she pinned the cap back onto her skull.

Throughout the procedure, Olivia was grinding her teeth. 'Higgins!' she called over her shoulder.

The coachman carried a faint cloud of tobacco aroma with him. 'Another message?'

'A package. I'm not certain, though, if Netty plans to hand it over or keep it for herself.'

Netty dropped the hairpin she'd held between her lips. A soft *ping* sounded from the marble floor. She excused herself, ran toward the parlour, and returned with a box tied with twine. 'It is heavier than it looks,' she provided, and blushed.

'Stop right there!' Higgins barked and snatched the package from Netty's hands. He held it up to his ear and shook it.

'Are you mad?' Netty asked.

'I read a story about a man who opened a package that was delivered by a stranger. A needle jumped out and pricked him. It was poisonous and he died.'

'Now really, Mr Higgins!'

'It was a detective story,' the coachman muttered, and held the box out to Olivia. 'Sounds like a stone to me.' He stuck another cigarette into his mouth, but didn't light it, just rolled it around between his lips.

Olivia undid the string, unfolded the brown paper and gingerly opened the box. She gasped.

Higgins eyed the contents. His cigarette dropped from his mouth. Netty's neck grew longer, she blinked and produced a tiny grunt.

Olivia curled her fingers around the yellow lump and weighed it in her hand. 'I'm not an expert, but this is heavy enough to be real.'

'There is a note at the bottom,' Higgins pointed out.

Olivia picked it up and read it.

*I am sorry.*

'What's that supposed to mean? Sorry for what? And why send me gold?' She dropped her hands, the lump of gold in one fist, the box and the note in the other. 'Higgins, we need to find a jeweller.'

----

'GOLD?' Sévère asked, as Olivia placed the lump into his outstretched hand.

'The note reads, *I am sorry.* The jeweller told me it's 3.8 troy ounces with a purity of more than ninety-five per cent.'

'That must be twenty, thirty pounds sterling,' Sévère mused.

'Twenty-seven.'

He rolled the metal around on his palm, held it up close to his eyes, and squinted. 'Could have come from anywhere. All one needs to do is melt down jewellery or sovereigns. The question is, *why.*' He looked up at her. 'Have you got an idea?'

'Not the slightest. But it certainly wasn't Frost.'

'No. The note is handwritten and not a sick threat.' Sévère scrutinised the note, sniffed the paper, and harrumphed. 'I smell no perfume. The hand looks as if it might be from a man.'

'William found out that the man from London Joint Stock Bank manages investments. He won't say what he's doing for Mr Frank. But if Mr Frank invests in gold, this might be his.' She snatched the lump from him. At

Sévère's amused glance she added, 'I do know this is conjecture. Investing in gold doesn't mean he has it lying around his house.'

Sévère patted his hammock. As she sat down, her shoulder pressed to his, he said, 'There was something in Mr Frank's statement that…' He scratched his stubbly chin. 'I will let it grow.'

'Excuse me?'

'I'll let it grow.' He tapped his chin. 'When the trial continues, the jury will see a new face and new evidence. I appear…good-natured with a beard. Less angles on which to cut oneself. It might help them *forget* all the incriminating details they heard during the first three days.'

'But the solicitor-general will remind them in his closing speech, will he not?'

His smile and his eyes grew soft. 'Look at the amiable man with his brace and his crutch. Do you believe what the evil attorney is saying?'

She poked his chest and grinned. 'Very amiable, very much the very poor, innocent man.'

His smile faded. 'About Mr Frank's witness statement. Have you noticed that he did not mention washing his wife's body? He was asked to describe the night his wife died. Mrs Appleton told you that he washed his wife's body, and after that she washed it again. Yet neither mentioned it in their witness statements. Not a word about it. You told me that you found her pushing about a bucket with towels and waxed paper which were later burned. If we were to assume that Mrs Frank was murdered and Johnston was…a calamity, we might also assume that aconitia was applied onto Mrs Frank's skin to kill her. When Johnston tried to revive her, he touched her frequently and intensely enough to transport poison from her skin to his own. We might further assume that Mr Frank or Mrs Appleton then washed the poison off Mrs Frank's body to avoid detection. And to avoid poisoning themselves, waxed paper was placed between the wet towel or flannel and their own skin as they washed hers.'

Olivia stared at her hands and sucked in a breath. She turned her wrists to gaze at her palms, and frowned. 'After the postmortem… Rose told me that she'd gone to Johnston and wished him good night. That she held his hand, and rubbed off a speck of blood. She came to my room, looking ill. Later, she vomited. It wasn't violent, merely a mouthful. As might be expected from a girl who had just witnessed something horrible. But what if she were experiencing the effects of aconitine? She kept scratching her hand. Her right palm.'

Sévère's spine snapped to attention. 'Go to Bicker at once. Rose has to give a witness statement. Should Dr Barry not be able to find aconitine in Johnston's skin samples, my release might hinge on the girl alone.'

Olivia snatched his hand. 'I believe… What if…' She felt the pressure of his warm fingers and her thoughts lined up, the jumble in her mind cleared. 'The rim of his hat was moist, Netty said. He arrived at the house sweating. The jury heard her say it. I'll ask Bicker to have Johnston's bowler hat confiscated and sent to Dr Barry for analysis.'

Sévère pulled her hand to his lips and kissed it, but abruptly dropped it like hot cinder. 'My apologies. I didn't mean to break my promise.' He seemed genuinely shocked.

'I'm not entirely blind, Gavriel. I do see the difference,' she said softly. 'A kiss given in joy and gratitude, not in… Not taken with greed and little thought.'

'There was little thought. And I might also be greedy.'

'I wish you would lie more often.'

When he opened his mouth to reply, she cut across him, 'I will make sure Rose gives her statement tomorrow. I also need to speak with the personal maid Mrs Frank employed up until a few months ago. She might have insights on the Franks that no one else has. I spoke to her brother — Mrs Frank's half-brother. He is the dye chemist at the fashion boutique on Sillwood Street, and he told me about Mrs Frank's many miscarriages, and her history of a weak heart. I asked him if Mrs Appleton warms Mr Frank's bed. He said he doesn't think so, and I believe him.'

Sévère was silent. The dripping noise seemed louder than the last time she'd been here. She looked up at the ceiling, and tried to find the source, but failed.

'You are a good detective,' he began. 'If you wish, you may keep my offices for your private detective agency.'

'Are you jesting? I heard Bicker mention that you wish to modify your will. How can you even *think* of the possibility of a death sentence?'

'I have to consider all possibilities. Don't tell me you haven't thought of it.'

She dipped her head. 'I… I have, of course.'

'The offer stands, whether I be released, or not.'

The *or not* hung heavily between them.

## NEW WITNESS

*H*iggins stood by the door, hand on the knob. 'They are still there. The whole horde of them. Would you like me to scare them off?'

Olivia came to an abrupt halt in the hallway. Rose bumped into her back.

'They can rot on the pavement for all I care.' She lifted her chin. 'I might need shooting lessons, though. Would newspaper men be an appropriate target, do you think?'

A flash of surprise. He doused it with a dry, 'The brougham is ready, Mistress.'

They went through the stables and climbed into the carriage. Olivia pulled the curtains shut. As Higgins steered them out of the courtyard, cries of 'Mrs Sévère! Mrs Sévère! Just one question!' made Olivia cringe. She was certain the servants had learned about her past *occupation* in the morning papers. Netty had not met her eye while serving breakfast.

She was surprised that it had taken days for the information to leak to the papers — information that wasn't supposed to leave the court room at all. She had expected it to be front page news within hours of the so-called Dr X letter being presented to the jurymen.

They alighted in front of the Leman Street police station. Rose's fingers felt clammy in Olivia's hand as they crossed the walkway. The girl had been fidgeting since Olivia had told her the previous night that her witness statement would be taken by Inspector Height at Division H Headquarters at ten o'clock the next day.

Two bobbies stood under the marble arch at the entrance, bickering through unkempt moustaches.

'Excuse us,' Olivia said as she pushed past them, tugging at Rose who had bent her neck to read a decree on a nearby billboard.

A scarecrow of a policeman received them, and led them up a staircase, into an office. He wore a jacket that was too large for his bony frame, and probably a third- or fourth-hand piece. It was clean enough, but the cuffs and collar were frayed, and the elbows patched. 'Inspector'll be here in a minute,' he said as a way of bidding his farewell.

'They *really* should let in fresh air,' Rose said, and pinched her nose.

Olivia shushed her, but walked up to the window and tore it wide open. Clouds of tobacco smoke gradually cleared.

The door was opened and Height walked in followed by…

Olivia braced herself on the windowsill.

'Good day to you, Mrs Sévère. May I introduce Chief

Magistrate Frost and Detective Sergeant Thick. PC Mizen will record the young lady's statement.' He pulled a chair out for Rose and bade her sit.

Olivia nodded at everyone in the room, dampening the urge to push between Frost and the girl, to shield her from him. All she could do was position herself behind Rose's chair, eyes on Frost and the Detective Sergeant, who had now arranged themselves along the wall.

PC Mizen found a stool and sat, back bent, bespectacled eyes intently on his pencil.

Height settled down at his desk, resting his elbows on the worm-eaten surface. He gifted Rose a brief smile, and said, 'The attorney of your master told us you have observed something peculiar regarding the death of Dr Johnston.'

A shy bob of her head. Her braids slipped off her shoulders.

Olivia patted Rose's arm. Height looked up at her and gave a minute shake of his head. She squeezed Rose once, then removed her hand.

'Will you tell me what it was that you observed?' he asked.

'I hid in the closet.' Her voice was so small, Olivia wished she could reach out and smooth Rose's hair. But it would appear as though she influenced the witness, which PC Mizen would write down at once, and the jurymen would get to read. So she pulled herself together. After all, no one would be harmed.

'You hid in the closet.' Height repeated, and it was enough to open the flood gates.

'I hid in the closet. In the laundry room. I wanted to

see him, but I didn't know…didn't know…' A small sob. 'They cut him up and there was so much blood. I squeezed my eyes shut and my ears but…it took so long. I was cold and hungry and tired and didn't want to sit in the closet any longer because everything hurt. And then all the blood was gone and I climbed out and he was… I swear I'll stop being so nosey!'

'It's all right,' Height said. 'So you climbed out of the closet and looked at Dr Johnston. What did you see?'

'He looked like he was sleeping. But there were awful stitches around his head and throat.' She motioned to her own face.

Height nodded.

'I *swear* I wanted to leave right away, but then I thought…I thought it's impolite. So I went to him and wished him a good night.'

PC Mizen snorted. Rose blushed and dropped her gaze.

'PC Mizen, you are not interrupt the witness.' Height said.

Mizen muttered an apology, and bent lower over his notes.

'That was very considerate of you, Miss Rousseau. And did you leave after you said your farewells to Dr Johnston?'

'Not right away. I saw that there was a small drop of blood on his hand. I didn't want to rub it off on my sleeve, because it leaves stains. So I…um…used spittle.'

'Where on his hand was it?'

She pointed at her right palm.

'What did you use to wipe it off if you didn't use your

sleeve?'

'Just my hand. I rubbed his hand till it was dry and clean. It even got a little bit warmer. He was so cold, you know. And then I told him I was sorry.'

'What were you sorry about?'

'That he was dead and cut up and laid out in our laundry room.'

Height was silent for a moment. Then he said. 'What happened after you wiped the blood off Dr Johnston's hand?'

Rose stared at her own palms and whispered, 'I went to Olivia's room and into her bed. I was so tired. I hadn't slept a wink. And I was afraid I would dream of it…of him. And then I… My hand began to prickle, and then it burned.'

Absentmindedly, she scratched her right palm. 'It burned terribly. And then I was sick.'

'You were sick?'

'Yes. On the…the carpet.'

'Where you very sick?'

'Only a little.'

'For how long?'

Rose answered so softly, Height asked her to repeat herself.

'I don't know,' she said. 'I… Olivia helped me sleep.'

'Did she give you sleep medicine?'

'She sang a lullaby.'

Height narrowed his gaze at Olivia, but addressed Rose, 'When you woke up, did you still feel poorly?'

'No, but I was very hungry and I missed Mr Pimley's lessons.'

'Mr Pimley of Pell Street tutors you?'

'Yes, but I'm not very good.'

'You are doing all right, Rose,' Olivia said, and looked up to find Frost's bored gaze directed at something outside the window.

Height asked a few more questions, basically making Rose repeat the main points of her statement. He prodded for weaknesses and lies, but found none. He asked Rose if she was prepared to repeat her statement at court, upon which she produced a tittering, 'Yes.'

Height leant back and nodded, satisfied. 'Thank you, Miss Rousseau. Mrs Sévère, as I understand, you are the girl's mistress and guardian?'

'I am. She is my maid.'

'Very well. I will need you to read her statement. Both of you will sign at the bottom, as will all gentlemen who witnessed Miss Rousseau's statement today.'

Before PC Mizen handed his notes to her, she said, 'May I ask why the Chief Magistrate is present? Surely, the statement of a little girl can't be worth his time.'

Frost smiled. 'Are you suggesting you know the responsibilities of a Chief Magistrate, Mrs Sévère?'

Olivia shoved down all the nasty replies that threatened to spill from her mouth. 'I suggested that your time is precious, Chief Magistrate.'

'It is, Mrs Sévère. It is.' With that, he placed his hat onto his head and made to leave.

He was half-way out the room when she called, 'You have not answered my question.'

'I see no reason to do so,' he replied and left.

Olivia's gaze slid to Height who kept his mouth shut.

'Can we go home?' Rose asked.

'Why did he not sign the witness statement? And why was he here?' Olivia asked Height.

The Inspector's gaze drifted to the door that stood ajar, and then back to Olivia. 'He's worried this case will throw a bad light onto our judicial system. He will sign the statement later today. Now if you would, please.' He nodded at the papers in Olivia's hand.

PC Mizen's script was clean and easy to read. She signed at the bottom of each page, asked Rose to sign as well, then handed papers and pen to Height.

As soon as Rose and Olivia exited the building, they were greeted by two newspaper reporters who effectively blocked their path. 'Mrs Sévère, our readers wish to know the truth—'

'Higgins!' she bellowed.

The coachman jumped off the brougham, swiftly covered the short distance, shoved aside the reporters, and held out his hand to Olivia.

Onlookers must have heard her name, for several were pointing at her, muttering excitedly.

She grabbed Higgins' hand, her other hand firmly wrapped around Rose's wrist, and together they fled the gathering crowd.

Once safely inside the carriage, Olivia said to Rose, 'You've earned a hot chocolate, my dear. I'll have one, too. And Mr Higgins can have a brandy.'

'Hot chocolate with brandy, if I may,' sounded from the driver's seat.

'You can have an entire ewer full, Mr Higgins!'

The wheels clattered noisily as the brougham turned

from Little Alie onto Commercial. Rose picked at her nails, her eyes darting out the window and back at Olivia.

And then Rose asked, 'Why was Mr Wednesday at the police station? And why did you call him "Chief Magistrate?"'

---

THEY SAT around the coffee table in the smoking room, William with a tray of cookies all for himself, Higgins and Alf smoking cigarettes, Rose eating a sandwich and drinking milk, and Olivia staring up at the ceiling lamp, rolling a glass of brandy between her fingers.

She cricked her neck and took in the room, the people waiting for her with various degrees of patience. 'In about a week, Dr Barry's chemical analysis will show if there is a vegetable alkaloid in Dr Johnston's skin samples. In two weeks, he might or might not be able to identify it as aconitine. He expressed his doubts, because of the embalmment fluids. But what we do know is this: It is highly likely that Johnston died of a contact poison. Sévère and I find it quite improbable that if his skin did come into contact with large amounts of poison, that he would have died of something else entirely shortly there-after. And there is the matter of the bowler hat. Mr Bicker asked Inspector Height to confiscate it, and send it to Dr Barry.'

William nodded at no one in particular. Higgins dropped a cylinder of ash into Sévère's crystal ashtray, and solemnly clamped his smoke back between his lips.

Olivia continued, 'Oh, and Barry sent a note that he

was unable to find a vegetable alkaloid in the ashes from the Franks' laundry room hearth. But that was to be expected. Now. What I need you...' she pointed her glass at Alf, '...to do is to trail the laundry maid to her home, and let me know as soon as she arrives there. I want to question her without Mrs Appleton or Mr Frank sniffing about.'

'Aye, Captain,' Rose said with a grin.

Olivia felt a pang of regret. 'Not you, First Mate. I will explain to you later.'

Olivia braced herself and avoided looking at William — the only man in the room who had known about her past long before the newspapers smeared it all over London. 'There's another matter I wish to address before we proceed.' She cleared her throat. 'If one of you feels unable to work with me now that you know what I used to do for a living, you should leave, for I lack the energy and time to discuss my past with anyone.'

No one said a word.

William bit down on a cookie, noisily chewed a few times, wiped his moustache, and said, 'Splendid. As to the more important things: I'm still working on our investment banker, and will notify you as soon as I learn anything new. Have you spoken to the personal maid, Olivia?'

She held up her hand. 'I'm not finished. You all know that I brought Rose here a day after the wedding. I assume you have already drawn your own conclusions as to her... upbringing.' She waited for the men's undivided attention.

Higgins coughed. Alf looked puzzled.

'Rose is the daughter of my former madam. What that

woman planned for her was unacceptable to me, so I stole her away. One of my former regulars — a man I will not name here — knows Rose's identity and where she grew up. As of this morning, he knows that she lives here.'

Rose kept her gaze attached to the carpet.

'That man is not to be trusted,' Olivia continued. 'He might tell Rose's mother where she resides, so that Madame Rousseau can retrieve her child and put her to work. This must be prevented. If any of you sees a stranger loitering near the house, notify me. And Rose,' Olivia rested her elbows on her knees, and waited for the girl to look up. 'Stay at home for a few days. Don't venture outside unless I or Mr Higgins accompanies you.'

Rose pushed out her lower lip. Behind her eyes, her brain visibly rattled. Then her expression brightened. 'No school?'

'No school.' Olivia nodded once. 'Keep an eye on the street. If you see Bobby or your mother, warn one of us or the servants at once. Do you understand?'

Rose produced a quiet, 'Aye, Captain.'

'Excellent.' Olivia emptied her brandy and set the glass down with a vigorous *clonk*. 'I will question the maid tomorrow. Mr Higgins, would you tail the dye chemist? I wish to know where he lives, if he has a wife and children, where he purchases his dyes, and which chemicals he uses.'

Higgins dipped his head in assent, and stubbed out his cigarette.

'Good,' she said, and rubbed her brow. 'Well, if that's settled, I should consider introducing myself to the new coroner.'

## MISS SHEPHERD

*O*livia took an omnibus to Percy Circus, went into a cobbler's shop at Vernon Street, and enquired after Mrs Muir.

'House at the corner, just across Baptist Church,' a bald man with white fringes and a sparse, grey beard told her. He sat on a three-legged stool. A wooden contraption between his knobby knees held a boot in place, to receive a new sole.

'Thank you,' Olivia said. 'Have a nice day, sir.'

She found the house and rang the bell. A servant admitted her, accepted her card, and led her into the parlour.

'The missus will be with you shortly.' The maid left with a curtsy.

The room was so stuffed that the small space left to accommodate a table, chairs, and a chaise seemed like mere concession. Olivia stood in the centre of the parlour and turned slowly, taking in the details. Vases stuffed with artificial flowers, porcelain figurines, and ebony statues populated the floor, the mantlepiece, cupboards and window sills. Terrifying masks hung all around the walls, rimmed with black and bristly hair, mouths agape in laughter or screams.

A creak pulled her attention to the door. A pinch of a woman sat there in a wheeling chair, her white hair neatly arranged on her head, her shoulders so bony they threatened to poke through the fabric of her flowery dress. Her voice was surprisingly strong. 'A young guest. Such a pleasant and rare surprise.'

A maid pushed Mrs Muir into the room, and Olivia introduced herself.

'A lady detective! How very unusual. I read about you, Mrs Sévère.'

The words hung in air, wafting about in beams of sunlight.

Mrs Muir pointed a crooked finger up at the walls. 'What do you think those are?'

'Masks?'

'Indeed they are. But they are also my memories. When I was young, I traveled.' She fastened her pale gaze — one blue eye, one milky — onto Olivia. 'I travelled without a husband.'

Olivia sank to the chaise.

'Imagine the outrage,' Mrs Muir said with glee, waved a hand at the maid, and ordered tea and biscuits.

The refreshments were swiftly delivered. Then the maid took a seat next to her mistress.

'Margot — the maid who admitted you — said you

wish to speak with Addie?' Mrs Muir patted the arm of the young woman next to her.

'If you allow, Mrs Muir.'

'Of course! Given the little entertainment I get these days, I wouldn't for my life forbid her to talk to you.' Mrs Muir clasped her hands in her lap, expectation and curiosity pulsing in every fibre.

'Well.' Olivia cleared her throat.

'Ah. You wish to talk to her in private.' So much disappointment in such a small woman.

The maid lifted her chin. 'We can speak here. I tell my mistress everything.'

Olivia looked at the two, cocked her head, and nodded. 'You are Miss Addie Shepherd, Mrs Frank's former personal maid who left her employ a few months ago, is that correct?'

'Yes, it is. Albert… Mr Perkin took me from a workhouse when I was eleven years old, and asked Mrs Frank, who is his half-sister, to employ me as a maid. At first, I worked in the scullery, but only a few months later, she asked me to be her personal maid. I was in her employ for nearly nine years.'

'May I ask why you left your post?'

Miss Shepherd dropped her gaze and frowned. 'It is… complicated. But then perhaps…not so much. Mrs Appleton was in love with Mrs Frank. A hungry, unrequited love. I can't be sure, but I believe she saw me as a child for the longest time, until one day, she found me tying Mrs Frank's corset, and she saw a woman — a competitor — and wished me gone. She accused me of stealing money, small amounts here and there. And then a piece of Mrs Frank's jewellery disappeared. By that time, Mrs Appleton has sown enough mistrust… But my mistress did not wish to report me. Perhaps she had doubts about Mrs Appleton's statements. Perhaps she didn't tell the police because there was no proof. But the mistrust was sown, and so I left and found a situation with Mrs Muir.' She smiled at the wizened woman.

'You had a room at the Franks?'

Miss Shepherd nodded. 'I shared a room with cook.'

'And Mrs Appleton?'

'She had her own room, of course. She's the housekeeper.'

'Of course.' Olivia licked her lips. 'Mr Perkin told me that he gave you a character. Did Mrs Frank not wish to do it herself, given the circumstances?'

'I believe so.'

'Interesting. Mrs Appleton told me that Mrs Frank sent you away because she couldn't bear being touched by anyone but her husband.'

At that, Addie Shepherd looked genuinely aghast. 'If that were true, I am sure I would have noticed.'

'Are you friends with Mr Perkin?'

'I would think so. He is a very amiable man.'

Olivia smiled. 'Yes, he is.'

'Women avoid looking at…'

'His mouth?'

'Yes.'

Olivia couldn't help but think that Miss Shepherd had kissed Mr Perkin's crooked mouth. 'You are in love with him.'

'I was. When I was young and foolish. We were…are friends.'

'I see. Could you describe the relationship between Mrs Frank and her husband?'

All air went out of Miss Shepherd. 'I honestly can't say. Perhaps I am too young to understand marriage. The Franks fought, they loved, they ignored each other.' She shrugged, lost for words.

'And how does Mr Perkin fit in? As I understand, he was a friend of the family and Mrs Frank's half brother.'

Miss Shepherd's expression darkened. 'He is one of the nicest persons I know. Respectful and kind. But Mrs Frank was…using him. When she needed a confidante, *he* was the first she would talk to, not her husband. As far as I could tell, that is. I wasn't privy to her thoughts. But whenever he needed something, anything, she ignored it.'

'For example?'

'Oh, there are plenty of examples.' Miss Shepherd waved a dismissive hand. 'I remember one winter particularly well. She sent me to fetch him. She *knew* he had a very bad cold and a high fever, and yet…she bade him come to her. When he finally arrived, all pale and weak, she bickered over trifles for an hour or more, then sent him away.' Miss Shepherd shrugged. 'Mrs Frank didn't know any better. She saw herself first. Others were to serve her. I am sorry. I shouldn't speak of her thus.'

'It's all right, Miss Shepherd. Perhaps this will be the piece of information that helps me solve this case, and saves the life of an innocent man.'

'Is your husband truly accused of murder?'

Olivia nodded. 'Now, pray tell, do you know anything about Mrs Frank's miscarriages?'

A whispered, 'Yes.'

Olivia waited. Miss Shepherd chewed on the inside of her cheek.

'Well?'

She heaved a sigh. 'It was terrible. She was with child five times, and every time — always around the fourth month, I believe — she would fall ill. She would be pale, feverish, and have bad stomach aches. And then she would bleed and lose the child. The doctors and midwives couldn't do anything about it.'

'Hum.' Olivia pinned a strand of hair behind her ear. 'You said you were accused of having taken jewellery from her. Do you know what the piece was, and if it was ever recovered?'

'It was a treasured family heirloom, handed down from her grandmother to her mother, and then herself. I saw her wear it only once. It was a golden necklace.'

'Could you describe it?'

'Yes, I remember it very well because it was so unusual. A broad choker necklace. From the colonies…India, she said.'

'And has it ever been found?'

'No, not as far as I know.'

'Does Mr Perkin have family?'

The change of topic seemed to startle Miss Shepherd. She hesitated, then shook her head.

'But?' Olivia tried.

Miss Shepherd looked up. 'There is no but. He doesn't have a wife. No children. I just wondered why.'

'You've never asked him?'

'I…did. He said he was unable to provide for them. I found this…odd.'

'A debt, perhaps? Is he a gambler?'

'No. He works hard. Very hard.'

'Odd indeed.' She looked to Mrs Muir, who had been listening silently throughout.

———

LATER IN THE AFTERNOON, Olivia was admitted to Coroner Baxter's offices, but the clerk told her that the coroner could not see her. Not this week, and not the following week. Seething, Olivia took a cab home, but halfway there she called up to the driver that she wished to go to the Leman Street police station instead.

'INSPECTOR HEIGHT, thank you for seeing me. I promise I'll take only a minute of your time.' Without invitation, she sat in same chair Rose had used the previous day, took off her bonnet, and placed it on Height's desk.

Height arranged his papers and gazed at her through a haze of cigarette smoke and the unmistakable stench of onion sandwiches.

'Now that we know that Johnston died of a contact poison, and that Mrs Frank was the last patient he attended to — a patient who died the same night he did — it might be prudent to confiscate the clothes Mrs Frank wore that night so we can send them to Dr Barry.'

Height merely grunted.

'Coroner Baxter won't see me. I wished to ask him about recent cases of poisoning with aconitine. There is a possibility that Johnston was accidentally poisoned, and that there might be other such cases.'

'There are none.'

'Are you sure? What about poison cases in other divisions?'

'I can assure you that there are none.' His gaze remained flat.

Sighing, she leant back in her chair. 'Mr Height, I do understand that you wish me to leave as quickly as possible. I also understand that all I might say has no credibility whatsoever because of how I was forced to live. But for the sake of my husband, I beg you to overcome your… aversions. Aid me in solving this case.'

Height rubbed his face. 'Mrs Sévère, I feel currently quite unable to care much about your beliefs on aversions or poison cases. All I know is that there are no new aconitia poisonings, and no deaths that appear similar to that of Dr Johnston. Should one occur, I will send word.'

Again, he arranged the papers on his desk. Obviously, Olivia had been dismissed.

'Very well,' she said and stood.

When she reached the door, she stopped and turned back to Height. 'You wouldn't know any particulars about Mr Frank's recent investments with the London Joint Stock Bank, would you?'

Height slowly lifted his head.

'Given that said investment happened shortly before his wife's demise.' She shrugged, placed the bonnet on her head, and turned the doorknob. 'But…it's probably not important. Have a good day, Inspector.'

'Shut the door.'

She forced the smile off her face as she pushed the door into its frame, and turned back to Height.

'Enlighten me, Mrs Sévère. What is the reason for the Chief Magistrate's interest in your husband?'

An unexpected question, especially coming from Height. 'He is not interested in my husband, and you know it.'

'A mere suspicion. So he knew you as a…prostitute?'

She kept her face blank. 'Did you believe I would throw myself onto Johnston?'

He jerked back in his chair. 'What are you talking about?'

'Your odd reaction to my presence at Johnston's exhumation. A naked man and a whore in one place can only mean one thing, can it not?'

A fleck of spittle flew from his mouth when Height burst out snorting. He rubbed his face, and said, 'My apologies, but did you think…' He gaped. 'You *do* believe that was why Dr Taylor was hesitant to undress Johnston, why his assistants were nervous, and I asked you if you needed assistance? Has it occurred to you that we were worried the sight of a weeks-old corpse might distress you?'

'I attended Dr Taylor's postmortem examination of Dr Johnston entirely without fainting.'

Height shook his head. 'And is one to deduce from this that nothing can faze you? Taylor and I have witnessed enough policemen faint or grow ill at the sight of a corpse. Even those who aren't novices to it. However, you are not entirely mistaken in your interpretation. I imagine it was somewhat disconcerting for the medical men to be with a former prostitute in the presence of one's peers.'

'You *imagine?*' She laughed.

Height leant forward and rested his elbows on his desk, 'Was the Chief Magistrate a regular client or lover of yours, before you married Gavriel Sévère?'

'It's of no importance,' she said and made to leave.

'Even if — purely theoretical, of course — a Police Inspector begins to suspect that Mr Frost's unusual interest in Mr Sévère's case might be a little…sinister?'

She froze. 'What did he do?'

'Nothing that would allow me to confront him.'

Olivia considered this, but didn't speak.

'At the very least tell me this: does he have reason for revenge?'

She cocked her head. 'Reason? No. There is no reasonable explanation for that man's behaviour. However, if I were to make a witness statement as to the past seven years of knowing a man carnally, and how I came to practice a particular occupation, would a jury believe what I had to say?'

She saw the cogwheels turn in Height's skull. He blinked once, then dropped his gaze. 'They might or might not. But now is not the time to find out.'

# COURTESAN

*D*earest Olivia,

*Please accept my apology for my failure to attend today's
assembly of the* detectives extraordinaire. *Although I'm quite
sure the suffering is exclusively on my side, for I do enjoy the
magic that comes out of your kitchen. By the by — is your cook
pretty and unmarried?*

*The excuse for my absence is rather dull: I'm currently repre-
senting a client whose true name must not be revealed, lest
certain criminal factions make my life a little less enjoyable.
But I can say this much — the man is giving me a constant
headache.*

*To get to the main point of these ramblings: Employing special
methods, I was able to extract crucial information from Mr
Winspear of London Joint Stock Bank. He tells me that his
client Mr Frank co-owns a small gold mine in some terribly hot
place in Africa, and that he purchased a pretty apartment at 82
Gloucester Terrace, Regent's Park, eighteen month ago.*

*Mr Winspear assures me that none of this is in any way as sinister as one might believe, although all of it has been kept from Mrs Frank's eyes and ears. Whenever Mr Winspear visits Mr Frank, their hushed conversations take place behind closed doors.*
*Yours respectfully,*
*William*

*PS: Oh, how I wish I could be a fly on your bonnet when you visit Mr Frank's lady at Gloucester Terrace. For a lady it must be!*

'Hum,' Sévère said and lowered the letter onto his thigh. Olivia was perched next to him on the too-short hammock, her hips and shoulders wedged against his.

She tapped the tips of her shoes to the puddle on the floor. 'Higgins is loitering at Gloucester Terrace to find out who lives there. It's easy to assume Mr Frank has a mistress, but what if…it's not what we expect?' Olivia shrugged. 'It's just that…there is this tangle of information, and some days I believe *everyone* is a suspect. And I wanted you to read this and share your thoughts with me before I talk to her.'

'It feels like walking on quicksand, doesn't it?' Sévère mused, observing the small splashes she made on the floor of his cell. 'It is always the next step that is the most important, but you can't quite decide where to place your foot.'

She ceased the tapping. 'An apt description.'

'Have you ever asked yourself why Mrs Appleton was so skittish?'

Olivia opened her mouth, but only a hollow, 'Ah,' came out.

'It would be easy to use Netty's behaviour as a reference point, just as it would be wrong. So tell me, Olivia, when did Mrs Appleton appear nervous?'

'She was nervous when we questioned her — when *you* questioned her — the day after her mistress died, and when I questioned her again a day later.'

'Under which circumstances precisely?' Sévère asked.

'In the laundry room,' Olivia whispered, and brushed her fingers over her chin, her mind wandering back to that evening. 'When she pushed the bucket with the towels and waxed paper into a corner of the room.'

'And when I interrupted her as she was washing her mistress' corpse, she all but fainted.'

'You don't think she...'

'One of several possibilities. Ask yourself, who had both a motive *and* the knowledge to kill Mrs Frank in this particular manner.'

'Mr Frank could have wanted his wife dead so that he could live with his mistress, if he *has* a mistress, that is. Mrs Appleton's motive might be revenge for her broken heart, if she indeed was in love with Mrs Frank.'

Sévère's jaws worked, his brows pulled low. 'Hum... You said Higgins is trying to find information on the substances Mr Perkin is using in his dye shop?'

She nodded. 'He's learned that Perkin is using salts and modern coal tar derivatives that he acquires directly from the manufacturer.'

'Wouldn't he know how to use plant toxins?'

'Why would he?'

Sévère scratched his short beard. 'As far as I know, fabrics were traditionally dyed with plants or plant extracts. As a dye chemist, Perkin should have some knowledge of extraction methods, I would think.'

'As would any chemist.' Olivia shrugged. 'But…hum. The poison was applied to the skin, and that bothers me. Why would Perkin, or anyone else for that matter, know more about poisons than one of the great experts in toxicology? Not even Dr Barry was aware that aconitine can be deadly when applied to the skin. As far as I know, the only person who might have been able to deduce the use of aconitine as a contact poison is Johnston's wife.'

'Hum…'

They sat in silence until a warden called through the peephole in the door, 'Five minutes.'

Olivia massaged her neck, and whispered, 'If you were only small enough to fit into my purse…'

Sévère bumped his fist to her arm. 'Next time. The food here is terrible enough.'

'Any suggestions as for the potential mistress of Mr Frank?'

'Find out if he promised her a future together, or if she's with child. Anything that could indicate why he might have wanted his wife dead, and why now. As to Mrs Appleton: Her behaviour was unusual. Find out why. You already know her nerves don't hold up well under pressure. Use this to your advantage. And keep an eye on Mr Perkin. If his sister did indeed treat him unfairly, that might be a motive.'

A SOFT KNOCK sounded from the door. 'Come in,' Olivia said.

Marion stepped into Olivia's private rooms and shut the door. Three strides in, she clasped her hands behind her back. Her white apron and cap were missing.

Olivia waited. It was simple enough to guess what was about to spill from the maid's mouth. Olivia wouldn't make it easier on her.

A high-pitched clearing of her throat, then Marion lifted her chin, and said, 'My parents do not wish me to remain in your services, Mrs Sévère.'

'I see.'

'I know it is an unfortunate time, but... May I kindly ask for a character so I may acquire a new situation?'

Olivia placed her pen into its holder. 'You said your parents want you to leave. But what do *you* want, Marion?'

The maid blushed. 'I, too, wish to leave.'

'And why is that, I wonder?'

She dropped her head. 'Because... Because...' And that was all she managed.

'You are worried what people will think of you, working for a woman who is said to have been a prostitute. Yet you seem unbothered asking me to be concerned about these immaterial problems of yours, even knowing that I must spend every moment fighting to save my husband's — and your master's — life. If you truly wish to leave your post because people gossip, you will soon be disappointed. People gossip everywhere. Stop aggravating me, stop wasting my time, and write that character yourself or ask Netty. I will sign it. You are dismissed.'

Marion opened and closed her mouth, curtsied awkwardly, and stumbled from the room.

'Well, that was one,' Olivia muttered, and turned back to her notes.

---

OLIVIA ALIGHTED FROM THE CAB, crossed the street and entered Regent's Park. She longed for a walk, for an hour or two without worries. But she only had time for a brisk stroll. As she walked, she collected her thoughts on what to say to the person inhabiting Mr Frank's secret apartment.

Higgins had seen boys delivering milk and meat, a maid leaving and returning, and had heard a child playing in the backyard. But he wasn't sure if the child lived in number eighty-two, or in one of the houses on either side.

Higgins's brief description of the neighbourhood hadn't done Gloucester Terrace justice. Olivia faced a row of pretty houses of bone-white plaster, large windows, and neat front yards. Not one pile of horse manure dirtied the street, not one ill-clothed person loitered. Roses and lavender spilled through picket fences, and bumblebees hummed summer songs.

Number eighty-two looked much like the neighbouring houses, except for a miniature perambulator abandoned on a path of stones flanked by flowers and ornamental grasses. Olivia stretched her neck and found a porcelain-faced, lace-trimmed doll that stared up at the blue sky. It gave her pause. Not the fact that she had finally found a motive for Mr Frank to kill his wife. No, it was the revelation that investigating this murder was granting her insights into the lives of strangers. It was intimacy she was forcing onto her suspects.

Olivia lifted her hand and rapped the knocker against the door. A peal of laughter sounded through a window that stood ajar, and a short moment later, a head peeked out through lace curtains, dark blue eyes blinked at Olivia, and then at the perambulator.

'Cecilia!' the girl squeaked and dove back into the room.

A servant opened the door, but before Olivia could introduce herself and state her business, she was interrupted by a white and yellow whirlwind that pushed past her and almost toppled into the pram.

'Bernice, your manners!' sounded from behind the servant. A shapely woman appeared in the doorway, her attention snapping from the girl to Olivia.

Olivia held out her card. 'Good day to you, miss. I am Olivia Sévère, private detective. I'm investigating—'

'I didn't expect you would find me so quickly.' Her hand went to her stomach, pressing down on it.

The servant's gaze flitted from her to Olivia and back.

'And when precisely did you expect me to find you?' Olivia asked, pretending she knew what the woman was talking about.

'I had hoped never.' She took a step back. 'You might as well come in. Bernice, bring in Cecilia. Cora, we'll take tea in the parlour.'

Bernice raced ahead of them, bouncing and screeching, and Olivia felt a wave of relief at her own childlessness. She stumbled over her own toes as she thought of

Rose. But the girl was more like a little sister than a daughter. And she wasn't half as annoying as Bernice.

Bernice ran circles around the coffee table until the maid snatched the girl's wrist and pulled her out of the room. There was some more screeching that threatened to shatter Olivia's eardrums, but finally silence fell and tea was delivered.

'I've forgotten my own manners, being so focused on the girl's,' the woman across from Olivia said, and held out her hand. 'Helen Warder. You probably wish to know why I did it.'

Olivia nodded, and said, 'Indeed,' but couldn't work out what Mrs Warder was playing at, for she seemed much too calm to be offering a confession of murder.

'I thought it unfair how the press was treating you, and…it all happened because of Hawley's wife—'

'Hawley?'

'Hawley Harvey Frank. Everyone calls him Harvey. Except me.' She smiled fondly. 'I'm aware that a little gold is nothing when one's reputation had been utterly ruined, but then…it was what I had, and after all it wasn't me who did it.'

'Did what?'

'Ruined your reputation.'

Olivia gazed out the window, then back at Mrs Warder. 'Did you melt a golden necklace, or did Mr Frank give you a gold nugget and tell you to send it to me?'

'Why would I destroy my jewellery?'

'I don't know.' Olivia shrugged. 'You sent a stranger a big clump of gold. That's rather queer, so why not make a habit of it?'

Mrs Warder ran her finger around the rim of her cup. 'Hawley doesn't know I sent it.'

'He doesn't?'

'I didn't tell him. He will notice, though, sooner or later.'

'Why?'

'It's a nugget he brought from Africa. One of the biggest they've found in the mine he owns. Well...he doesn't own it. He invested into it.'

'When was that?' Olivia asked.

'When we fell in love. Four years ago.' Mrs Warden touched a ring on her finger, then settled her gaze on Olivia. 'I was a prostitute, and he a client. He gave me the gold so I could buy my freedom. I never used it. I didn't want to leave, I...wanted *him*. A few weeks later he presented me with this.' She motioned at the room, the garden outside the window. 'I was already carrying his child.'

'Why didn't he divorce his wife?'

Mrs Warder snorted. 'He believed she would die of a broken heart. He is too soft-hearted. It's one of the reasons I love him.'

'It must have been rather inconvenient for you.'

'Sometimes it was. I despised her for the nights I spent alone. Despised her for her right to call herself his wife.'

'And now you can have it all,' Olivia said softly.

'It should make me content, shouldn't it?' Mrs Warden tilted her head. 'But he grieves. I didn't think he would.'

'You believed he would *not* grieve the death of his wife?'

'There was no love between them.'

'Did he say that?'

'At times. But even if he had never mentioned it, it was obvious from how he talked about her.'

'I see.' Olivia stood and walked to the window. 'May I ask if you grow wolf's bane in your garden?'

EVIDENCE

*O*livia woke with a start. Alf stood above her, a finger tapping her cheek. 'Missus! Missus!'

She swatted him away and sat up 'What is it?'

'The laundry maid is about to leave.'

'The…what?'

'The laundry maid. You wanted to talk to her. She's about to leave her home and go to Mr Frank's house.'

Olivia blinked out the window. The sun was up and birds were blaring, but the usual street noises were missing. 'What time is it?'

'Half past five.'

She yanked the covers aside, and sent Alf off to tell Higgins to ready the brougham. She dressed, rushed down to the kitchen to snatch a cup of tea, and then hurried to the stable to find Higgins waiting by the gate, holding the brougham door open for her.

'I'm in need of fresh air and information,' she said, and climbed up onto the driver seat. 'I hope you don't mind.'

In answer, Higgins folded up the steps, snapped the door shut, and took up his seat next to her. He snapped the reins and clicked his tongue. The brougham made a lurch.

'Mr Perkin doesn't seem to have a family. That is, he's not living with wife and children,' Higgins said, and fumbled around in his jacket, extracted a tobacco pouch, and began to roll a cigarette.

'You can do that *and* steer?'

'I'm not steering right now. We are going straight and not very fast. You can hold the reins if you wish.' He dropped the leather straps in her lap. 'Grab them, but don't pull. Use them to tap the horses once in a while. They need to know you're in charge and awake.'

Olivia picked up the reins, trying not to look like a dolt.

'Take the next right,' Higgins said. 'Pull the right side in, gently. A bit more. There.'

They made the turn, and Olivia exhaled. 'I'm glad I didn't tip us over.'

Higgins chuckled. 'For that, we would need more speed.' And then he grabbed the whip and tapped the horses. At once, they fell into a trot.

'Higgins, I doubt this is a good idea!'

'It's only a trot. Look straight ahead, and don't run over the old ladies.'

'Higgins, really!' She slapped the reins back to him.

He grinned, stuck the cigarette into his mouth, and took over. 'Mr Perkin seems to be a hard working fella,' he spoke through the corner of his mouth. 'He is at his workshop from six in the morning till eight or nine in the evening. He rents a small room up in the attic of one Dean Knapman at 21 Ravey Street. Cheap place. And I was thinking about what you said earlier. About shooting practice. It's a good idea. You need to get a feeling for the recoil, else you'll hurt your wrist, and then you might hesitate to pull the trigger a second time.'

'Do you think…'

'That you'll need to fire more than once? Yes, I do.'

'I don't want to shoot anyone accidentally.'

'You might shoot someone accidentally if you don't practice. You can use the basement. Send the servants away. Alf especially. And then…put up a target of some sort. A door, maybe. I'll show you later. Ah, here we are.' Higgins thrust out his stubbly chin and pulled the horses to a stop.

At first glance, the house Higgins had indicated seemed covered in rust and flour. Its dark red bricks were withered. White crusts were blooming around the base. The air swelled with scents of dew and ammonia.

Olivia picked up her skirts, climbed off the brougham, and made for the house. She rapped knocker against cracked wood, and waited. The tapping of heels, the whining of a key in a rusty lock. A middle-aged woman with creases around her mouth and a flowery kerchief covering her brown hair opened the door.

'Mrs Eloise Hibbert?' Olivia asked.

'Who is it?' a male voice thundered from the depths of the house.

'Well?' Mrs Hibbert said to Olivia.

'I am Olivia Sévère, private investigator. And I have a

few questions regarding the death of your mistress, Mrs Frank.'

'Is it the strumpet?' sounded through the corridor. 'Bring her in, Elli, I need a—'

Mrs Hibbert hastily stepped outside and shut the door. 'I am so sorry. My father, he is…um… Age has made him unkind.'

Olivia merely nodded, then motioned to the brougham. 'Shall we walk, or may I convey you to Sillwood Street? '

'Oh, I…I never…' A smile spread on her face. 'If I may?'

They entered the carriage, and Olivia said, 'You weren't present the night your mistress died, but I wonder if there's anything peculiar you observed the following morning?'

'Peculiar?'

'There was a bucket with towels and waxed paper in the laundry room. Do you know anything about it?'

'It's from Mrs Appleton what washed the mistress.'

'And Mr Frank?'

Mrs Hibbert frowned. 'He was feeling poorly. I mean…his wife died. He grieved, but… He'd already felt poorly the evening before, that's what Mrs Appleton told me. So it was her what washed Mrs Frank's body.'

Olivia squinted at Mrs Hibbert. 'Are you quite sure?'

'I saw Mrs Appleton come from the Missus' room with a bucket and towels. I didn't know why she had need of the waxed paper, but then I thought maybe it was to prevent the sheets from getting too wet.' She shrugged, and continued, 'Later that morning, she did it again. I heard her tell Mr Frank to rest and that she would take care of it. The...corpse.'

'And then you left the house? I'm asking because you weren't present when the Coroner and I came to the house, and Mrs Appleton was washing your mistress.'

'I was at Mrs Bixby's, and then at Mrs Greenham's, where I also work as laundry maid.'

'I see. Hmm...' Olivia tapped her lower lip. 'Did you find it peculiar that Mrs Appleton washed Mrs Frank's body?'

'No, not really. Mr Frank was ill and Mrs Appleton was ever so helpful when it came to anything the mistress needed. But...' Mrs Hibbert's hand trailed from her chin down to her stomach. 'But I was so very sorry to see her beautiful chemise burned. I've never seen such a fine piece of undergarment in all my life. That chemise was fit for a queen.'

'You saw Mrs Appleton burn Mrs Frank's undergarments?' Olivia kept her voice calm, but inside, she felt something contract sharply.

'Yes, it was...' Mrs Hibbert looked out the brougham's window into the pale morning. 'About this same time. I came through the servant's entrance, not knowing what had happened. Mrs Appleton dragged a bucket into the back yard and tipped it into the privy.' Eloise Hibbert chewed on her lip, thinking. 'She used laundry tongs to drape the towels over the rack. Then she pumped water into the bucket, rinsed it, and dumped that into the privy, too. Hum... I think there was a flannel in the bucket when she poured it out. I'm not sure. I asked her what she was doing, and she told me to mind my own business. I went inside and she followed. When I entered the laundry room, she sent me away to take breakfast.' Mrs Hibbert looked up, eyes large, head bobbing. 'She *never* does this. She ever only tells us to *work work work*.' Her hands made quick shooing motions.

'So you took breakfast.'

Mrs Hibbert snorted. 'I just had breakfast, and I…was curious. I poured myself a cup of tea and tiptoed to the laundry room. And there she was, shoving clothes into the fire. I was shocked to see her put Mrs Frank's pretty evening dress into the hearth — it barely even fit. Such a nice dress. Mrs Appleton heard me gasp and scolded me. Explained that the missus had died in those clothes and that the master wanted them burned, because of the smell. They smelled of death, she said. I didn't smell anything but the burnt fabric.'

Mrs Hibbert put a hand to her mouth. 'But the chemise! By God, I couldn't help myself. I jumped to snatch it from her. But it was of no use.'

'Did she touch the chemise with her hands?'

Mrs Hibbert cocked her head. 'No, she didn't. Strange, isn't it? She used the laundry tongs for everything.'

'Even the heavy dress?'

'Yes, and her…shoes.'

'That must have been a sight,' Olivia said.

'Oh, it was. It was.' Mrs Hibbert rubbed the back of her right hand. 'She whacked me with the tongs when I tried to grab the chemise.'

'Would you describe Mrs Appleton as a woman of delicate nerves?'

Mrs Hibbert burst out laughing. 'Among the other servants she's called the badger.'

'The badger?'

'Prod her once and she'll eat you alive.'

---

SÉVÈRE STARED AT THE CEILING — his favourite pastime now that there was nothing else to do but sleep, eat, worry, and piss into a bucket.

His mind went in useless circles, as it often did these days. Poison — skin samples — Johnston's bowler hat — the clump of gold.

He longed for exercise, for a walk, for open air. But most of all he worried about Olivia's absence. Was it a good or a bad sign? Was she already chasing the killer, or did she not dare come to see him because she hadn't found anything that might help?

He would go mad, indeed he would. There was a constant dripping noise just outside his cell, echoing through the peephole. Its frequency was just a tiny bit faster than his pulse, and when he tried to sleep, it seemed to quicken his heartbeat to match, so that he never truly rested.

Nor would rest have been possible even without the *drip drip drip*, for the men in the neighbouring cells rarely kept their mouths shut. They prayed for their souls, begged for someone to spare their lives, cursed judge, police, and magistrates, or masturbated with abandon.

Sévère had tried praying, but it felt ridiculous. He had tried stuffing corners of the threadbare blanket into his ears, but then chill went into his bad leg and the ache grew too intense to be ignored. He tried to pleasure himself to find sleep, but grew even more frustrated once the edge was taken off and his mind pounced on his case, on solving this problem and that, and then finding even more problems.

Noises rose in a cell to his right — one of his fellow prisoners was taking up his angry prayers once more. The man had been pleading his case since the previous day, at times angry, other times desperate. And then, his prayers turned to sobs.

Sévère found no pity in himself. After all, he was the only innocent man in this place.

But…was he?

Somewhere, a door was unlocked, words were muttered. Keys scraped through various locks. His cell door sprang open and Bicker stepped in. He had to stoop not to knock his head against the low door frame. Sévère's eyes went to Bicker's hat, which he gripped hard in front of his stomach.

Sévère wondered how bad the news might be.

Bicker waited for the warden to leave them alone, and then he heaved once, twice, and pinched the bridge of his nose.

'Dr Barry could not find vegetable alkaloids in Johnston's skin samples,' Bicker began. 'He wasn't even able to find vegetable alkaloids in the organ samples the second time he analysed them. It's the embalmment fluids. They render an analysis impossible.'

Sévère felt his spine go soft. He sagged forward and buried his face in his hands.

Bicker went on, 'He did find traces of vegetable alkaloids on the rim of Johnston's hat, though, which he will analyse further. However…' And here he stopped.

In the silence, Sévère looked up.

Bicker's eyelids drooped. His mouth was working up the words. 'The prosecution will point out that both the hat and Johnston were in your house, and that you had ample opportunity to manipulate both.'

'But…what for?'

'The point is that the hat would have helped your case only if it had never entered your house.'

'Then my release hinges on Rose's statement.'

Bicker rubbed his face and gazed up at the ceiling that was mere inches from his face. 'Well… There's her upbringing.'

All joints felt too loose on Sévère. He had the faint impression that his very substance was falling apart, and dripping from his frame. 'Does the prosecution know?'

'It doesn't matter. She'll be asked the usual questions: her name and residence, how long she has worked for your wife, how she came to know the prisoner, *et cetera*. And because she is so young, the prosecution will enquire about her mother and her upbringing.'

'But all this taken together — the burning sensation on Rose's palms after she touched Johnston's hand, the poison on the rim of his hat, the fact that I *told* the surgeon to send organ samples to Dr Barry — all this is evidence that I did not commit the crime. Yes, it is circumstantial evidence, but so is the evidence that was brought up against me.'

Bicker slowly nodded, but Sévère saw that it was done for his benefit only.

'Sévère, the problem is that the statements of Mrs Johnston and your housekeeper weigh heavy against you. Your wife's past gives you a strong motive. Your unusual interest in postmortems and all medical matters relating to suspicious deaths gives you the expertise to accomplish such an extraordinary killing. Forgive me for being so blunt, but sending samples of Johnston's organs to Dr Barry is only a sign of the arrogance you are well known for.'

If Sévère had been able to stand, he would have punched Bicker's face. 'Bicker, forgive *me* for being so blunt, but you are a horse's ass. You don't have to prove my innocence. You only need to show that there is reasonable doubt as to my guilt.'

'Is there?'

Sévère's jaw unhinged. 'You believe I killed him.'

Bicker's expression softened. 'No, I do not. But enough people do.'

# THE HORSEMAN

*A* narrow beam of sickly-yellow light dropped through the peephole of Sévère's cell door, and fell directly into the jar with unguent. He moved it in and out of the light, the unguent's greasy reflection appearing and vanishing, just as hope had done these past days.

God, how he embraced that feeling every time it returned! No matter how small or insignificant, he could weep every time hope showed its lovely face once more.

And how hollowed out he felt every time it left.

He exhaled, listened to the hiss of breath through his nostrils, watched ghosts of condensation rise, and wondered how death at the end of a rope would feel.

He touched his throat. How tender the skin was there.

His gaze dropped back to the unguent. Half a grain of aconitine in a dollop the size of a bean or nut. He had much more at his disposal. Judging from Johnston's death, he wouldn't have to suffer long.

He dipped his index finger into the jar, and lifted it up

to his face. Such a curious little thing, he mused, and stuck it into his mouth.

His tongue began to prickle. Hot shame washed through him. He spat out, and washed his mouth with tepid water, rubbed his sleeve across his tongue, and spat again.

Cowardice had, until this day, never been one of his traits. Nor was witlessness. For if he were found dead in his cell, poisoned by a substance his wife had smuggled in, she would face the consequences.

---

GNARLED shadows twitched in the candlelight. Olivia's nerves felt raw and exposed. Whenever she answered one of the many questions Sévère's case raised, another dozen seemed to appear. It was maddening.

How the deuce could she get Mr Frank, Mrs Appleton, or Mrs Warden to confess to the murder of Mrs Frank before it was too late? She didn't even know where to begin.

Olivia placed the pencil aside and stared at the useless scribbles in front of her. The clock on the mantle told her it was nearly two in the morning. She rubbed her face and went to check on Rose.

The girl wasn't in her bed.

---

OLIVIA BLASTED INTO THE KITCHEN. 'Have you seen Rose?' she barked at cook who almost dropped the bowl of late supper she must have planned on sneaking into her room.

'Seen her around noon. Surely she's in bed now.'

Olivia dashed from the kitchen and made for the coachman's quarters above the stable. She banged her fist against the door until Higgins opened, dressed only in a long grey shirt that reached to his hairy knees, his face a question mark.

'When was the last time you saw Rose?'

He blinked. 'In the morning.'

'What was she doing? Was she distressed? Did she say anything about a man or woman loitering on the street?'

Higgins shook his head, then his eyes flew open. 'Is it about the man you warned her about?' Before Olivia could reply, he said, 'I'll get dressed and find her.'

He was about to slam the door shut, but she blocked him with her hand. 'I'll search the attic. You start in the basement. We'll meet in the middle.'


Rose was nowhere to be found. Not in her pirate shack up at the attic, not in any closet, not under a bed or table. The servants stood in the corridor, Netty kneading her apron, cook staring into her bowl of cold supper, Alf pulling his ear. Olivia rushed from Sévère's office, her purse stuffed with her gun and whatever money she could find in her haste. Higgins came back from his rooms, slipping a revolver into a pocket of his jacket, his face utterly calm. 'Alf,' he said to the boy, 'go to the police and—'

'No.' Olivia grabbed Higgins' arm. 'We'll decide about that later.'

They summoned a cab, and rode to a place Olivia had

no wish to ever see again. She sorely missed Johnston. He was the only one she would have trusted for this.

They alighted not in front of the brothel, but about fifty yards from it. 'Higgins, you must stay close but hidden for now. I might need you to play the client if the madam doesn't let me see Rose.'

A nod from him, and she strolled off. The revolver in her purse felt heavy. She hadn't had time to practice much. One evening, fifteen shots. That was all. Now she desperately wished she were a legendary gunfighter from the Wild West.

She burst into the brothel without knocking. Bobby jumped from his armchair. 'Where is she?' Olivia barked, and only then took in the lobby. Two clients sat stiffly at a table, a bottle of wine and two glasses between them. They were unfamiliar to her.

She turned back to Bobby. 'Well?'

Bobby straightened, cracked his knuckles, and stared down his nose. Then he lifted his arm and tapped the small bell above his head. The madam arrived a few heart-beats later.

'Oh, look who graces us with her presence. Miss Mary, what a pleasant surprise. But if you are looking for work, I must dissapoint—'

'Where is Rose?'

'Are you referring to *my daughter*? The one you abducted and kept locked in your house for six months? She found her way back home and is doing very well.' The madam smiled, and casually tucked a dark curl behind her ear. Her pearl earrings glittered in the lamplight.

Olivia's blood was coming to a boil. 'You have two

options. One: You hand Rose over to me and never see her again, except when she wishes it. Two: You rot in gaol.'

'Why don't you ask her what *she* wants?' The madam winked, sauntered to the stairwell, and called, 'Rose, my dear, would you come down for a moment?'

A door opened and a redhead stepped out. Her eyes flared with surprise when she saw Olivia. *Mary*, she mouthed, beaming.

'Claire, fetch Rose,' the madam said.

Claire's expression shuttered. 'She's asleep.'

'Well, wake her then!'

Claire descended the stairs, her eyebrows tilted toward sarcasm. 'Wasn't it *you* who gave her the laudanum?'

Olivia stomach roiled. Her hand itched to grab her revolver and shove it into the madam's face.

Madame Rousseau waved a dismissive hand, and said to Olivia, 'There you have it. She can talk to you tomorrow.'

'Very well, gaol it is then.'

The madam snorted. 'The girl resides here, she is my daughter, and she offered herself to a man. Told him she was thirteen years old. What can I do?' She shrugged. 'No one will arrest me for this.'

Olivia snapped her fingers, a cruel smile on her face. 'Well, dammit. I would have liked to see the six months for seduction of an underage girl added to the three years for concealment of death. Because that's what you and Bobby will get for dumping Alexander Easy into the Thames. Hum... And who knows if he was *really* dead when he was thrown in? It all depends on my memory which is a little…scattered. At times.'

Still, the facade did not slip from the madam's face. 'Claire, dear, please take those two gentlemen up to your room.'

Claire put on a seductive smile, and the men rose. As they passed Olivia, one of them whispered, 'Is there a chance you would join us?'

Olivia gifted him a cold stare that made him flinch. She watched Claire hooking her arms around both men, and walk them upstairs. As they disappeared, there was a softly spoken, 'Bobbie,' from the madam, and two thick arms dropped around Olivia.

'You will go to gaol. I'll make sure of it!' Olivia hissed as she struggled against Bobby's grip.

'I wish you a pleasant night, *Mary*. If you dare show your visage here again, you will regret it.' She nodded at Bobby, and his arms tightened around Olivia, and lifted her up.

Olivia struggled, tossed her head back and whacked Bobby's nose. He boxed her ear in retaliation. The pain and screeching noise in her head made her vision swim.

'Higgins! Higgins!' she hollered, kicking Bobby's legs. 'HIGGINS!'

A dull thwack sounded behind her, somewhat above her head. Bobby froze, and dropped like a sack of flour, taking Olivia down with him.

Higgins grabbed her shoulder. 'Where?' he hissed, his eyes black and furious.

'Upstairs. First door to the right, I believe.'

Higgins whirled around, and took the stairs three

steps at a time, closely followed by the madam who was struggling with her voluptuous skirts. Bobbie lay prone, his eyeballs rolling about beneath his lids, a line of spittle lolling from his half-open mouth.

A screech and a thump sounded from upstairs. And then Rose's small voice, pleading.

Olivia pushed herself up, a hand pressed to the wall to keep the room from spinning away from her. She fumbled for her revolver, pulled it from her purse, and approached the stairs.

Higgins appeared, Rose in his arms. 'Out!' he bellowed.

Olivia backed away and stumbled over Bobby's bulky form. He grunted and swatted at her. She kicked his side for good measure, then made for the door.

As Higgins ran past her, the sight of Rose — dressed only in a sheer nightdress, her small arms wrapped tightly around his neck, her face pressed to his throat — broke Olivia's heart in two.

They covered a few hundred yards by foot until they found a cab. Rose was transferred to Olivia's lap, and the girl clung to her like a barnacle.

'Is she dead?' the girl whimpered.

Olivia threw Higgins a glance. 'What happened to her mother?'

'A small tap to her chin. She should wake soon enough.' And then gently to Rose, 'I did not kill your mother.' He turned away and muttered, 'Although I very much wanted to.'

ONCE AT HOME, Olivia ordered a bath to be drawn in her

bedroom. She held Rose's hand as Higgins carried the girl up the stairs, and then laid her down onto Olivia's bed.

Silently, she sat by Rose's side as the small tub was set up and filled. She watched her dilated pupils and half-open eyes that seemed unable to focus on anything for more than a fleeting moment. The faint, sweetish scent of opium clung to her lips.

Once Netty had left, Olivia touched Rose's cheek, and said with a nod toward the tub, 'The ocean is all yours, First Mate. Although it might be a bit boring, for I ate all the sharks.'

Rose blinked at Olivia's face. 'Claire washed me.'

'Good.' And after a moment, she asked, 'Are you hurting?'

Rose's lids fluttered. She pulled her knees to chest, her body stiffening. 'I want to bathe,' she said, voice adrift.

'All right. Let me help you with the nightdress. It is a rather un-piratey garment.'

Rose looked down her body, and plucked at the frills.

'Shall we?' Olivia asked.

Rose pushed herself to a sitting position, her shoulders slumped.

Careful, Olivia lifted off the nightdress. There were bruises around Rose's neck, shoulders, and hips. She didn't dare touch them.

'Come, I'll carry you,' she said, slid her arms under the girl, and conveyed her to the tub. As she lowered her into the warm water, Rose flinched, but did not protest.

'All right?' Olivia asked.

Rose stared at her knees that were sticking out of the water like white twin islands.

'Shall I fetch our ships while you wrestle the sea monsters?'

A small nod.

Olivia made for Rose's adjoining room and searched the cluttered windowsill for the armada of walnut shell pirate ships. She picked them up one by one, and returned to Rose.

'The cowards were hiding behind a half-dead cactus,' Olivia said, and set them down in the lagoon formed by Rose's knees and chest.

Rose's throat was working. A tear scuttled down her cheek. 'I'm sorry,' she whispered.

'No, no! Don't be sorry! Be angry. Furious. Scream at others, not at yourself. None of this,' Olivia took Rose's chin in her hand and made her look up. 'None of this is your fault.'

Rose's gaze dashed away.

'This is *not* your fault. Do you understand?'

'But you told me to stay inside,' she said with a trembling voice.

'And that gives Bobby the right to take you away?'

'My mam took me.'

'It still doesn't give anyone the right to do this to you. I'm so sorry, Rose. I'm your captain and I should have protected you better.' Olivia caressed the girls's cheek, and smoothed a strand of her hair behind her ear.

Rose shrugged, dropped her gaze to the boats, and systematically sank them.

One by one.

WHEN OLIVIA ENTERED HIS CELL, Sévère thought for the shortest of moments that he had never before seen this woman, that this wasn't his wife, but a brittle, empty husk of her. An impostor.

The next moment, he thought he was going to die. Whatever news she brought must mean he would, with utter certainty, face the gallows. He dared not breathe.

She told him about the statements of Franks' laundry maid and the former personal maid. He knew these new developments should give him hope, but the way Olivia spoke — detached, like an automaton— he all but waited for a blow. But it did not come.

When she fell silent, he croaked, 'Something horrible must have happened. Tell me.'

She turned her face away. 'Rose was taken to her mother.'

Relief blasted through him — the fatal blow, the thing that would get him hanged, did not exist. Not today. At once, the feeling of relief was swept away by fury. Fury that he was locked up here and couldn't prevent, couldn't revenge, couldn't protect. He felt the bite of his nails against his palms. The small pain tethered him to sanity.

'Higgins and I retrieved her.' Olivia clapped a hand to her mouth. In the dim light her eyes began to glitter. Silver trailed down her cheek. 'I told that swine of a mother I would make sure she rots in gaol. But...' Olivia dropped her hand and lifted her head to the ceiling, gulping for breath.

Sévère pulled tight the buckles of his brace, and made to stand. Olivia threw her hands out. 'No! Sit down. 'I'm all right. It will pass. It will pass.'

He lowered himself back onto his hammock, watching Olivia adjust her armour. Her chin lifted, her spine straightened. Her gaze emptied.

'Rose spoke very little. She blames herself. Judging from the things she *doesn't* say, it's clear she is protecting her mother. And even if she weren't... Madame Rousseau would tell the police that Rose offered herself to the man and lied to him about her age. The police won't expect much else from a girl who grew up in a brothel.'

Sévère had no words.

'But there's still the concealment of death she's committed. Rose has...injuries. Her body will heal. As for her soul...' Furiously, Olivia dashed tears off her face. 'She's convinced she's the stupidest and weakest girl in the world, because she believes that all of this is normal and she's the only one who didn't do it right and so...she deserved the pain.' She dropped her gaze and balled her fists. 'It's what he told her, the bastard.'

'Who?'

'Mr Wednesday.'

Sévère cocked his head. 'Do I know him?'

'One of my clients preferred to visit me on Wednesdays. It was such a regular occurrence that Rose called him Mr Wednesday. They rarely gave their real names, anyway.'

Sévère felt tension grow in his stomach. He leant forward. 'Who?'

'Frost.'

# FALLING

*S*évère watched the clenching and unclenching of his hands. There was a trembling of the distal two digits whenever he stretched his fingers. It disappeared when he curled them. You are weak when you open yourself up, he thought.

And yet, maybe that's what he would do.

What had been done to Rose drove chills down his back. But the way Olivia talked about it was incomparably worse. It had given him a clear view of the darkness curled up in the depths of her soul. It terrified him how brittle her armour had become. He feared what might happen when she broke — when *it* broke out.

Something inside him stirred. He wondered if Olivia was feeling the same. As if a beast had been roused. Was that the birthplace of monster stories — one's own soul? It must be, for what else would a storyteller weave if not his own tapestry?

Chief Magistrate Frost was a black thread in Sévère's

tapestry. The man had inserted himself into Olivia's life, and with that, into Sévère's. And now into the life of Rose. He had seen her in Height's office, and must have notified her mother at once. Rose had turned nine in spring. Sévère hadn't known that until Olivia told him. She also told him that for Madame Rousseau, nine was an appropriate age to be sold to the highest bidder. Her own daughter!

Disgusted, Sévère spat on the floor.

The attack on Rose felt like an attack on himself. A girl who was under his protection had been taken from his own home, and raped. But shouldn't he be outraged that this was an everyday occurrence in this city? Shouldn't everyone?

He had tried to convince Olivia to report the crime to the police. She turned him down with a cold glare and two short sentences: Frost *is* the police. Rose will not be violated again.

Her mother had drugged the girl with laudanum to make her pliable. Olivia had drugged her again in the early morning hours when the pain and nightmares came.

He touched his throat. He was in gaol, but a serial rapist wasn't and never would be.

Sévère curled his hands to fists. What were the things he desperately clung to? His freedom. His ability to walk.

He unfurled his fingers.

He listened to his fellow prisoners, their moans, prayers, and curses. 'I've lost all fear,' he whispered, the sudden clarity shocking him.

He gazed at the peephole in his cell door. A smile tugged at his lips.

Mrs Appleton sank against the door frame. One hand fluttered to her mouth and lingered there. 'Perhaps…' She looked up at Olivia, who was waiting on the doorstep. 'Perhaps it is best if we retreat to my room.'

They walked down a staircase, past the kitchen and laundry room, and through a door at the end of the corridor. Mrs Appleton offered Olivia a chair by a narrow window that was set high up in the wall, but she herself remained standing, fidgeting with her apron.

'I did not steal it,' Mrs Appleton said, eyes fastened to her shoes. 'I returned the necklace to my mistress' jewellery box.'

'You took the property of your mistress. That's theft. And then you went on and falsely implicated Miss Shepherd for the theft that you committed, knowing she might be taken to the police.'

Mrs Appleton licked her lips. 'But she wasn't.'

'Hmm,' Olivia said, and scanned the room.

'You won't find it here. I returned it.'

'I wasn't looking for the necklace. In fact, I didn't come here to enquire about it.' Olivia rested her gaze on Mrs Appleton. 'Where do you keep the poison?'

All the blood drained from Mrs Appleton's face. She methodically shook her head.

'I know what you did,' Olivia lied. 'As does my attorney. He and I have an appointment with Inspector Height of Division H at noon today. It is of no use to lie or to delay, Mrs Appleton. The evidence against you speaks clear enough.'

Mrs Appleton stumbled two steps back. 'I didn't do it. I didn't do it. I swear I didn't!'

'You were seen burning the clothes of your mistress,' Olivia said softly. 'And then you laid out fresh clothes for her before you washed her a second time.'

Mrs Appleton took another step back, bumped into the bed frame and sank to the mattress. 'He wants to kill me.'

'Excuse me?'

'He wants me dead. The Spider wants me dead! Or a man who's paid the Spider for his services. All he needs to do is place an ad in Reynolds's Newspaper. Don't you *see?*'

'I… No, I don't.' Olivia had never expected Mrs Appleton to be raving mad. Does one call a doctor or does one drop off insane people directly at the gates of an asylum?

Mrs Appleton's chest was heaving. She gripped her hair and began rocking back and forth, muttering, '*Spider silk sought*, that's all one has to write. *Spider silk sought.* And where and when. Don't know how much it is, but it must be expensive. Very expensive. It must be a rich man who wants me dead.' She looked up. 'Why would a rich man want me dead?'

'Who is the Spider? And what is spider silk?' Olivia asked, mostly to calm Mrs Appleton down and get her to make some sense.

It was as if lightning struck the housekeeper. She shot out her arm, wrenched open a drawer of her night stand, and picked up a piece of paper. A newspaper clipping. 'It's from the Daily Post. From Tuesday.'

Olivia took it and read.

**Fleming heir dead!**

*The police and trustworthy sources close to the Fleming family have informed us that on Sunday night last, Mr Rupert Maximilian Fleming, heir of Sir Robert Maximilian Fleming, did commit suicide by firing a bullet into his own heart. In a letter to his parents, he listed his reasons for ending his own life: The loss of his fiancé, Miss Edwine Mollywater, and the false and cruel rumour connected to her death — that she had taken a lover. The rumour arose when it became known that she did receive a package on the day of her death, that contained an extraordinary undergarment as well as a note that read, "Wear this and meet me by the tigers." The ceremony for Mr Rupert Fleming will be conducted within the circle of his closest family.*

Something niggled in the back of Olivia's memory. 'I don't understand,' she murmured.

---

'OH, this is so much more fun than attending to Mr Anonymous and his many criminal friends,' William said, and scratched his belly. 'Did I hear you right? You did place the ad already?'

'Well…yes,' Olivia answered.

'But you don't seem to be overly convinced that this will work?'

'I honestly don't know, William. This is too absurd to be true. A man who fashions poison undergarments as murder weapons, to sell them to killers? If that were true, he should have been discovered much sooner. Let's assume Mrs Frank wore a poison chemise fashioned by a serial killer. Johnston examined her, and died. Mr Frank was affected as well. The killer would soon discover that dead people cause more dead people. Not only members of the household, but the physicians and surgeons who perform postmortems would be dying, too.' She slapped her forehead. 'It simply can't be! It was Johnston who performed the postmortem on Edwine Mollywater. He would have noticed the effects of aconitine, had her chemise been poisoned with it. But I remember him saying that Miss Mollywater's death was natural. There was nothing much suspicious about it, other than the swiftness of it, and her youth and good health.'

'Hum…' Willian said, and tapped the edge of the table. 'Maybe the chemise was accidentally overdosed? Murderers can get carried away. Especially when the motive is love, envy, hate, revenge. Passion can turn a planned clean death into a bloody massacre.'

'But are you willing to go? Even if I might be wasting your precious time?'

'Waste precious sleep for an adventure? Anytime, my dear!'

Olivia smiled at him. 'You are a good friend. Thank you.'

---

AT TEN MINUTES PAST MIDNIGHT, William and Olivia walked through Victoria Park toward its fountain. She kept whispering instructions, and he kept waving them away.

'If you don't stop your sermon, I will resort to a

screaming attack,' he whispered back. 'We're almost there. Time for you to be invisible.'

A few yards from the fountain, Olivia hid in a copse, pulled her cap down low, and the collar of her dark jacket up. Squatting in the underbrush, she pricked her ears.

Crickets clicked and rasped. An owl screeched. And occasionally, William coughed. It was their signal that he was all right and still alone. It was early yet. He was to meet the poisoner at one o`clock.

Olivia thought of Rose. The girl walked about the house like a wraith, avoiding everyone but Olivia and Higgins. She played quietly. She'd smashed the shack in the attic. And then she'd returned to her silent, hollow state.

Olivia wished Rose were furious instead.

Olivia knew precisely how she would kill Frost. She wasn't sure yet what to do with the madam. She didn't want to hurt Rose. But Frost's fate was sealed. She would follow him, wait until he was done with whatever girl he was assaulting, and then she would put a bullet into his belly, gag him, and watch him die slowly. She would make him suffer.

There was a faint crack. A twig breaking under the weight of a boot. Olivia narrowed her eyes to slits, worried the whites would make her visible. She silenced her breath, but could not silence her heart that threatened to jump out of her throat.

A crunch of footfalls on the walkway. Not far away now.

She heard William's voice greeting the person, enquiring about spider silk.

The answer must have been a nod or a shake of the head, because Olivia did not hear the stranger speak.

William explained about his nonexistent wife, that he wished her dead because she was an evil hag who had not shared his bed for twenty years.

There was still no answer from the stranger, and Olivia grew nervous. What if William was in danger? He was too slow to dodge the slash of a knife or the swing of a fist.

William kept on prattling. He asked about the price.

'One hundred pounds,' the stranger said. His voice seemed familiar, but Olivia couldn't place it.

'When will it be delivered? And…how? I don't want it to be sent to my home, you see.'

'You will give me your name and your address, and I will send you a telegram with directions when and where you can pick it up.'

*That* voice! Olivia pressed her knuckles to her mouth.

William chuckled. 'I'm no fool, dear man.'

'Very well,' the man said, and the scrunch of boots retreated.

After a moment, William called, 'Wait!' and ran after the man, huffing like a steam engine.

---

'Do you remember Edwine Mollywater?' Olivia asked Sévère after she'd taken a seat next to him.

He cocked his head. 'Yes, I remember. She died in the zoo. I found her death suspicious.'

'And you were right. She was poisoned by the same man who killed Mrs Frank and Dr Johnston.'

Time ceased to exist. Sévère acutely felt the clenching of his throat, the thudding of his heart.

He forced himself to breathe, and then he said, 'Inform Height at once. You cannot catch a serial killer.'

She snorted. 'Really, Sévère, you should hear yourself. Wouldn't it be appropriate to say, "Thank you," and "Who the bloody hell is the man?"'

He huffed a laugh. 'Thank you, my sweet wife. Who the bloody hell is the man?'

'The dye chemist of the fashion boutique on Sillwood Street.' And she told him how she learned about it, what had occurred the previous night, and that the Spider's voice sounded familiar to her. And when she asked William if the man had a harelip, he told her that he had a moustache and that it was too dark too see if it was fake or not. But the voice was the slightest bit muffled in a way that is peculiar to people with a harelip. William described the man's stature and manners, and it was just how Olivia would have described Albert Perkin plus moustache.

'And you are waiting for his note now.' Sévère nodded slowly, then raked his fingers through his beard.

'It suits you well,' Olivia said and touched a hand to his cheek. 'Will you need a barber?'

'It's courtesy of Newgate. Every prisoner is offered a grooming before facing the court, lest the honourable judge and jurymen believe the prison conditions *dreadful*. How is Rose doing?'

Olivia dropped her head. 'It's as if she's half-dead. And

she's easily frightened. I left her alone in my room last night, and when I returned she was bathed in sweat, terrified I had left forever...' She trailed off and Sévère felt an iron tension settle around her.

---

WHEN THE TRIAL WAS REOPENED, William still hadn't received a telegram from Perkin. Olivia felt as if she might burst into flame as she took her seat by the jury box.

The judge entered the court room and everyone was asked to rise, but Sévère wasn't in the prisoner's dock, and Olivia knew something was wrong. She willed Bicker to look at her, to explain what this was about. But the attorney gazed straight ahead, bowed slightly to the judge, and took his seat.

'The prisoner's poor health prevents him from attending today,' the judge announced. 'The trial will commence without him.'

'What?' she cried. The judge narrowed his eyes at her, and Bicker turned and signalled her to be quiet.

Dr Barry was called in, but Olivia barely listened as he reported on the small amounts aconitine found on Johnston's bowler hat, and the inconclusive results of the skin sample analyses. The prosecution established that the poison might have been applied in the home of the prisoner, and that there probably wasn't any poison on Johnston's hands after all.

She wished she could read Bicker's mind. Or better yet Sévère's, so she would know what had happened to him.

If only Perkin had finished the chemise already and had sent word to William!

She was startled out of her thoughts when the judge rapped his gavel and announced that the trial was adjourned for the day, that all evidence had been heard, and that the attorneys were to prepare their closing speeches for the following day.

The solicitor-general stood. 'My Lord, I wish it to be noted that the prosecution has reason to believe that the prisoner is planning to influence the jury.'

The judge raised his eyebrows.

The solicitor-general turned to the jurymen. 'Tomorrow, the prisoner will enter the court room in a wheeling chair. He will claim that he has lost the ability to walk. But a warden tells me that Mr Sévère is heard shuffling about his cell at night.'

'I object!' Bicker cried out, and smacked his palms flat on the desk.

Justice Hawkins gaze grew icy as he looked from Bicker to the solicitor-general. 'Mr Hanbury, your behaviour is appalling. You use rumour to discredit the prisoner. Shall we enquire if the audience would provide a few rumours of their own as to *your* nightly activities?'

Bicker snapped his gaping mouth shut. Never in his entire career had he heard a judge grind the solicitor-general so effectively under his boot.

Mr Hanbury had the presence of mind to blush, drop his head, and retract his statement.

## LAST DAY

*S*évère sat in a wheeling chair in front of the prisoner's dock. He ignored the glances the audience threw down at him, those of mistrust, accusation, and pity. He was bored senseless by mankind's predictability. It was no feat to deduce what they were whispering: How can he end up in a chair so quickly without visible injury? Does he believe he can wrap the jurymen around his finger with this charade? Does he believe the judge won't send him to the gallows for all that he's done?

He wanted to set the court room on fire.

There'd been no word from Olivia.

Sévère looked down at his knees, observed the trembling of his bad leg, mildly fascinated about how little like himself he felt. It was as though his body weren't made of flesh and bone, but wood. He could almost hear the creaks and groans of old planks. A ship sinking fast, the killing wave rolling in to pull him to the bottom.

When he'd been taken from the condemned ward, sent through countless corridors, and through the domed hall of the Old Bailey — its entrance doors wide open and the sky a distant flash of blue — he'd filled himself with scents of summer and sun and life and freedom, and almost wept.

That small moment had lost its meaning the instant he laid eyes on Frost.

There was movement up on the dais. The judge was making an announcement. Was this already the summing-up? Had he missed the closing speeches of Bicker and the solicitor-general? Sévère blinked, and took in his surroundings.

'…to call in new witnesses. In order to protect an ongoing police investigation, the court room will now be closed to the public.' The judge rapped the gavel against his desk. The ushers promptly shouldered the protesting masses and newspaper men out of the room.

Sévère twisted around, searching for Olivia. There she was, sitting in the very back of the room, her expression pinched and exhausted, her hands clasped tightly in her lap. This wasn't the look of a woman who'd caught a murderer.

The last wisp of Sévère's courage vanished.

Bicker's voice rang through the court room. 'Please accept my apologies for the delay.' He offered a small bow to the jury, and another to the judge. 'Only a few hours ago, fresh evidence was brought forth which allows me to outline to you how precisely Dr Johnston was killed. It is of utmost importance to the case, as I will demonstrate to you in but a moment.'

Bicker coughed once. 'The defence calls Mrs Eloise Hibbert onto the witness stand.'

Sévère felt himself return to the present, as a woman in her mid-thirties placed her right hand upon the Bible, and swore to tell the truth and nothing but the truth. She told Bicker her name and occupation, and went on to detail how Mrs Appleton had burned Mrs Frank's clothes — those her mistress had worn when she died. And that she felt very sorry about the beautiful chemise being burned.

'Was it a chemise such as this one?' Bicker walked over to his desk and picked up a package. He unfolded the waxed paper and showed its contents to the witness.

Mrs Hibbert reached out. Bicker took a step back. 'Please don't touch it. It is extremely toxic.'

The jurymen murmured. Justice Hawkins grumbled, 'Mr Bicker, what is this?'

'The murder weapon, my lord.'

Hawkins' jaw tensed. 'And when, pray tell, did you come upon it?'

'I received this final piece of evidence in the early morning hours, a few minutes past three o'clock.'

The judge huffed and dipped his head.

Bicker continued, 'Mrs Hibbert, you may look at it closely, but it would be very unwise to touch it.' He placed the package in front of her.

Her eyebrows drew together, and she said, 'It looks very much like the one Mrs Frank wore that night.'

'The night she died?'

'Yes.'

Bicker folded two edges of the waxed paper over the

chemise, grabbed the garment through the paper, and held it up. The silk unraveled.

Mrs Hibbert clapped a hand to her bosom. 'It's the same. Extraordinary!'

'Thank you, Mrs Hibbert.' Bicker stepped away from the witness stand and held the chemise up for the jurymen to see. 'I have no further questions for the witness.'

The solicitor-general prodded Mrs Hibbert as to her belief whether or not this chemise really was precisely like the one Mrs Frank wore, and if she'd ever seen Mrs Frank's chemise up close. Yes, she had seen it up close, but Mrs Appleton wouldn't let her touch it, just as Mr Bicker wouldn't.

Next, the defence called in Mr Arthur Adams of Adams & Sons Finest Undergarments for Ladies.

'Mr Adams, do you recognise this chemise? Please take your time examining it, but I must insist that you refrain from touching the evidence.'

Mr Adams pinched a pair of glasses onto the bridge of his nose, and narrowed his piercing gaze at the chemise laid out before him. 'No doubt. This is one of ours.'

'Would you please tell the jury how you arrive at this conclusion?'

Mr Adams patted his waistcoat, and then asked if he might borrow Bicker's pencil. He inserted one end of the pencil into the neckline of the chemise and drew it up a few inches. 'There is the material itself. Finest mulberry silk which we purchase from Bengal. The type and origin of the material is evident from the sheen and how it refracts the light. Then there is the neckline which is trimmed with hand-made bobbin lace, or — to be precise — Chantilly lace, which we personally select from a small manufacturer in France. And then…' He used the pencil to spread out the chemise. '…there are Miss Muddy's pink silk roses. She makes them for us and no other.' He tapped at the delicate flowers sprinkled below the lace of the neckline. 'And if that were not enough to identify the maker, you will find a small embroidered *A&S* at the hem of each item we make.' He lifted an end of the sheer fabric

Bicker stepped forward and squinted, then said, 'Indeed. Thank you, Mr Adams. Now, can you recall who purchased it?'

'I couldn't tell you, precisely. Unless there were a name embroidered into it, which, in this case, there is not.'

'Have you sold an identical chemise a few days, weeks, or months ago?'

'Of course, we have. This is one of our most priced items.'

'Can you recall how many you have sold this year?'

'Easily. As we use only highest quality materials and the best tailors, we produce only to order. Of these chemises we have sold a good two dozen this year.'

'You mean to say that they are expensive?'

'Very much so.'

Bicker waited, but when Mr Adams did not elaborate, he prodded for details.

Mr Adams cleared his throat and said, 'Forty-five pounds.'

'Thank you, Mr Adams,' Bicker said. 'Would you please tell the jury the names of the clients who have purchased this precise chemise from you?'

Mr Adams squirmed in his seat. 'I prefer to not intrude upon my clients' privacy.'

A *bonk* sounded from the dais that made Mr Adams jump. 'The witness will answer the question.'

'Please accept my apology, my Lord. I merely wished it to be noted that Adams and Sons is *very* discreet.' Mr Adams pulled a small booklet from his waistcoat, snapped it open, read off a handful of names, and then handed the booklet to Bicker.

Mr Bicker presented it to the jury. 'One man has purchased five such chemises this year. He gave the name of Alf Perks.'

Bicker kept his gaze on the jury when he asked the next question. 'Mr Adams, did you find anything peculiar about Mr Perks?'

Mr Adams mumbled at his hands, threw a nervous glance at the judge, then said, 'We hold Mr Perks in highest esteem. He has been our client for the past four years and has purchased undergarments of the best quality.'

'And as to his peculiarities?' Bicker prodded.

'I wouldn't dare venture—'

'Allow me to rephrase: Is there anything about Mr Perks' face that makes him stand out?'

The witness touched his own mouth. 'A harelip.' Then he frowned. 'Well, I guess I should add that his bearings don't appear to be those of a wealthy man.'

'Thank you, Mr Adams. I have no further questions for the witness.'

Sévère's heart was hammering so hard, he feared it might kick him off his wheeling chair. He turned to

Olivia, willing her to look at him. And she did. With a strained smile and a stiff nod.

He didn't pay attention when the solicitor-general addressed the witness, for his mind was a noisy mess. When Bicker announced a re-examination of Mrs Appleton, Sévère managed to pull himself together.

'My apologies, Mrs Appleton, for calling you back onto the witness stand,' Bicker said. 'But there are a few small things that need clarification.'

She nodded meekly.

'Does this look familiar to you?' Bicker presented her with the chemise.

Mrs Appleton squeaked and clapped her hands over her face.

Sévère felt a grim calmness settle upon him.

Bicker placed the chemise back onto his desk.

'Mrs Appleton,' the judge said. 'Please compose yourself.'

Her hands dropped onto the Bible in front of her, fingers fidgeting around its edges. 'I received a package a day before…before the death of my mistress.' A sob squeezed through her windpipe. 'I swear I didn't know. I swear!'

'You received a package,' Bicker repeated. 'What was in it?'

'This chemise.' She pointed her chin at the embroidered silk.

'Do you mean to say a chemise identical to this one?'

'Yes, identical to the one you have. Not the same, because the one I received was burned after…'

'Please begin with the package, and explain in chronological order what precisely occurred.'

Mrs Appleton's chest heaved. 'I received a package. My name was on it, and so I opened it. A chocolate and a typed note lay on top of the...the chemise. An extraordinary piece such as I would never be able to afford. The note read, "From a secret admirer." I laughed when I read it. I thought someone was jesting or accidentally had put my name on the package when he must have meant to send it to my mistress. Whichever the mistake, I was sure it was for her...for Mrs Frank. And so...I gave it to her.'

'What did she say about the note?'

'She looked at it, and...said that I'd done right, that the chemise must be for her, not for me. That...no one would present me with such an expensive present. And then she folded the wrapping back over it and placed it aside.'

'Did you touch the chemise?'

'Oh, I did not dare to touch such a fine thing.'

'I see. When was the next time you saw the chemise?' Bicker asked.

A hand fluttered up to Mrs Appleton's throat as she said, 'When Dr Johnston tried to revive my mistress.'

'And what happened then?'

'She...died.' Mrs Appleton fell silent.

The judge tapped a finger onto his desk and said, 'Mrs Appleton, you have been asked to describe the events. If the attorney of the defence has to pull every single sentence out through your nostrils, I will lose my patience.'

Abruptly, Mrs Appleton sat up straight, wiped her

nose, and continued. 'Dr Johnston gave the certificate of death and left. The master, Mr Frank, wept. And after some time, he decided to wash his wife's body to make her presentable. But he was feeling ill, and then I thought about the chemise and what...what my brother had told me... You must know that my brother is a warden at Millbank Prison, and he once told me a horrid story that's whispered there. They say that there is a man in London who would fashion a piece of clothing that would kill. For a price. They call him the Spider. And that one could only ask for the Spider's services by placing an ad into Reynolds's Newspaper. An ad titled, "spider silk sought." And then a time and place to meet this man.'

She cleared her throat several times. 'When I saw the chemise on my dead mistress, and the weakness of Mr Frank that had come about earlier that evening, I recalled my brother's story and was struck by terror. What if someone had paid the Spider to fashion this poison chemise for me? What if the Spider *himself* wanted me dead? What if I it was I had killed my mistress, and made Mr Frank ill? And would he try again? And then I...thought that if I wouldn't take it all away, someone might believe I killed her. So I washed her body taking care that I didn't get too much of the poison upon my skin. If it was indeed poison. I couldn't be sure. But I was afraid. So afraid that it was all my fault. I burned her clothes. The night after, I burned the towels, flannels, and waxed paper I used for washing her.'

'Did you feel a prickling or burning sensation on your palms?'

'Yes,' she whispered. 'A faint burning and a queer yellow flickering at the corners of my vision.'

'And you simply forgot to mention this when you gave your witness statement.'

She dabbed a handkerchief at her nose, and answered, 'I was terrified.'

'Of what, Mrs Appleton?' Bicker bellowed. 'We all witnessed you being utterly unconcerned about an innocent man being led to the gallows!'

Justice Hawkins rapped the gavel against his desk. 'Mr Bicker, control yourself.'

'My apologies, my Lord.' Bicker straightened his lapel with a snap. 'Mrs Appleton, do you believe it possible that a man in love with the woman you have hurt by implying she stole a necklace from your mistress might have wished to poison you with the chemise?'

Mrs Appleton's eyes bulged. A croak issued from her. The solicitor-general stood to protest, but Bicker waved him away, retracted the questions, and announced, 'I am done with this witness.'

The judge threw him a warning glare.

The solicitor-general said, 'My Lord, given the new developments I respectfully ask that you grant an additional day for the prosecution to prepare its closing speech.'

'Granted. Does the prosecution have questions for the witness?'

Of course they had. Was Mrs Appleton absolutely certain that her mistress wore the same chemise that was sent to Mrs Appleton the day before her mistress died? And was she absolutely certain about this and that. Would she give the name of her warden brother so that the prosecution might call him onto the witness stand, because they had great doubts that this queer story about a man who killed with poison undergarments was true. Honestly, who came up with such fairytales?

When Bicker announced he would now call his final witness, he added that the prosecution might find it unnecessary to question Mrs Appleton's brother, and that an additional day for the closing speeches might not be needed after all.

'The defence calls Mr William Burroughs onto the witness stand.'

Sévère's skin began to buzz. He felt as though he were waking up after long, cold months of hibernation.

'Mr Burroughs, you are barrister-at-law with offices at Oxford Square. Would you please tell us how you came about this chemise?' Bicker asked, and held up the chemise, careful to touch only the waxed paper.

'I purchased it to poison my wife.'

Voices rose in the court room. The jurymen whispered to one another, and even the ushers looked terrified.

Justice Hawkins struck his desk and demanded silence. After three echoing raps, the room quieted down.

All the while, William Burroughs looked as content as a piglet in a mud puddle.

'Mr Burroughs,' Bicker said, 'have you placed an ad into Reynolds's Newspapers seeking the services of a man known as the Spider?'

'Ah, no. Mrs Olivia Sévère did it. I acted in the role of…bait.'

The resulting ruckus was enough for Justice Hawkins

to ask the more composed ushers to remove their noisy colleagues.

'Mr Burroughs, my patience is wearing thin. If you keep insinuating that you and Mrs Sévère set the stage for a murder — and I am certain your sole aim is to put on a good show — I will remove you from the witness stand and let you cool down in a holding cell. You, of all witnesses, should know best not to aggravate me.'

'My apologies, my Lord,' William said.

At the slight twitch of Mr Burroughs' mighty moustache, Sévère couldn't help but think this man was having an unhealthy amount of fun in the court room. And that he'd also had fun with Olivia. For years.

'What reason did Mrs Sévère give you for placing this ad and asking you to procure a poisoned chemise?' Bicker said.

William turned to the jury, and said, 'Mrs Sévère is the prisoner's private investigator. The evidence laid out at court has demonstrated that Dr Johnston died of a contact poison, specifically, aconitine. Mrs Sévère discovered that much of the evidence that might have unburdened her husband had been destroyed. The clothes Mrs Frank wore, and the towels and flannels used to wash her corpse were burned. The skin samples from Dr Johnston's hands were rendered unusable owing to the presence of embalming liquids. We concluded that an exhumation of Mrs Frank would be equally useless.

'However, Mrs Sévère discovered that Mrs Frank's former maid had had relations with Mrs Frank's half-brother, and that the maid was sent away when a family heirloom of Mrs Frank's disappeared. According to Mrs

Frank's maid's statement, Mrs Appleton spread the rumour that the maid had taken the necklace. Upon Mrs Sévère confronting Mrs Appleton, she admitted that she had hidden the necklace but couldn't find it anymore, and that—'

'Mr Burroughs,' the judge interrupted. 'Would you mind telling me where this is going? I fail to see the connection between a missing necklace and Dr Johnston's death.'

'The necklace leads us directly to the murderer, my lord,' William answered, and winked at Sévère.

'The murderer?'

'It will be all clear in a minute, if you allow me to continue.'

The judge nodded.

William twirled his whiskers, and went on, 'You see, we — that is, Mrs Sévère, Mr Higgins, who is her assistant detective, Mr Sévère, and I – we first suspected Mrs Appleton, for she harboured an unrequited love for her mistress, which was what led her to falsely implicate Mrs Frank's personal maid with theft so that the maid would be sent away and Mrs Appleton could have her mistress all to herself. However, as I said already, Mrs Frank did not return Mrs Appleton's romantic feelings, and a broken heart is as good a motive for murder as any. When presented with our conclusions, Mrs Appleton was much distressed, and revealed that she had received a package with a chemise, which she gave to her mistress. And that she feared a man wanted her dead. She told a queer story about a man who poisons undergarments and sells them to men who might wish a wife or lover dead. She also produced a short article reporting on the suicide of Mr Rupert Fleming, the fiancé of Miss Edwine Mollywater.

'Miss Edwine Mollywater received a package with a typed note that read, "Wear this and meet me by the tigers," and a chemise of embroidered silk. She put it on and went to the zoo. Perhaps she believed she would meet her fiancé, Rupert Maximilian Fleming, the son of Sir Robert Maximilian Fleming. All we know is that the young woman arrived at the zoo but didn't make it to the cats. She fell, and died on the spot. Witnesses stated that they heard her say, "Why does it hurt so much?" A few weeks later, Rupert Fleming took his own life, for he could not live without Edwine and with the rumours that she had planned to meet a secret lover on the day of her death. You see, both the note and the chemise suggested an affair, for neither her parents, her maid, nor Mr Fleming had ever seen the undergarment. May I have a sip of water, please?'

An usher poured a glass of water for William, which he noisily drank. 'Thank you, my dear man. Now, where was I? Ah, Miss Mollywater. Unfortunately, Miss Mollywater is long embalmed and in the ground, together with her chemise. Exhuming her would probably lead to the same disappointment we experienced with Dr Johnston. Except, of course, should anyone wish to see whether she wore the same chemise as this one.' William pointed at the package on Bicker's desk.

'However, it became clear that we might have a serial killer plaguing London. One who is extraordinarily skilled and clever. One who probably overdosed the chemise he intended that Mrs Appleton wear. The question was: Why did he overdose it? Was it an accident? Was it intent? To answer our questions and find the killer, Mrs Sévère placed an ad into Reynolds's Newspaper titled, "spider silk sought." We were very curious to see who — if anyone — would appear at the suggested meeting place.'

William paused to look at the jurymen. Satisfied that every single one of them was in rapt attention, he continued, 'The man who met me in the dead of night in Victoria Park was unknown to me. But Mrs Sévère recognised his voice. When, late yesterday night, I met him a second time and was given this package…', he motioned to the chemise on Bicker's desk, 'Inspector Height was hiding among the trees. He then followed the man to his home and arrested him. Mrs Sévère and I conveyed the package to Dr Barry and asked him if he would place one or two tiny threads of the fabric onto his tongue. Dr Barry did so and confirmed that he experienced symptoms identical to those of aconitine. He is performing further analysis as we speak.'

The judge had scooted so close to the edge of his desk and was pushing out his elbows so far that the dried flowers that had been scattered there dropped one by one onto the floor. The court room was eerily quiet. Sévère felt something building in his chest.

'By god, Burroughs, if you don't give them the man's name at once, I fear I might throttle you.'

All eyes went to Sévère.

'Did I say that aloud?'

'You did, indeed,' Bicker said. 'Mr Burroughs, I agree with the prisoner. Would you please spare us the torture?'

'Mrs Frank's half-brother, Albert Perkin, dye chemist

at the fashion boutique on Sillwood Street. He has a harelip — as did the man Mr Arthur Adams described as the one who purchased several chemises identical to the one Mr Perkin sold to me. Mr Adams should this moment be on the way to Leman Street to corroborate the identity of—'

The entrance door was pushed open and Inspector Height stepped through. He handed a note to one of the ushers and whispered to him. The usher rushed to Bicker, offered the note to him, and an apologetic glance and half-bow to the judge.

Justice Hawkins leant back in his chair, and tugged at his ermine cuffs.

'I'm begging your pardon, my Lord.' Bicker held up the small piece of paper. 'Inspector Height informs us that Mr Perkin has confessed to having sent a poisoned chemise to Mrs Appleton which resulted in the deaths of Mrs Frank and Dr Johnston—' Bicker was interrupted by the jury's shuffling and muttering.

The judge demanded silence, then bade Bicker continue.

Bicker nodded his thanks. 'Furthermore,' he said, 'Mr Perkin confessed to having assisted more than two dozen murderers, and is asking for leniency in exchange for their names and addresses. All of them.'

Bicker had to shout over the swell of voices, 'The defence demands that Mr Sévère be released at once.'

# AFTER

*T*o Sévère it felt like falling into empty space. The vast expanse in front of him, the too-bright light, the press of onlookers — all penetrated him like so many knives through his temples. Faintly, he felt Olivia's presence by his side.

He knew it had to be this way, knew that he couldn't allow himself the easy way out through the backdoor. London had to see what had become of him. And yet, shame burned white-hot when Higgins carried him down the marble steps of the Old Bailey, and sat him into the wheeling chair.

Sévère felt warm fingers entwining with his. Olivia. A gentle tug, then Higgins began to push him forward. The brougham was waiting by the gates.

'Excuse me. Excuse me!' Olivia called out, negotiating them through the crowd. Questions were fired at them, and remained unanswered. Sévère longed for the carriage, the small enclosure. Privacy. When they finally reached it, and Higgins opened the door and folded down the steps, the courage Sévère had managed to summon vanished. The obstacle was unsurmountable.

Olivia moved to his side and unfurled her umbrella, effectively shielding him from view, as Higgins moved to his other side and slid his arms under Sévère's back and legs, and deftly manoeuvred him inside. Olivia followed, snapped her umbrella shut, and bade farewell to the Londoners, the Old Bailey, and Newgate prison with a crude gesture of her hand.

Higgins jumped onto the driver's seat, and instructed two men to deliver the chair to Sévère's lodgings. A flick of the whip, and the horses began to trot home.

*Home.* Sévère gazed out the window and wondered if his home would look as different to him as London now seemed. A hundred yards from the Old Bailey and they reached anonymity, among omnibuses, cabs, and carts of all kinds.

A sigh left his chest. He pinched his eyes shut and thought of his home. After all this time of longing for his own bed, for the warmth of the fireplace in his private rooms and good food, he suddenly felt that he couldn't face the walls surrounding it. He lifted his gaze and called to his coachman, 'Higgins, drive us to the countryside. A hill or a meadow. I don't care where. Just make it quick.' And then a little softer, 'If you don't mind, Olivia.'

A smile played around her lips. 'Well, you never took me on a honeymoon. Better late than never, I say.'

'By God, I wish I could take you to a dance,' burst from his throat, followed by a hoarse laugh. He shut his mouth, leant against the back rest, and closed his eyes again. The clacking of hooves soothed him.

After a long moment Olivia said, 'I can imagine... What I mean to say is...'

He opened his eyes, and she began anew, 'I can imagine you wish to be alone after all this. Higgins could drop me off at home. Take a holiday, Sévère. Get drunk.'

He inclined his head. 'I asked a lot of you in these past weeks. Allow me to make one last request: come with me today, sweet wife.'

Her features hardened, but she nodded assent.

They rode on in silence, only exchanging occasional glances, which were soon dropped. He wondered if he'd gone too far.

An hour and a half later, Higgins stopped the carriage, tapped on the roof, and enquired if Furze Down was acceptable.

Before Sévère could answer, Olivia said, 'Could you bring us to Mitcham Common, please? It's not far from here. If you follow the Peckham and Sutton Line south, you'll see it in a few minutes.'

The two horses snorted as Higgins tapped the whip to their flanks, and the brougham was set in motion once more.

THEY ALIGHTED ON A HILLSIDE. After Higgins had helped Sévère down onto the grass, Olivia asked him to make arrangements for a private dinner at the nearby inn.

And then Sévère was alone with her. The setting sun painted fire onto the gently sloping hill, a pond, a church, a windmill, trees. He plucked a handful of grass, rubbed it between his hands and inhaled its fresh scent.

Squinting against the red sun, he said, 'When I was a boy, when I was paralysed, I read a lot. My mother gave me a new book every other day or so. When the pain was unbearable, I stared at the ceiling, wondering why life was so unfair. What had I done to deserve this? Father gave me a slingshot and paper. Hundreds of flies succumbed to missiles of pulp and spittle.'

He chuckled, and abruptly grew sober. 'Newgate had neither library nor slingshots. At times, I wondered who had done this to me. Who wanted me gone so badly? I felt as crippled as when I was a boy. I fancied myself a victim of conspiracies, caught in a web of lies the Chief Magistrate had spun to cause my downfall, perhaps even my death. I blamed even *you* for a moment, because it was you who asked me to investigate his heinous crimes.

'Watching justice go so wrong and yet, seeing that there was no great fault, that no one in court was spinning obvious lies, that the judge, the jury — everyone — was interpreting the limited evidence just as I would have interpreted it...'

He gazed at the bunched up grass in his palm. 'To know that there could only be one conclusion, was... I don't even have the words for it.'

He turned to her. Anger made his voice rough. 'Can you imagine that I began to doubt myself? I *knew* I was innocent. But there were moments... Listening to the evidence being laid out, I thought, perhaps I am wrong and they are right? It was maddening.'

Olivia opened her mouth to reply, but he cut her off

before she could utter a word. 'I know it makes no sense. I did not kill Johnston. I know that as surely as I know my name. But there I was, in the prisoner's dock, and everything the prosecution put before us allowed only one conclusion: I must have done it.'

He took off his hat, clamped it between the fingers of his left hand, and rubbed his scalp vigorously with his right. Then he placed his hat back onto his messy hair that now contained bits of crushed vegetation. 'I wonder who, of all the men and women I have sent to goal, experienced what I experienced. I wonder how many innocent people are in Newgate, how many have been hanged, how many sent to the colonies. I wonder...' He inhaled a shudder. 'I am not sure my occupation suits me any longer. Or rather, if I suit my occupation.'

Frowning, he looked at his hand, opened it and closed it, then dropped it.

'Do you believe the Crown would...' she trailed off when he shook his head.

'Of course not. Baxter is the new Coroner. The office will certainly not be given back to a man with a questionable reputation.'

'I am sorry,' she said softly.

'Don't believe for a moment it's your fault!'

'And you? Do you believe it's *yours?*' She scooted closer to him, took off his hat, and picked the grass from his hair. 'No one is perfect. No judge, juryman, coroner, or solicitor is without fault. If they were all to grow tired of the struggle of seeing justice done, we'd soon live in chaos. All anyone can do is to try one's best. You excel at what you do. Don't throw it away now. You've worked hard to be what you are today.'

He huffed. 'And what am I?'

She smoothed back his hair with her fingers, and put his hat back on. 'Solicitor Gavriel Sévère.'

'And what am I to you?' he asked, his voice low and dark.

She looked away, her gaze settling on the last scratch of sunlight. A blackbird began to sing nearby.

'I wonder how long it will take until it leaves me,' he said. 'The sight of the iron door, the stone walls. The feeling of cold moisture in the marrow of my bones. The noise. I believed I would go mad. Day in, day out, every night. *Drip. Drip. Drip.* It was as if the world had shrunk to this one noise. As though the ocean were slowly emptying itself into me. Drop by maddening drop. It was worse than the solitude, worse than being locked up. Worse than waiting for the gallows. It felt as though the dripping water were carving a hole into my brain.

'When I knew...' He cleared his throat. 'When I knew I would live, all I could think was that I'm finally rid of that awful dripping noise.' He pinched the bridge of his nose. 'And yet, I still hear it. It's burned into my mind.'

Olivia was silent for a long moment before she said with a voice so warm it made his skin prickle, 'Listen.' She pointed to a large bush nearby. 'A blackbird.'

She paused, then directed her attention a little farther west. 'I don't know the name of this one, but it sounds very pretty, don't you think?' She indicated a tree that emitted brilliant birdsong.

'Are you sure it's only one bird?' he asked.

'I don't know. But that one over there sounds like it's had too much of your brandy.' She nodded toward a rough scraping noise that came from a mass of reeds belting a pond.

She slid her hand into his. Sévère felt as though his world were slipping away, and that she was the only thing he could hold onto. He entwined his fingers with hers and brought her hand to his lips. He fell utterly still, eyes shut, mouth pressed to her skin, his breath a wild battle. And just as suddenly, he released her. 'It is better you leave now. Go to the inn, send Higgins to come and get me. Eat something. You must be starving.'

'Hm,' she said, but didn't move.

'I beg you, Olivia.'

Still, she did not move.

He exhaled a groan. 'I want to punch a hole into a wall. Goddammit, I want to tear down a building with my bare hands! I want to scream until I lose my voice. I want to rip out that part of my brain that keeps mocking me with this dreadful dripping noise. But most of all…' His sharp gaze held hers captive, then dropped to her lips. After a moment, he dipped his head, saying nothing.

His eyes roamed the expanse. All conscious thought seemed scattered by the breeze. A small part of him had accepted the seemingly inevitable, the other part — that with an iron will to survive — had been pushed beyond the breaking point.

He wasn't quite sure how to put himself back together.

And then she squeezed his hand, and said, 'Take me to a dance.'

'I…what?'

She took off her bonnet and dropped it into the grass, then leant back to lie on her side.

He watched her brush a lock of hair from her face, and hold up one hand while sliding the other toward his shoulder. A small tune came from her lips.

'A waltz?' he asked.

'Would you care for a dance, sir?'

He couldn't help but smile as he followed her example and lay back in the grass. One hand reached out to touch her waist, the other took the one she offered.

His stomach seized as she moved closer. He felt her breath flutter across the exposed skin of his throat. The warmth of her body. Surely, she must hear the ruckus his heart was making.

'Olivia, you don't have to—'

'It is only a dance, Gavriel,' she whispered.

'I don't want you to feel obligated.'

'I don't feel obligated. Shut your eyes now.'

He did as she asked, and she continued humming a slow waltz.

'Have you ever attended a ball as grand as this?' she asked.

'N…no.'

'Nor have I. Do you think the others will notice our lack of dancing skills?'

He opened one eye. 'I don't think the birds care.'

'Hush! Lady Gainsbury is already looking in our direction.'

He threw a glance over Olivia's shoulder and snorted. 'The fat crone can get a heart attack for all I care. By the by — are we just standing here or are we going to dance?'

'Don't ask *me*, you dolt! A stupid rule demands that the lady wait for the gentleman to take the lead.'

'Hum. Shall we be cocky tonight and break all the stupid rules?'

Seeing her frown, he added. 'Let's throw ourselves into the moment. Who cares what others may think. Why don't you take the lead, Olivia?'

A small laugh erupted from her, and he wondered if it came from a place hidden deep inside, a place she kept locked and secured.

'If you wish it,' he added softly.

'Only if you don't step on my feet.'

'I'll do my utmost not to.'

---

CHAINS HUNG from his shackled wrists down to his ankles, which were secured with heavy iron bands. Olivia's gaze traveled up to his face, searching his eyes, then dropped to his lips. She had been granted half an hour with the prisoner, for it was she who had caught him. But now that she faced Perkin, she failed to see a monster. All there was, was a man whose chains seemed larger than himself.

'Why didn't you grow a moustache?' she asked.

He threw back his head and laughed. 'Of all the things you could ask me. No "Why in God's name did you do it?" Instead you wish to know why I didn't hide my harelip.'

She shrugged. 'It is as good a question as any.'

'Why did you come, Mrs Sévère?'

'I wanted to know if there was something I missed. The first time we met, I found you to be an amiable man.'

'And now? Now that you know me better?'

She cocked her head, considering. 'I find you amiable still.'

The policeman who stood by the door looked up sharply. Olivia ignored him.

'He probably believes you are insane,' Perkin said with a wink toward his guard.

'He wouldn't be the first,' she replied. 'Who purchased the poison chemise for Edwine Mollywater?'

'Her sister. She wanted what was Edwine's.' He shrugged. 'The undivided attention of a handsome young man with money.'

'I see.' Olivia paused. 'When did you begin poisoning your sister? Was it when she confided in you that she was with child, or before that?'

Upon his flash of surprise, she added, 'It doesn't matter now, does it? You killed her.'

'I didn't mean to.'

'You didn't mean to kill her? You killed her unborn children. All five of them. Killing *her* instead might have caused her less suffering.'

A cold flicker brushed past his gentle, brown eyes.

'Ah,' Olivia said. 'But why did you hate her so much?'

He leant back, and sighed. 'I was deeply saddened to hear of Dr Johnston's death. I hope you can forgive me one day. The procedure... I modified it and did not test the toxicity of the chemise. I was in a hurry and made a mistake.'

'Molly Johnston will never forgive you,' Olivia said,

growing impatient and tired. 'You didn't answer my question.'

'Ah, my sister. It was a well-nurtured hate. My father instilled it, cultivated it, and my sister made it flourish. I was the bastard child, made to sleep by the kitchen hearth, looked down upon as though I were a thing hawked up by the dog. Was it *my* fault my father tumbled countless women and got one with child? Apparently, it was. That's what they all decided.'

'He paid your tuition, did he not?'

'Ah, yes, he did. He couldn't bear the shame of having fathered a bastard *and* an idiot. Minnie and I were tutored together. Yet, while her education was a natural thing, freely given, mine was…a loan. He demanded I pay back every ha'penny he spent on my clothing, education, and food. Every plate I broke. Every piece of cutlery that went missing. He wrote it all down in his small black notebook. He even put the amount I *owed* into his will. I was to pay my debt to Minnie. My own sister, my friend, and his sole heir. She didn't need my money. Not a farthing of it.'

He smiled a bitter smile. 'Yet she gladly enforced our father's rules. She couldn't live without a certain…order of things.'

'But why kill her unborn children?'

'Because of her, I could not have a family of my own. There was…a sweet young woman. We wished to marry, but her parents did not agree to the match. You see, I was unable to provide for her. I was to provide for my wealthy sister instead. I begged Minnie on my knees. Can you imagine what she said?'

Olivia shook her head.

'"You are better off without her."' He looked up at the ceiling. 'Mrs Appleton was of the same caliber. She tried to destroy Addie, and was almost successful in her endeavour.'

'Addie Shepherd. She loves you, I believe.'

A soft smile. 'Yes, she does. A rare creature. Not a single egoistical fibre in her.'

'She seems quite content with her new mistress.'

'Yes.' He frowned and turned his wrists. The black iron chains clanked. 'She'll be…unhappy now.'

'And you?'

He snorted, and lifted his arms a few inches. 'What do you think?'

'You asked for leniency. Your freedom in exchange for the identities of more than a dozen poison murderers.'

'Freedom, what does that even mean?' He huffed. 'Are *you* free, Mrs Sévère?'

She took in his face, the paleness of his cheeks, the crookedness of his mouth, and the slight dent in his nose. His warm, brown eyes, tinged with something she knew all too well.

'My brother had a harelip,' she said softly. 'I loved him very much.'

------

THE AIR between Sévère and Olivia had been strangely charged since the previous evening. Was it because he had kissed her hand? Or because they had…danced? It hadn't been a real dance, of course. They'd barely moved at all. And yet, he would never forget the magic of that moment.

This queer and wonderful dance he'd danced with his wife, lying in the grass, holding hands, and listening to the music of her breath.

Later, when he'd told her they needed to discuss a case, she appeared reluctant to meet him in the smoking room. He hadn't lied outright. It was his own case that needed discussing.

He watched her from the corner of his vision. Wet hair spilling over her shoulders, a wool blanket hugging her form, fingers wrapped around a crystal glass, the brandy iridescent in the firelight. He would miss this sight.

He moved his wheeling chair over to the desk, and picked up a thick envelope. 'For you,' he said, and placed it onto her lap.

Frowning, she looked at him.

'I arranged this when an acquittal appeared unlikely. Read it, please.'

She pulled a stack of papers from the envelope and scanned the first few lines. 'Divorce?' she whispered. 'Wh…what have I done?'

'I purchased under your name the house and premises your grandfather was renting. I've arranged for a divorce and a release from the contracts we made. Mr Burroughs helped pen the papers you are holding, and he approved the final version. You'll find his initials on every page. It has no date on it, because at that time I was unsure of… everything. The outcome of the trial. Whether you preferred to be divorced or widowed. All you need do now is sign and put a date on them.' He held out a fountain pen. 'I spent enough time in prison to know how captivity feels.' He nodded toward the papers. 'You are free. Open your apiary, Olivia.'

He was surprised at the exquisite pain in his chest when her slender fingers picked up the pen. The sweep of her neck as she read every page. The swiftness of her hand as she signed without hesitation. She blew dry the ink, set the papers orderly onto her lap, and slowly nodded. 'You are tired of me.'

'No! That's not the reason for—'

'Well, in that case, you must believe me to be entirely without loyalty and honour. It is only natural to expect nothing else of a whore. Allow me to explain something to you: I have agreed to be in your employ for three years. Difficulties will not deter me from it. So, as long as you do not violate our agreements, I will remain here for another two and a half years. And *only then* will I put a date to these papers and ask William to file the divorce. Should this not be to your convenience, tell me so now.'

He felt as though he'd been kicked in the groin. 'It is to my convenience,' he croaked.

She stood and made for the door.

As her hand reached for the doorknob, he asked, 'Do you know what the word *whore* stands for?'

Her fingers curled to a fist and dropped to her side.

'It derives from the old Germanic word *horon*, and means *one who desires*. *Horon* derives from an even older word, *ke-roh*, which means *dear*, *loved*, or *friend*.'

Silently, she stared at the door. Sévère feared she might hear his thundering heart and laugh at him.

'I should thank you for your efforts.' She turned back to face him. 'Thank you, Sévère. But I cannot accept your gift. Instead of paying the former landlord, I will now pay you until the whole sum is covered. You must understand that this is something I have to accomplish by myself. And I... I will *not* be bought.'

He slammed his fist onto the armrest. 'You are insulting me, Olivia!'

Hastily, she dropped her gaze.

'You saved my bloody life, goddammit! Can you not imagine that I would like to repay you? Don't you think that giving you what you most wish for — even if it is only a decrepit little stone hut with a gorse brush-infested back yard — might be a small gesture compared to what you did for me?'

'It is *not* decrepit!'

'Have you seen it recently? Have you seen it with your own, adult eyes? Or are you purchasing a dream, a child-hood memory from when your childhood was still intact?'

'You are aiming very low, Sévère.'

'Am I? I believe *you* are aiming very low. You believe you must fend off all offered help in order to be strong. Have you not fought alone all these years while the world conspired against you? And most of all, you seem to believe that a friendly gesture offered by a male can only mean one thing — that he wants your legs wrapped around him. While you expect me to not hold your past against you, you hold my upbringing and my sex against me. And that, Olivia, is insulting.'

He bit his tongue so as not to say, *You believe that throwing away all that you have accomplished will bring you peace.* Instead, he narrowed his eyes at her, waiting for her to throw a barrage of insults at him.

She spoke to the tassels of the rug, her voice cracking. 'You do want my legs wrapped around you.'

'Look at me, Olivia. Do I strike you as a delusional man? I think not. My offers to you are intended to see you happy. Why else would I let you go?'

Her jaw set and her skin tightened over her cheek bones. 'It is only natural, I expect. You haven't had a woman for weeks. It will pass soon enough.'

He paled. 'You believe this is all I am able to feel? You believe me an animal in a suit?'

'I believe that you are convinced there is more to it. Some…meaningful, deeper emotion. As soon as you've seen a prostitute, you'll realise your mistake and you'll be all right.'

Oh, how he wished he could jump out of his damned chair, grab her shoulders, and give her a good shake! He exhaled, trying to relax his clenched muscles. 'Take a holiday. The Isle of Wight must be beautiful now. Should you attempt to pay me back, I will put the money into a trust fund for Rose.'

Her chin began to quiver. She straightened her spine in an attempt to keep her composure. 'I will pay you for the decrepit stone hut and the gorse brush-infested back-yard. What *you* do with your money is your concern.'

'Well, obviously, it isn't,' he muttered, annoyed.

'Gavriel, you… You must know that… That after I was abducted, I… The first months with Mrs Gretchen were the most…the most…'

Her hand came up to her throat, and her gaze grew unfocused. 'I spent long days, weeks, locked in a cupboard. She pulled me out for clients, then put me back in. I was terrified of the clacking of her heels on the floorboards. When she came to get me, it was like…dying. It's why I…why I was barely able to breathe when I was in your cell and you spoke of personal matters. It was like your words ripped me open.'

She pressed her fist against her heart. 'I wish… I wish you would talk to me as you used to. Distanced. Indifferent. But most of all I wish you hadn't bought my grandfather's house. You don't understand what it means to me to… That was the *one* thing that kept me alive. The other girls, they had nothing. They hoped a client would take them away, make them his mistress. I have seen those girls lose their hopes, their dreams, their…future. One after the other, after the other, after the other. When there was nothing left for them, they died inside or took their own lives because what else is left if there's no hope? The men who came to me, I used to…beg them to take me away. They told Mrs Gretchen. I was punished. And then I begged another, and another.'

Her chest was heaving as she battled for words. 'Eventually I learned that I can rely on no one but myself. I clung to the dream of my own apiary. One day, I would have it. I would work for it. Hard. I *would* have my future, and *never* would I need a man to give it to me.'

She looked up, her dark-brown eyes turning black. 'Do not take that from me.'

He was gripping his armrests so hard his fingers hurt. 'I am giving it to you, Olivia. Freely. If you must, see it as payment rendered. Payment for saving my life.'

'But you are taking *everything*!' Desperation rang through every word.

Sévère blinked, and shook his head. 'I don't…understand.'

Unspeaking, she wrapped her arms around her ribcage. Her shoulders trembled.

'I put a nick in your armour,' he said, baffled. 'And you hate me for it.'

Her nostrils flared and her stance changed. Ready for battle, he realised.

'I have a question for you,' she said. 'Why do you think I insisted on consummating our marriage?'

'You needed to seal our contract.'

'Precisely. And I tried my best to bind you to me. That night, I presented to you a small part of me. The vulnerable, insecure part, because that was the one you needed to see. Else you would have only seen the whore and not your wife, not someone whom you should treat with respect.' Her voice was harsh, a grating of rusty metal against stone. 'I gave you what was necessary to instil hesitation in you. The hesitation to take me against my will or discard me before the three years were up.'

He had to admit that she was right, partially. He would have seen the prostitute in her had she not been shy, vulnerable, and as lovely as she had been that night. But that she mistrusted him so deeply was…disconcerting.

'I understand,' he managed to say, although understanding seemed far from his grasp.

'Gavriel, whatever you believe you feel for me is based on lies. My lies.'

He huffed. 'You are an exceptional crime investigator, but you know nothing at all about the heart.'

'Oh, I do know plenty and wish I didn't,' she snarled.

'Would you feel better if I treated you the way you've been treated for years? Do you want me to throw a coin on your night stand and tell you how to serve me?'

'I would expect it. But I would never accept it.'

He frowned at his knees. 'I would expect to be shut away. A man in a chair is not fit for society. But would I accept it? Never.'

He looked up at her, a glittering in his eyes. 'Perhaps that is what makes you a warrior. Even when you are broken, you never allow the crack to run all the way through. You bravely stand in the way of whatever tries to destroy you.'

*S*évère sat by a window, staring at the notes in his lap without really seeing them. His mind was going through the past two hours, ticking off the factors he needed in place, and the ones he needed out of his way.

The servants had retired. Higgins had been dismissed for the evening. Sévère resolved to decide within a fort-night whether his coachman would make a trustworthy steward. Olivia was sleeping upstairs. The cane was hidden behind the curtains. A simple, brown cane.

The bells struck one o'clock. Sévère rolled his chair to his desk. He stretched his left leg, then his right, and pulled off his trousers. He fetched the customised brace and strapped it onto his bad leg. He grabbed the corner of his desk and pulled himself up, then bent his legs several times. He adjusted the buckles, went down to a crouch, straightened up and shifted his weight from one leg to the other. The edge of the top-most buckle cut into his groin.

He folded a handkerchief and wrapped it around the leather strap.

Satisfied, Sévère pressed his knuckles against the top of his desk, and walked around it once. He tried again without supporting himself, then took three unaided steps to the curtain and retrieved the cane.

He twisted the head of the cane a fraction, and pulled. Lamplight reflected off a blade. He pushed the weapon back into its sheath, then dressed himself in tattered corduroys, and put a pair of glasses onto his nose. A red necktie would pull glances away from his eyes and his limp. Witnesses always remembered the most useless features, and he knew how to use this to his advantage.

He turned down the lights, pushed the curtains aside a few inches, opened the window, and made sure no one was about on the pavement.

He slipped out and landed heavily on the grass. His knee gave a twinge of pain which he swallowed before setting off along the road. He turned onto another road after a hundred yards or so, summoned a cab and rode it to an arbitrary place, alighted, and summoned another cab for a return to Whitechapel. He picked his way through narrow alleys and slunk into a doorway opposite a nameless boarding house.

And then he waited.

The sweat that coated his spine gradually cooled as wind eddied into his hiding spot. His left foot began to feel chill, then his calf and knee. A prickling followed.

He put more weight on the cane and his right leg, pressing his shoulder harder against the doorway.

Puzzled by his own aloofness, he stood in the dark and

observed the fog — how it rose in ribbons from puddles in the alley, how it was pushed back as the sky began to spit lightly.

Black windows. Black walls that seemed to melt into black puddles and Sévère's black doorway. Only a street lamp twenty or so yards away outlined houses and gutters.

There was a creak, and a wedge of light fell onto wet pavement as the door to the boarding house was opened. A man stepped out, straightened his lapel, unfurled his umbrella, pushed his hat farther down over his face, and was swallowed by the dark as the door shut behind him.

He started in Sévère's direction.

Odd, how familiar Frost's movements had become. Odder yet that Sévère felt nothing. No trepidation. No anticipation. Not even guilt.

As Frost entered the alley, Sévère stepped out of his hiding spot as if he'd just come out of his home, planning to go about his nightly business. Casually, he walked a few steps ahead of Frost.

And then Sévère stumbled. He swore like a sailor, and gripped his cane hard as his knees buckled. Frost kept walking, starting to swerve so as not to brush against the drunkard.

Sévère hurried the hidden blade out of his cane, stood and rammed it into Frost's chest. Just below the ribs. Angled upward a little.

He was surprised by the effort it took to penetrate several layers of clothing, skin, and flesh, but Sévère had attended enough postmortems to know precisely where to strike.

Frost's heart received the metal. His face contorted, his eyes wide and incredulous. His mouth fell open, preparing for a scream. Sévère let go of the blade and punched Frost's throat. The man collapsed in a puddle of rain and piss. His legs began to twitch.

With a soft hiss Sévère retrieved the blade. He wiped the weapon on Frost's lapel, and stood with difficulty. The pain in his left leg was growing intense.

He froze as something moved in the corner of his vision. Sévère looked up, readying himself. Come what may, he would *not* go back to Newgate.

His gaze met Olivia's.

She stood only a few paces away, in trousers and jacket, moustache and corduroy cap. A cigarette at the corner of her mouth lit part of her face. She held a pistol in her hand. The weapon trembled. Her eyes were stuck to Sévère's legs.

'I should have known,' he said.

'You...walk?' she muttered.

'Would you mind taking his valuables? I need this to look like a mugging.'

She cocked her head.

'I doubt I'd be able to get back up. My knee is a little... tired.' He knocked his cane against the brace, and slipped the blade back into its sheath.

Olivia exhaled a cloud of smoke, bent over Frost's still-twitching body, and dropped to one knee. She rifled through his pockets, took his wallet, and spat her cigarette in his face.

Sévère felt his hackles rise as she drove her thumb into Frost's wound, and hissed, 'God created you for me, my

313

sweet. Do you feel me stretching your flesh? Do you enjoy it as much as I do? Say yes, my sweet.'

Frost's feet jerked in response. A faint grunt issued from the man, and Sévère swore to himself to never again use the word *sweet* on her.

'Olivia, we need to leave.'

She put her full weight onto Frost, driving in her thumb to the hilt. 'So tight, my sweet. You are so tight. And so hot. You do love it, don't you?'

Sévère grew sick to the marrow of his bones. 'Olivia!' He grabbed her shoulder, but she shook him off.

'I can make your curls bounce, and your mouth form a perfect "o." Would you like me to do that for you, my sweet?'

No sound and no movement came from Frost, yet Olivia did not stop.

Sévère grabbed her by the collar and yanked her back. She threw out her arms to keep balance, and almost took him down with her.

'Don't wipe your hands on your clothes. Use his lapel,' he said.

Finally, she did as he asked. When she rose, he took in the contours of her mouth, nose, and eyes, and it seemed to him she'd been carved from ice.

'It's over,' he whispered hoarsely. 'It's over.'

'Is it?' She looked up at him.

'We need to leave.' He took one step, staggering. 'Check his pulse, please.'

She touched his throat. 'He's dead,' she said and stood. 'Gavriel?'

'Hmm?'

She wrapped her arm around his waist. 'Lean on me.'

'I'm too heavy.'

'Lean on me anyway.'

They turned away from the alley, from the monstrous act they'd committed, and onto a street dotted with gaslight and frosted with mist.

A pair of sleepy crawlers grunted in protest when two drunkards — one with a cane and a red necktie, the other long-limbed and moustachioed — hobbled past a decrepit doorway they called home.

**END**

Olivia & Sévère will return in spring 2018. Check out my Book Club for pre-publication access at
**anneliewendeberg.com**

ACKNOWLEDGMENTS

To write Sévère's poison murder trial, I relied heavily on the 1882 trial of George Henry Lamson — recorded in the Old Bailey archives, the book "Notable English Trials: G.H. Lamson" edited by H.L. Adams, and "Leaves of a Life" by Montagu Williams. Although quite entertaining, the scientist in me recoiled at how aconite tests were performed (also: yuck!), and how swiftly — despite the unreliability of the analyses — Mr Lamson was led to the gallows.

A huge number of people have helped create this story:

My lovely Patreon patrons, Kim Wright - the queen of ugly blankets and turn of the century Boston background research, Robyn Montgomery, Michael G. Morrison, Valancy, Chris Stevens, Andrea Ward-Kelly, Sandra Stehr,

Donald, Nancy, Bernadine Yeghoian, Carrie Pandya, Emily Shirley, Gudrun Thäter, Rey Arbolay, Victoria Dillman, as well as Sabrina Flynn & Rich Lovin who are also faithfully beta-reading every single manuscript I throw at them.

Mercutio Jones for insightful information on 1800s embalmment fluids and alkaloid tests, and Irina Kraft for stunning Victorian undergarments.

My prime test subject and husband (isn't that the same thing?), Magnus, who only complains about my stories when I write too slow, and my children Béla and Lina who make sure I occasionally partake in "real life" (jumping in puddles and all that).

Tom, my patient and sharp-eyed proofreader who keeps offering his help and friendship, and I keep wondering how I deserve it (I'm a grump, you know); and Nancy DeMarco who miraculously found time to edit this book while renovating her house from top to bottom.

68005967R00182

Made in the USA
San Bernardino, CA
29 January 2018